AWARDS AND ACCOLADES FOR THE
CRITICALLY ACCLAIMED AND BESTSELLING
PASSPORT TO PERIL MYSTERY SERIES

Bonnie of Evidence

"[A] delightfully deadly eighth Passport to Peril mystery."

—*Publishers Weekly*

Dutch Me Deadly

"*Dutch Me Deadly*, the latest adventure of [Hunter's] endearing heroine and zany Iowan seniors, offers nonstop humor and an engaging plot woven so well into its setting that it could take place only in Holland. Despite the danger, I want to travel with Emily!"

—Carrie Bebris, award-winning author of the
Mr. & Mrs. Darcy Mystery series

"The cast of characters is highly entertaining and the murder mystery mixed with good humor!" —*Suspense Magazine*

"A bit of humor, a bit of travel information and a bit of mystery add up to some pleasant light reading." —*Kirkus Reviews*

Alpine for You

An Agatha Award finalist for Best First Novel
and a Daphne du Maurier Award nominee

"I found myself laughing out loud [while reading *Alpine for You*] ..."

—*Deadly Pleasures* Mystery Magazine

Top O' the Mournin'

An Independent Mystery Booksellers Association bestseller

"No sophomore jinx here. [*Top O' the Mournin'*] is very funny and full of suspense."

—*Romantic Times BOOKclub* Magazine

Pasta Imperfect

An Independent Mystery Booksellers Association bestseller

A BookSense recommended title

"Murder, mayhem, and marinara make for a delightfully funny combination [in *Pasta Imperfect*] . . . Emily stumbles upon clues, jumps to hilarious conclusions at each turn, and eventually solves the mystery in a showdown with the killer that is as clever as it is funny."

—*Futures Mystery Anthology* Magazine

G'Day to Die

"The easygoing pace [of *G'Day to Die*] leads to a satisfying heroine-in-peril twist ending that should please those in search of a good cozy."

—*Publishers Weekly*

Norway to Hide

"*Norway to Hide* is a fast-paced, page-turning, highly entertaining mystery. Long live the Passport to Peril series!"

—OnceUponARomance.net

Fleur de Lies

Fleur de Lies

A PASSPORT TO PERIL MYSTERY

maddy
HUNTER

MIDNIGHT INK
WOODBURY, MINNESOTA

FIRST EDITION
First Printing, 2014

Book design by Donna Burch
Cover design by Kevin R. Brown
Cover illustration: Anne Wertheim
Editing by Connie Hill

Midnight Ink, an imprint of Llewellyn Worldwide Ltd.

Library of Congress Cataloging-in-Publication Data

Hunter, Maddy.
  Fleur de lies : a passport to peril mystery / Maddy Hunter. — First edition.
      pages   cm
    ISBN 978-0-7387-3798-0
    1. Andrew, Emily (Fictitious character)—Fiction. 2. Tour guides (Persons)—Fiction. 3. Older people—Fiction. 4. Tourists—France—Fiction. 5. Americans-—France—Fiction. 6. Murder—Investigation—Fiction. I. Title.
    PS3608.U5944F58 2014
    813'.6—dc23
                                                                                        2013050724

This is a work of fiction. Names, characters, places, and incidents are either the product of the author's imagination or are used fictitiously, and any resemblance to actual persons living or dead, business establishments, events, or locales is entirely coincidental.

Midnight Ink
Llewellyn Worldwide Ltd.
2143 Wooddale Drive
Woodbury, MN 55125-2989
www.midnightinkbooks.com

Printed in the United States of America

DEDICATION

In memory of World War II veterans Frank Mayer, Gardner Holmes, and George Foley—three ordinary men who left ordinary lives in ordinary towns to save the world ... and did.

With thanks and admiration ~ mmh

ACKNOWLEDGMENTS

I'd like to extend special thanks to Gail McDonald for suggesting the title for the French adventure. Gail's great title inspired the awesome cover. *Merci beaucoup*, Gail!

Thanks to my editors, Terri Bischoff and Connie Hill, for allowing me to write in my own voice. Ask any author. This is invaluable.

Heartfelt thanks to my loyal fans who continue to follow the misadventures of Emily and the Iowa gang with such wonderful enthusiasm. I've said it before. You're the best.

My trip to France was something of a "bucket list" holiday. I'm a huge WWII buff, so it's been a lifetime dream of mine to visit the D-Day beaches and surrounding villages.

I wasn't disappointed.

My most memorable moment took place at Pointe du Hoc. As my husband and I waited our turn to climb down into one of the craters caused by Allied bombings on the morning of June 6, 1944, we smiled at a grammar school teacher who was trying to herd her class out of the crater. She was most apologetic that her wayward children were causing a delay, but then she looked at us and asked, "Are you American?" To which we replied, "Yes, we are." She looked us both in the face and said simply and sincerely, "Thank you."

My eyes welled with tears. I got a knot in my throat. And I was truly never so proud to be an American.

This book is my humble tribute to the servicemen and women who fought so bravely during that terrible time. They truly were... the Greatest Generation.

ONE

On June 6, 1944, Allied forces from the United Kingdom, Canada, and the United States stormed the beaches of Normandy, France, in the greatest single-day troop movement in recorded history. The operation was called "Overlord," and its purpose was to establish a beachhead from which troops could punch through German lines to recapture the cities and towns that had lived under Nazi occupation for four horror-filled years.

The British landed on a five-mile crescent of beach code-named "Gold," which sat in the middle of the string of five D-Day beaches. At the far west end of this sandy crescent, flanked by towering limestone cliffs, lies the seaside village of Arromanches, which boasts an invasion museum, carousel, souvenir shops, and a parade of once-stately homes perched at the lip of the seawall. The houses look long abandoned, their windows boarded up, but in June of 1944, their location would have afforded them panoramic views of the spectacular white sand beach that stretched halfway to England when the tide was at its farthest ebb.

Having just led my group of a dozen Iowa seniors down a flight of stone steps onto the beach, we stood at the base of a high bank of large broken boulders that were stacked against the seawall in an obvious attempt to lessen the destructive force of English Channel storms. "Is the tide in or out?" asked Alice Tjarks as she glanced seaward.

I regarded the half-mile expanse of dry sand and rippled tidal flats that stretched before us. "Based on pure observation, I'd say it's out." Iowans can scan a field of budding green leaves and tell you what crop is growing, but asking us to speculate on the status of coastal tides is even more absurd than asking us to demonstrate how to eat a live-boiled lobster.

I'm Emily Andrew Miceli, who, with my husband, Etienne, is co-owner of Destinations Travel Company in Windsor City, Iowa. I leave the office quite frequently to escort a core group of seventy-, eighty-, and ninety-year-olds who'd rather spend their retirement years seeing the world than knitting or playing golf. Etienne sometimes accompanies us, but this go-round, he's hosting a five-day travel seminar at the agency. So while we cruise the Seine River, traveling from Normandy to Paris aboard a small river ship, with optional tours available to explore historic sites in the French countryside, he'll be pretty much incommunicado. At least for a few days.

Eleven sets of eyes riveted on ninety-something Osmond Chelsvig, who, as a member of Windsor City's Board of Elections for longer than half a century, usually settled the group's most divisive flaps by requesting a show of hands.

Osmond nodded thoughtfully. "Yup. Tide's out."

Jaws dropped. Eyes widened.

"You can't agree with her," Helen Teig protested. "What happened to a show of hands? You *always* ask for a show of hands."

Margi Swanson's voice rose with sudden panic. "Helen's right. If we can't voice our opinions on really stupid things, our whole social dynamic will be destroyed."

Gasps. Nods. An errant belch.

"C'mon, Osmond." Dick Stolee delivered a playful punch to Osmond's bony shoulder. "Call for a vote."

"Nope."

Dick paused, his eyes narrowing with suspicion. "*Oooh*, I get it. Very clever, but don't think you're gonna get away with it. I'm onto you, fella. I wasn't born yesterday. None of us were. And we know exactly what you're doing."

"We sure do." Dick Teig nodded emphatically before shooting his friend a quizzical look. "What's he doing?"

"We've come to expect underhanded stuff like this from Bernice." Dick Stolee patted the shoulder of a woman with a dowager's hump misshaping her back and sparkly Mary Janes dazzling her feet. "But we expect better from you, Osmond."

Bernice Zwerg fluffed the wiry bristles of her over-permed hair and smiled sourly. "Stow the flattery," she snapped in her ex-smoker's rasp. "I'm immune."

"He didn't mean it as a compliment," deadpanned Lucille Rassmuson.

Dick Stolee let out a disgusted snort as he thrust an angry finger at Osmond. "He doesn't care what the rest of us think anymore. He's decided our opinions don't have any value. He's trashing the democratic process we've practiced all these years in favor of a dictatorship that lets him call all the shots. Do you know what this is a sign of?"

"Maturity?" I suggested.

"Armageddon!" whooped Grace Stolee, whose glee at providing a likely answer quickly dissolved into worry. "Except it better not be Armageddon, because I have dry cleaning to pick up when we get home, and I'll be slapped with a stupid handling fee if I leave it there for more than a month."

"Voter suppression!" thundered Dick. "Osmond Chelsvig is guilty of the worst political dirty trick in the book. He's denying us access to vote!"

More gasps.

George Farkas removed his Pioneer Seed Corn cap and rubbed his bald head. "I thought stuff like that only happened in places that are hotbeds of seething dissention and political unrest, like Egypt ... or Florida."

My grandmother, whose name tag identified her as Marion Sippel, slid her wirerims up her nose to better see our own homegrown political trickster. "Gee, playin' fast and loose with votin' rights don't sound like Osmond."

"It sure doesn't," he admitted. "Show of hands. How many people think I'm trying to suppress the vote?"

I checked my watch and smiled. Back to the old routine in under one minute. There really was an upside to short-term memory issues.

Osmond was exonerated in a classic squeaker—six votes to five. Bernice abstained on the grounds that voter suppression is a fiction invented by left-wing radical extremists and liberal morons, so she refused to vote on a flawed premise.

Tilly thumped the beach with her walking stick, sending up a geyser of fine-grained sand. "Normandy beaches are renowned for their twenty-foot tides," she announced in her former professor's voice.

"So we're safe." Grace Stolee exhaled a relieved breath. "The water's out more than twenty feet, isn't it?"

"Looks like it's out about a hundred miles," said Dick Teig, squinting toward the water's edge.

"Good." Grace kicked off her shoes and rolled up the hem of her pants. "I have an uncontrollable urge to dip my tootsies in the English Channel. Anyone else game?"

Graduating at the top of her class from Beginners Swim at the Senior Center pool had turned Grace into an unabashed daredevil.

The eleven nonswimmers in the group eyed her with various degrees of envy.

"Showoff," teased Margi.

"I wouldn't be caught dead anywhere near that muck," whined Bernice as she positioned her foot like a ballerina modeling toe shoes. "Not in my new walking shoes." She rotated her ankle to provide us with both left and right views. "Did I mention they were ridiculously expensive?"

Dick Stolee flung his hands palms up into the air. "That swimming certificate of yours has gone straight to your head, Grace. Where's my wife? The one whose only uncontrollable urge is to put the toaster away before I've finishing using it?"

"Point of order," Osmond spoke up. "Tides aren't measured in distance. They're measured in depth. Vertical depth. Kinda like what happens to the water level of a fish tank when you drain it."

I blinked at Osmond. He lived in a landlocked state. How could he possibly offer an analogy to explain coastal tides?

"We shouldn't be asking if the tide is in or out," advised Tilly. "We should be asking where the high water mark is located."

Alice ranged a curious glance up and down the beach. "There's a mark?"

"There should be a long, narrow field of debris on the sand somewhere," Tilly said as she scanned the immediate area. "Seaweed. Seashells. Crustacean shells. Empty beer bottles. The tide deposits everything at the high water mark."

"So if we stay above the high water mark, we won't get swept away by no rogue waves?" asked Nana.

Tilly nodded. "In theory."

"Spread out!" shouted Dick Teig as he directed the gang left and right, "and if you find any of the crap that Tilly is talking about, give a holler."

"What if we all find it at the same time?" fretted Margi. "Should we appoint a spokesperson to give an official holler so we're not all sending out mixed messages?"

"Do we have an official holler?" puzzled George, looking a bit lopsided as his wooden leg sank into the sand.

"My Dick was always fond of 'Balls'!" Lucille reminisced, hand pressed to her heart out of respect for her deceased husband. "Remember? No one could hold a candle to my Dick when it came to cussing."

"I found it," offered Nana.

"*Eww*, did everyone hear what Marion just said?" Alice used her KORN radio voice to be heard above the din. "She's got a winner."

"What'd she say?" asked Dick Teig.

"I said, I found it," Nana repeated.

"Works for me," agreed Osmond. "Show of hands. How many people think we should call out, 'I found it!' when we—"

"We don't need no show of hands," Nana blurted in exasperation. She held up her new and improved iPhone and jabbed the screen with her forefinger. "It's right here on YouTube. Some fella downloaded a bunch of photos showin' what Gold Beach looks like at high tide." She touched her fingertip to the screen. "Check your messages."

Like gunslingers going for their guns, they went for their phones. I would have gone for mine, but I was guessing I wasn't in Nana's "Golden Oldies" email loop, so my inbox would probably be empty.

"This has gotta be a different place than where we're standing," scoffed Dick Teig as he studied the photo Nana had sent him. "Where's the beach?"

I peeked over Dick's shoulder at a stunning image of white-capped waves swallowing up the sand all the way to the seawall.

"I think it's under the water what's crashin' against them rocks there," said Nana.

Heads swiveled toward the seawall, causing eyes to widen with fear as the reality of the situation set in. Helen dropped her gaze to her shoes, regarding them with mounting alarm. "Do you know what this means? If we stay where we are, when the tide comes in, it's going to roll over all of us. We'll be buried under twenty feet of water!"

"You better hope your eyebrow pencil is waterproof," Bernice taunted her.

Helen gasped as she touched her painstakingly drawn brows. "It's nonsmear and hypoallergenic, but I don't know if it's waterproof."

Her husband pulled a permanent marker out of his shirt pocket. "I gotcha covered," he snorted proudly. "Green's not your normal color, but it was the only one left on the shelf. Close enough, right?"

Sure, if she were an avocado.

"Well, *I* won't be under water," boasted Grace, clacking the soles of her shoes together to rid them of sand. "I'll be doing my award-winning dog paddle to that ramp over there. I told you people it was time we learned to swim, but *nooo*. Swimming was too *boring* for you."

Alice frowned. "I thought we said it was too wet."

"Low-impact breakdancing had a much better time slot," defended Lucille.

"And we got to wear them slinky spandex unitards." Nana gave her eyebrows a little waggle.

"And we couldn't complain about the reduced rates we got when our instructor made a group appointment for us at the chiropractor's," conceded Margi.

"Okay, people, listen up." I waved my arm above my head to indicate a time-out. "No one's going to get buried under twenty feet of water."

"Nineteen point four feet to be exact," amended Tilly. She held up her iPhone and shrugged. "I just Googled it."

"None of you are going to be buried by a sudden flood tide," I reiterated. "It's going to take hours for the water that's down there"—I threw my hand in the direction of the Channel—"to work its way up here." I nodded toward the seawall.

"Six hours and thirteen minutes," said Tilly, eyes glued to her iPhone.

"Over six hours!" I repeated. "So you need to lighten up. You're on one of the most historic beaches in the world. Do a little beachcombing. Take a few pictures. You're safe."

"How do *you* know?" argued Bernice. "Are you the resident expert on Normandy tides?"

"No, but I'm the resident expert on schedules, and according to ours, we have to be back on the bus in a little over an hour, so we'll be gone before the tide becomes an issue."

Panic swept over them like a flash fire.

"Why didn't you tell us that earlier?" chided Dick Stolee as he wrapped his hand around his wife's arm. "C'mon, Grace, put your shoes back on. We've gotta get back to the bus. We're late."

Feet shuffled. Arms flapped. Sand flew.

"You are not late!" I pleaded as they stampeded back toward the stairs. "You have a whole hour. The bus will not leave without you!"

"We can make it on time if we don't lallygag," Dick Teig exhorted the troops.

"How far away is the bus parked?" Lucille gasped out from the back of the pack.

Nana charged up the stairs in her size 5 sneakers, muscling out Bernice and Dick Teig to arrive at the top first.

Wow! That low-impact breakdancing class of hers had really improved her range of motion and stamina.

"Hold it, everyone!" Margi paused against the handrail halfway up the stairs. "I wanna get a picture of the high water mark." She took aim at the beach with her iPhone. "Did we ever find it?"

When they were all safely off the stairs, I called out one last essential nugget. "If you need to use the comfort station, the entrance is on the outside of the museum." I gestured to the building beyond the carousel that called itself the Musée du Debarquement. "And don't be surprised if you have to cough up some money to use the facilities. I warned you about this before we left home, so have some coins ready."

"Shysters," groused Bernice. "I'm not paying to use their dang potty."

"So what are you going to do?" asked George. "The toilet on the bus is out of order."

"I'll just cross my legs until we get back to the ship."

All color drained from Margi's face as she appeared to realize how she might be affected by her seatmate's threat. "Would someone *not* wearing white linen pants like to change seats with me on the bus ride back? I'll reward you with a free bottle of hand sanitizer." Ever since winning the grand prize in our church raffle, Margi had been wearing linen and bamboo rather than polyester and nylon, proving that a five thousand dollar gift certificate to Farm and Fleet can turn even a fashion-challenged Norwegian into a stylish clotheshorse.

While Margi lobbied to exchange her seat for one in a potentially less hazardous location, I untied the ribbon straps from around my ankles, stashed my sandals in my shoulder bag, and headed for the tidal flats, determined to investigate a gargantuan platform that was marooned on the sand like an alien spacecraft.

It was the size and shape of a tennis court and reminded me of an above-ground pool that had collapsed and tilted. Strands of slick green seaweed hung like dreadlocks from its concrete shell; rust bled red along its steel reinforcing bars; algae devoured large chunks of the outer skeleton and looked to be spreading like a flesh-eating virus. Holes punctured the structure's skin like open wounds, some no bigger than a basketball, others the size of a two-car garage. A warning was painted across the concrete in large white letters: *Access Interdict*, followed by a word I had no trouble understanding: *Danger*. I had no idea what the thing was, but it was obviously really old, and probably linked to the slew of other odd structures that were strewn both across the beach and in a semi-circular formation farther out to sea.

I shot a picture of the leviathan with the iPhone Nana had given to me for my birthday, then with my feet slapping wetly on the rippled sand, circled around the platform to view it from the side that faced the Channel.

"I don't care what it is or why it's here," drawled a honey blonde in a strapless sundress and alligator cowboy boots. "It's just plain nasty."

"I'm with ya, hon," agreed a Swedish blonde in white leggings, halter top, and a wide-brimmed Western hat that was woven from straw. "If this thing washed ashore on Padre Island, we wouldn't put it on a postcard. We'd blow it up."

"With what? Dynamite?" The third person in the group, a platinum blonde in a sleeveless cowl neck and half boots, flipped her silky locks behind her shoulders and cocked a hip that was intimately outlined beneath skinny snakeskin jeans. "I wouldn't need dynamite. I bet I could break that thing up into a million pieces with my AK-47." Making a muzzle of her index finger, she sprayed a flurry of bullets into the platform with her invisible weapon, blasting it into a million imaginary chunks.

The booted blonde in the strapless dress gave her wrist a sassy flop. "AK-47s are so common. Shoot, everyone has one." She arched her eyebrows and smiled coyly. "Did I tell you about my new subcompact semi-automatic? It's a Kahr P380." She paused for effect. "And it's *pink*!" She screamed the word, tossing her head back and doubling her fists in a shameless display of ecstasy.

"*Ewww!*" cried the blonde who'd advocated blowing up Padre Island.

"Get *out!*" cried the blonde who'd riddled the platform with invisible bullets.

"Did y'all hear about that blue state that has a referendum to outlaw the sale of all forms of ammunition?" asked Alligator Boots. "If it passes, folks'll still be able to stockpile as many weapons as they want, but they won't be able to fire them. Idn't that just criminal?"

"Is that constitutional?" asked Snakeskin Jeans, wrinkling her nose in an adorable gesture.

"Heck, no." Western Hat puffed out her bottom lip in thought. "There's an amendment protecting ammo, isn't there?"

"Tenth!" threw out Alligator Boots, her expression growing serious. "That's the one that comes after the Ninth, right?"

Western Hat coiled a strand of her long, glorious hair around her finger. "I thought the Tenth was the one that abolished alcohol."

Snakeskin Jeans gasped. "The government abolished alcohol? No kiddin'? Even during Happy Hour?"

I suspected the trio would have to do some serious cramming to qualify for an appearance on *Jeopardy*, but they possessed a quality that was far more marketable than instant game show celebrity.

They were jaw-droppingly beautiful.

Their hair was so blonde that it looked like liquid sunshine shot through with skeins of spun gold. It cascaded around their shoulders in the kind of long, sexy waves that invited a man's touch and roused a woman's envy. They looked to be related by either birth or sorority affiliation, flaunting toned muscles, even tans, and complexions so flawless their faces looked airbrushed. Their cheeks were tinted the perfect shade of pink; their eyelids dusted with shadow that created depth and allure; their full, collagen-injected lips so highly glossed that looking at them in direct sunlight might cause blindness. I'd noticed them aboard ship, so I knew they were part of our tour group, but this was the first time I'd seen them without a wall of men forming an impenetrable circle around them.

"Group photo, group photo!" Western Hat waved her camera above her head, then, spotting me, brandished it in my direction. "Honey, would you mind doin' the honors?"

Flattered to be acknowledged by the fetching threesome, I flashed a smile that I hoped was every bit as blinding as their lip gloss. "You bet."

Western Hat sashayed toward me in her bare feet, walking with the kind of hip swivel that could eject both joints from their sockets. I met her halfway, so dazzled by her looks, I couldn't help staring.

She handed me her camera.

"Thanks." I fought off a twinge of jealousy that my gene pool hadn't included Rapunzel's hair, spray-on leggings, and a cowboy hat worthy of a Vegas pole dancer. "Nice hat," I said in a burst of chattiness.

"Idn't it though?" She trailed her fingers around the brim. "I have a whole closetful back home. And they're crushable, so I packed a slew of 'em for the trip." She glanced at my name tag, her exquisitely plump lips curving into a smile. "Well, butter my buns and call me a biscuit."

I didn't normally wear a name tag, but I'd grudgingly hung one around my neck this morning to give guests a chance to see that I was one of them.

"You're on our tour?" she tittered. "Shame on me for not noticin' you sooner, sugah."

"No problem." If I had to fend off a crush of admirers every time I poked my head out my cabin door, I might not notice anyone else with mammary glands on the tour either.

"Hey, y'all, this is Emily. She's on the tour with us."

Waving. Half-hearted smiles. Quick mirror checks to remove errant particles of food from their teeth before the big photographic event.

"I'm Bobbi," said the blonde, "and you're a real doll to do this."

Her guest ID indicated her full name was Bobbi Benedict, from Corpus Christi, Texas. I couldn't guess her age, but unlike movie stars whose fading youth can be masked through the miracle of soft focus camera lenses, Bobbi Benedict was even more gorgeous up close than she was far away. As she sashayed back to join her friends for a group shot, I studied the settings on her camera and wondered how my hubby would react if I flew home as a blonde.

"Bobbi!" cried a voice from across the beach. "Dawna! Krystal! Wait up! I want to be in the picture, too!"

The woman running toward us was dressed in a skintight mini-dress that inched higher up her thighs as she raced across the tidal flats, splattering wet sand with the abandon of a child jumping into a mud puddle. Her legs pumped like pistons. Her mane of long hair whipped straight out behind her as she gained speed. Her oversized metallic handbag banged against her hip with every footfall, calling into question her choice of fashion accessories today. She was six feet tall, shaped like an hourglass, boasted the kind of beauty that most women could acquire only through heredity or expensive plastic surgery, and. unlike her girlfriends, was unabashedly brunette.

Her name tag identified her as Jackie Thum, and years ago, when she'd been a Broadway actor named Jack Potter, I'd been married to her.

TWO

"I stopped at the souvenir shop to buy a booklet," she choked out as she sprinted toward the platform to join the blondes.

"*Ewww*, you're spraying gunk," yelped Bobbi, ducking behind her companions to avoid the mud splatter.

"Cut it out!" snapped Alligator Boots as she swiped a glob of wet sand from her designer footwear.

"Sorry." Jackie shrunk visibly beneath the unforgiving glares of the toothsome threesome. She dropped her shoulders and hung her head with proper contrition before bouncing back in a burst of excitement. "So, where do you want me?"

Snakeskin Jeans flashed a squinty look that said, "Anywhere but here," but to Jackie's face, she said, "You know something? I don't think the light's quite right anymore. So let's just skip the photo for now and try for a better shot later."

I focused Bobbi's camera and captured all four of them within frame. "The light looks great to me," I called out.

Bobbi hustled out of frame as if her feet were on fire. "I'm all in for waitin' on the picture takin'. We can find a better backdrop than a piece of rusty old junk."

"It's not a piece of junk," Jackie enthused as she whipped a booklet out of her shoulder bag. "It's part of the artificial harbor that the British—"

"How about we saunter through some shops to see what kind of cosmetics our competitors are peddling?" Alligator Boots proposed, sending her two companions into fits of glee.

"*Ewww!*" cried Bobbi. "You think we have time?"

Snakeskin Jeans clapped her hands with excitement. "Yes! I don't know why we're lookin' at all this sand anyway. It's borin'."

Jackie waved her booklet with the zeal of a cheerleader waving her pompoms. "But it's one of the D-Day beach—"

"We've only got an hour," interrupted Bobbi, "so we better get our tushes in gear."

"We can skip the shop where I bought my booklet," Jackie offered helpfully. "It's the one directly across from the museum. They had *no* beauty products whatsoever. It was really disappointing."

"Jackie, sugah." Bobbi smiled sweetly. "Since you've already hit some of the shops, would you do me a Texas-sized favor and take some pictures of the beach so I can show the folks back home? Emily will give you my camera." She nodded toward me before bobbing her head back and forth with abbreviated introductions. "Emily, Jackie. Jackie, Emily. And lemme tell ya, I'm happy to entrust it to another Mona Michelle rep, 'cause I know you'll take good care of it. You wouldn't believe what I paid for the thing."

"Of *course*, I'll take care of it." Jackie splayed her hand over her chest as if pledging an oath. "I'm honored that you asked me. This is *such* an historic beach. It's where—"

"Come *on*," Snakeskin Jeans urged, prodding her companions with a meaningful look.

"The three of you scoot," Jackie insisted, as if she were playing mother hen to her baby chicks. "I'll take some pictures, and then I'll catch up with you."

"You're just an ever-lovin' doll," Bobbi called over her shoulder as she and her friends scurried away like cockroaches escaping the glare of an overhead light. "We'll flag you down when we see you!"

Oh, sure. Like that was going to happen.

"I won't be long!" Jackie waved to their retreating backs before exhaling an immensely satisfied sigh. She stashed her booklet in the outside pocket of her bag, then turned to me, aflutter with anticipation. "Aren't they the best? I mean, I've only known them for half a day, but we've already bonded like this." She twined her middle finger around the knuckle of her highly lacquered forefinger. "The four of us are going to be best friends forever!" Clasping her hands, she steepled them against her heart like a music idol about to burst into song. "It's so awesome being part of a clique, Emily. Overnight, I've become one of the beautiful people—the ones who get immediate seating in restaurants, wolf whistles from construction workers, upgrades to the exit rows on airplanes. It makes me feel *so* much better than everyone else." She paused, her eyes suddenly narrowing with a hint of self-awareness. "Do I sound like a snob?"

"Yup."

She arched her exquisitely waxed brows and smiled. "You're such a kidder." Readjusting her minidress over her hips, she struck a wistful pose, as if recalling her life before facial hair remover creams and PMS. "You know, Emily, guys are so clueless about this whole bonding thing. I mean, I'm not knocking the really deep discussions I used to have with my buds about football and beer, but it's so much easier to bond when you're talking about really intimate things, like eyebrow threading and breast implants. Not to toot my own horn, but if you noticed the way the girls were fawning all over me, you might have to agree that I'm taking to this bonding thing like a diva to the red carpet."

Unwilling to break the news that her clique had just ditched her like the butt-end of a stale cigar, I forced a smile. Her gender reassignment surgery might have allowed her to become female, but she was way behind the developmental curve when it came to recognizing cold shoulders. "Yup," I agreed. "You're a natural."

"Really? You're not just saying that because you always avoid conflict and we used to sleep together?"

I crooked my mouth and held out Bobbi's camera. "You're going to need this if you plan on taking any pictures."

"BE CAREFUL!" She sucked in her breath and rushed over to me. "Bobbi might not like me anymore if you drop her high-end, state-of-the-art camera."

"It's a single-use disposable."

"What?" She lifted it from my grasp as if it were a live grenade and cradled it in her palm, assessing the shiny buttons on the plastic casing. Puzzled, she turned it over in her hand. "Okay, but … it looks like a really expensive disposable."

Jackie might be lagging behind her female counterparts on the cold shoulder graph, but she was off the chart when it came to denial. "Bobbi probably didn't want to fuss with any complicated equipment," I said in a charitable attempt to explain away the woman's subterfuge.

"Well, if simplicity is what she wanted, she bought the right camera, because this model only has one button."

As Jackie got off a shot of the chalky cliffs to our west, I ranged a long look toward the seawall, eying the three blondes as they climbed the stairs to the promenade that fronted the beach. "So your new best friends are the women you wrote to me about, hunh? The reps with the highest company sales?"

"They've been the top income grabbers for years, so imagine their surprise when yours truly joined their ranks by outselling the gal who used to set the gold standard for the northern region. I executed quite a coup for an inconsequential upstart."

Which might explain why the ladies were "fawning" over her so much.

In her torturous quest to find the perfect job, Jackie had quit her gig as a life coach to try her hand at something for which she was uniquely qualified: beauty consultant for the country's largest independent cosmetic manufacturer, Mona Michelle. As a Mona Michelle representative, she was responsible for convincing scores of average Janes that their pathetic lives could turn on a dime and explode with excitement simply by using the right foundation to match their skin tone. She threw makeup parties. She demonstrated the proper technique for applying eyeliner without poking your eye out with the liner brush. She explained the need to buy really expensive skin care products that only her company could supply. She handed out free sample-size lipsticks whose labeling attested that no animals had been harmed in the testing of this product.

And she rocked at it.

After only one year on the job, she was being rewarded for her stellar sales record with an all-expenses-paid holiday to France, which included a chance to rub shoulders with her company's esteemed president, and an opportunity to pal around with the three other regional winners. Apparently, when her sales topped the million dollar mark, she'd be awarded the company's highest honor—a pink Porsche with a Swarovski crystal-encrusted steering wheel, but according to her last email update, she hadn't quite reached that pinnacle yet.

"So if you're the regional winner from the north, what parts of the country are the other three women from, because they all sound like they're from the same place to me."

"You're *so* good with accents, Emily. They *are* from the same place. Texas!"

I cocked my head, flashing her a squinty look. "How is it geographically possible that three winners from different regions of the country are from a single state?"

"Because more cosmetics are sold in Texas than in the other forty-nine states combined, so our national map is basically an oversized map of the Lone Star State. Why do you think women in Texas look so great all the time? Two words: Mona Michelle."

Swinging around to face the Channel, she snapped several photos of a series of boxcar-shaped structures situated about a half-mile off shore. They formed an incomplete semi-circle around the beach, like a passenger train missing some of its cars, and were so massively big, I suspected if they were covered in artificial turf, the NFL could play Sunday football on them. Angling around forty-five degrees, she took aim at another seaweed-sprouting curiosity that lay on the tidal flats like the carcass of a prehistoric sea serpent.

Click.

"*Fini,*" she said as she dropped the camera into her bag. "Bobbi might have a bird if I use up all her film."

"Do you have any idea what all these structures are?" I asked, wishing I'd done more research before leaving Windsor City.

"You don't know?" She gave her hands a little pattycake clap. "*Ewww*! I'm *so* glad you asked."

Whipping her booklet out of the side pocket, she flipped open the cover and held it at shoulder level while the interconnected pages accordioned downward like paper dolls. "Grab the end there, would you, Em?"

I caught the tail end of the booklet before it landed in a tidal pool, then stepped away from her, stretching the pages between us. I scanned it from left to right. "A panoramic photograph?"

"Of the very beach we're standing on, only it was taken in 1945, three months after D-Day."

I looked from the photo, to the beach, back to the photo, comparing the "here and now" to the "then and there." "Wow, this place was really humming back then."

"Well, duh? This is where the British built their artificial harbor so ships could deliver supplies to the troops, so of course it was humming."

The photograph depicted a moment, frozen in time, when ingenious engineers had cross-hatched the beach with floats, pontoons, and roadways, and created a working harbor farther out to sea with piers, loading docks, floating cranes, and mooring facilities that serviced ships that were anchored outside the staging area.

Jackie trailed a finger along the photo. "Once a ship's bow doors opened up, a fleet of jeeps and trucks whisked the cargo over the floating roadways to the beach, and from there, everything headed inland. Fuel. Ammo. Tanks. Guess how long it took to empty the cargo hold of a landing ship?"

I shrugged. "Twenty-four hours?"

"Eighteen minutes. Can you believe it? I can't even blow-dry my hair in eighteen minutes."

"How do you know so much about World War II naval logistics?" I regarded her one-eyed. "Military History Channel?"

She arched an eyebrow and tapped a finger against her earlobe. "Grampa Potter. Did you ever meet Grampa Potter?"

I mined my memory for an image of Jack's grandfather. "*Uhh...* cigar stuck in the corner of his mouth? Cute lisp? Smelled like mothballs?"

Jackie frowned. "That was Gramma Potter. Grampa didn't have a lisp. Anyway, he was a navy Seabee who actually helped build this harbor."

"No kidding?"

"Yup. You should have heard the stories he told about how his unit blew up old merchant ships to form the breakwater out there. You wouldn't believe the great sound effects he came up with, Em. Even with the cigar in his mouth. And you see those boxcar-shaped things? They're made of concrete and were towed across the Channel from England to be the primary building blocks for the entire operation. Would you believe they weighed as much as six thousand tons apiece?" She regarded the photograph. "Gramps never could figure out how a six-thousand-ton concrete box could float while a four-ounce bar of Lifebuoy soap couldn't."

She chuckled. "Poor Gramps. The relatives used to get so tired of listening to him repeat the same stories that they'd sneak out of the room one by one. But I hung in there with him. Gramma, too. She'd just yank out her hearing aid, light up a stogie, and smile at him through a haze of cheap cigar smoke."

"That was really sweet of you, Jack." Even as a child, his kinder, gentler feminine side had come to the fore.

"I couldn't leave. What if he remembered some gory details that involved shooting, stabbing, or blasting something sky high? No way was I gonna miss that."

I rolled my eyes. "Why are guys so obsessed with loud noises and gore?"

She exhaled a long breath. "I dunno. But I have it narrowed down to either testosterone or political affiliation." She peeked at her watch. "Are you ready to head back? I don't want to lose track of the girls. They're so helpless without me." She executed a shimmy that rippled all the way down her body. "I'm their guiding force."

After collapsing the photograph back to its original booklet size, we struck out across the sand, aiming toward the stairs that fronted the carousel. "Which home visit are you scheduled for?" Jackie asked as she dug a sheaf of papers out of her shoulder bag.

"I'm in group one."

"Shoot." She made a face at the information on her itinerary. "I'm in group three."

One of the unique features of our river cruise was an opportunity to visit a French family in the Normandy countryside. Guests were being divided into groups of eight and would be dropped off at designated farms, villas, and chateaus where they'd be encouraged to discuss anything from local cuisine to politics with the host family. I didn't know who else would be joining me in group one, but I hoped that whoever they were, they'd prove themselves to be worthy ambassadors of the United States and not ugly Americans.

Please let Bernice be in someone else's group. Please let Bernice be in someone else's group.

At the foot of the stairs, I paused to brush sand off my feet and slip back into my sandals. "I wonder which group the girls are in?" Jackie asked as she watched me retie the ribbons around my ankles.

"Why? Are you planning to surprise your host family with a group demonstration of tone-correcting wands and cucumber facial masks?"

She went statue-still for a long moment before shoving her itinerary back into her bag and grabbing her cell phone. "Ohmigod! Why didn't *I* think of that? You're a genius, Emily. An absolute genius! Mona Michelle goes international. Do you mind if I say it was my idea?" She tapped her screen and pressed her phone to her ear, bobbing her head impatiently.

"Jack! I was teasing! You can't pitch your cosmetic line on your home visit."

"Why not?"

"Do the words 'inappropriate' and 'tacky' mean anything to you?"

She pulled a long face. "How can Bobbi's number no longer be in service? She gave it to me right before we boarded the bus."

Unh-oh. I didn't like the sound of this.

She punched her screen again and waited. "Well, this is really weird. Krystal's number isn't available either."

"Try blonde number three. Third time might be the charm."

"Can't. Dawna couldn't remember her number." She clutched the device in both hands and stared miserably at the screen. "Do you suppose there's something wrong with my phone?" She seized up with panic. "Or my hearing?"

"You probably entered the numbers wrong, Jack. It happens."

Her eyes suddenly brightened. "Initializing Plan B." Scrolling through her phone book, she hit another number and gnawed her bottom lip as she waited for someone to pick up.

"Who're you calling now?"

"Your grandmother. She gave me her number yesterday, so if I got that one right, then maybe— Mrs. S.? I'm *so* glad you answered. This is Jackie. Quick question. Is this the right cell number for you?"

She broke out in a giddy smile. "Well, thank God. I thought— *Uh-huh… Uh-huh.* Can you speak up a little, Mrs. S.? What's all that yelling in the background? *Uh-huh. Uh-huh.* You're where? No kidding? Yup. She's right here with me. Oh, sure. No problem. Thanks."

She waved her phone at me in a celebratory gesture. "I knew I wasn't the one who screwed up." She exhaled a long, relieved breath before breaking out in a wince. "But now I'm really in a bind."

"Why?"

"Because someone's going to have to tell Krystal and Bobbi that their memories suck, and if *I* tell them, it'll probably ruin our friendship. Women really resent other women pointing out their flaws. So"— she flashed a hopeful smile—"would you tell them?"

"No!"

"Please?"

I stared at her, stonefaced. "Where's Nana?"

"In the public restroom."

"Who was yelling?"

"Oh, yeah, I almost forgot. Bernice's hand is stuck in the donation box, so you better get over there fast because the attendant has the place in lockdown until they free her, and the line is backed up around the building."

THREE

"Why are you looking at me like I'm a new species of mold?" demanded Bernice.

"Because you nearly started a restroom riot in Arromanches." I spoke to her firmly, but kept my voice low to avoid humiliating her in public. "Do you know the anxiety you created? Seniors with plumbing issues cannot afford to waste precious minutes standing in a line that's been shut down because of something *you've* done."

She bobbed her head nonchalantly. "They've got medications to take care of that now, you know."

"That's not the point."

"That moron attendant started it. I told her that I accidentally dropped the wrong coin in the box, but she wouldn't give me change."

"Did she understand English?"

"How should I know? Why is that important anyway? Hey, I'm not taking the blame for this. It was all her fault."

Of *course* it was the attendant's fault. In Bernice's world, it was *always* someone else's fault.

We were seated in the parlor of a three-hundred-year-old farmhouse that had survived the French Revolution, the Napoleonic wars, the German invasion of World War I, and the Allied bombings of World War II. The decor was an eclectic blend of antique and shabby chic with memorabilia-filled china cabinets, gilt-framed oils of grazing cattle, a sideboard glutted with photos, and sofas and chairs modern enough to have been purchased at IKEA. The windows were tall and narrow and afforded us excellent views of the apple orchard at the back, the impenetrable stone wall at the front, and the jungle of pink and purple hydrangea that grew in unruly banks across the lawn. Our hostess had introduced herself as Madeleine Saint-Sauveur, and before she'd disappeared into the kitchen to retrieve refreshments, she'd invited us to tour the ground floor to acquaint ourselves with the layout of the house.

Osmond ambled into the parlor, seated himself in the chair beside me, pulled out his iPhone, and cued up a site. "You wanna see the video Margi shot in the little girls' room? You know the subject matter has gotta be something special when Margi decides to shoot video instead of hand out sanitizer. She's calling it the Princess and the Potty."

"*Uhhh*—"

"It's nothing racy. Just Bernice trying to pull her hand out of the donation box before your grandmother destroys it with a jumping reverse hook kick."

"There's footage of Nana?"

"Yup. And a real good closeup of her sneaker."

29

"Can you send the video to my phone so I can show Etienne when I get home?" I knew I'd be able to figure out the pool of data relating to cell phones if the technology would remain the same for more than a minute, but until then, I continued to need expert advice from either a random teenager or an old person.

"Don't need to send you anything, Emily. Margi posted it on YouTube, so it's there for the whole world to see."

"I'm on YouTube?" Bernice leaned across me and snatched his phone from Osmond's hand. "Have I gone viral yet?" She started the video, her eyes suddenly spitting fire. "Idiot. She didn't shoot me from my good side."

Osmond regarded her blandly. "Does she know you got one?"

"Margi posted a video of Bernice's restroom disaster on YouTube," Tilly announced as she strode into the parlor from the entry hall. "Have you seen it yet, Emily?"

Bernice clutched Osmond's phone, refusing to give it back. "Does anyone know how to delete other people's videos from YouTube?"

Tilly headed for an armchair across from us. "Try to appreciate the cultural implications, Bernice. Imagine what future generations might think when they view it. Why, among the Akuntsu, if a woman makes a fuss like you did in the communal toilet, it means she's just discovered she's entering the Change." She bobbed her head thoughtfully. "In rarer instances, it indicates she's being eaten alive by fire ants."

"*Bonjour, mes amis.*"

Madeleine Saint-Sauveur was a dark-haired beauty in her mid-thirties who seemed to shun makeup in favor of plain old soap and water. She was simply dressed in tight jeans and a short-sleeved

T-shirt, but the scarf she'd wrapped around her neck in a half-dozen interconnecting loops bespoke a sense of style that was both effortless and elegant. "I think this is not all of you," she said in charmingly accented English as she placed an oversized serving tray on the coffee table in front of us. "Perhaps the smell of brownies will prompt them to join us. Yes?"

As if on cue, the missing guests made their way into the parlor and took their seats, save for one straggler—a cadaverously thin man wearing dark glasses—who shuffled halfway into the room before discovering that all available seats had been taken. Feet braced apart and cane anchored in front of him to steady his balance, he swayed dangerously left and right before asking, "Where'm I s'posed to sit?"

"Why don't you sit here?" I said as I popped out of my chair. He was either drunk, infirm, or both, but I didn't want to see him faceplant on the floor.

"Mush obliged," he slurred as I escorted him to my seat. "You're okay, honey."

"Don't get tricked into thinking she did that out of the goodness of her heart," cracked Bernice. "She gets paid big bucks to be nice to old geezers like you."

"I don't understand." Madeleine did a quick head count. "There are nine of you. I was told to expect eight. My mistake, yes? Let me fetch another chair from the kitchen. And please, pour yourselves some cider. Made from the apples grown in our own orchard. Or if you prefer something stronger, I invite you to sample the Calvados." She gestured to the liter bottle next to the pitcher of cider. "Apple brandy. One of the specialties of our region."

"Shounds good," boomed our inebriated guest. "Make mine a double."

"Hey, bud, looks like you've had your fill already," said the man in the chair next to Tilly.

"Were you assigned to group one?" demanded a woman whose silver hair was styled in an upsweep that looked stiff as starch.

"Don't know. When the bus shtopped, I got off. Wasn't I s'posed to get off?" He angled his head in a slow arc from left to right, taking in the entire room behind his sunglasses. "How come the rhest of you got off?"

"Because we're in group one," snapped the silver-haired woman.

"Braaa-vo." He raised his hand in a mock toast and bowed his head. "I'm pleazhed to make the acquaintance of all you good people. I'm Irvin, but you can call me Irv. So... ish anyone gonna sherve that brandy, or do I have to pour it myshelf?"

Madeleine bustled back into the room with an extra chair. "Your tour company would frown on my seating their guests on the floor," she teased as she placed the chair next to me. "Please, madame, sit," then to the room at large, "If I dig out my map of the United States, would you tell me your names and show me where you live?"

We spent the next several minutes introducing ourselves to our hostess and locating our hometowns on the map. "So many of you from the same state," Madeleine commented as she highlighted Windsor City with a pink marker. "How nice that you enjoy traveling together."

"That's a matter of opinion," snorted Bernice.

"Is the name 'Osmond' a common one in Iowa?" Her voice grew animated as she questioned Osmond. "We have several in our family. Did you know it can be traced back to the time of the Norman Conquest? Although back then it was spelled A-S-M-U-N-D-R. The invading Norsemen had more of an influence on our language than we often realize."

"I vishited Iowa once." Irv knocked back his second apple brandy, sucking in his breath at the aftertaste. "And once was enough. *Woo*! This shtuff's good."

"Honestly." The lady with the stiff hair drilled him with a look that oozed disgust. "Is it too much to ask you to conduct yourself with a little more dignity?" She'd introduced herself as Virginia Martin from Houston—a well-preserved socialite type with rhinestone reading glasses hanging from a rhinestone chain around her neck and stunning rings gracing every finger of her unblemished hands. And surprise, surprise, she was married to Victor Martin, who just happened to be Jackie's boss and the founder of Mona Michelle cosmetics. "Do something, Victor," she insisted. "He's making a mockery of this lovely woman's hospitality."

"What would you have me do, my pet?" Victor Martin, financial mogul and cosmetic magnate, was an exceedingly old man. He still boasted a full head of hair, but that's where Father Time's generosity had ended. His skin was loose and wrinkled and ravaged with liver spots. His posture was stooped, his shoulders rounded. His gait was so unsteady, he couldn't take a step without clutching his cane in one hand and his wife's arm with the other. On his back he wore a portable oxygen pack that allowed a continuous flow of air to be pumped into his nostrils. I admired his pluck, but I questioned the wisdom of his decision to lead a bevy of beautiful blondes through France when he looked as if he'd be more comfortable resting in a skilled nursing care facility.

33

"Hey, Irv, why don't you try the cider?" suggested the man who occupied the seat next to Tilly. "Guaranteed to be easier on your liver." He'd introduced himself as Cal Jolly from Minnesota, a self-effacing guy in his fifties who was traveling with his dad, Woodrow Jolly the Third, a spry octogenarian of Victor Martin's generation, but without Victor's cane, oxygen pack, wife, or hair.

"Maybe he doesn't *like* cider," Woody spoke up in a voice that was surprisingly strong and confident. He scratched an ear that had grown too big for his bald head and fixed his son with a frosty look. "Would you stop trying to save folks from themselves? You young people have gone way overboard with the health issues. He's not gonna live forever, Cal. None of us are. So if the man wants to pickle his organs in a sea of booze, let him."

Irv tipped his head. "Thank you for that, shir."

"You're very welcome. And speaking of living forever"—Woody's eyes twinkled as he addressed his captive audience—"have any of you failed to take advantage of the pre-planning options offered by your local—"

"Dad!" Cal went red-faced. "Will you give it a rest? You're on holiday. We're *all* on holiday."

"Misfortune can strike at any moment," Woody fired back. "Even on holiday. Which is why it makes so much sense to make those important end-of-life decisions *before* the need arises." He probed our faces like a kindly grandfather, lecturing us in a hushed, almost hypnotic voice. "Advanced funeral planning is a gift that eases the emotional trauma of a loved one's passing by enabling the grief-stricken family to focus on the more personal aspects of the event. The staff at Jolly's Funeral Home has treated families with the utmost dignity and respect since my great-grandfather embalmed his first corpse in 1869."

We stared at him, dumbstruck.

"Oh, I get it," Bernice piped up. "The cruise company hired its own undertakers because they heard Emily was traveling with us. Someone finally wised up. Now we won't have to make any unscheduled stops to offload bodies."

"Bodies?" Virginia Martin's gaze darted between me and Bernice. "What bodies?"

Tilly shook her head. "You don't want to know."

"Oh, yes, I do. Why did the cruise company hire undertakers because of Emily?"

"We prefer to be called 'funeral directors,'" interrupted Cal, "a term that polls much more favorably with focus groups than undertaker, which ranks a notch below garden slug and three notches above Congress. And no one hired us. We're just a group of ordinary businessmen who decided to take our annual conference on the road. Or the boat, as the case may be."

"Would anyone like a business card?" Woody pulled a small leather case out of the inside pocket of his jacket. "It lists our 1-800 phone number, FAX, email, website, Facebook page, Twitter account, blog address, Pinterest accoun—"

"No one needs our business card," said Cal as he leaned over to swipe the leather case out of his father's hand.

"Shoo!" Woody knocked his son's hand away. "Here's the problem with you, Cal. You're not willing to market. Everyone in this room is a potential client, but *nooo*. You don't even want me to hand out our damn business cards!"

"This is neither the time nor the place, Dad. You can't meet people for the first time and launch into a spiel about advanced funeral planning."

"Why not?"

"Because it depresses people!" Cal flung out his hand. "Look at the effect you've had on Bernice. Have you ever seen a more miserable face?"

Osmond flicked his hand in an "aw, go on," gesture. "Don't blame that on your dad, son. She always looks like that."

"I don't care how miserable she looks," bristled Virginia Martin. "I want to know why Emily is working in collusion with undertakers."

"Funeral directors," repeated Cal with a hint of impatience.

Victor Martin cleared his throat with such force, he nearly popped the oxygen tube from his nose. He stabbed his cane in the direction of the coffee table. "While my wife conducts her inquisition, would someone be kind enough to pour me a glass of the Calvados?"

I couldn't quite figure out Victor's accent. It was so subtle as to be undetectable to the untrained ear, but I was pretty sure he hadn't been born and raised in Houston.

Virginia swung her head around in slow motion, pinning her husband with her gaze. "Are you insane?"

"Does it matter?" he wheezed. "I want a drink."

A spark of temper flared in her eyes. "Really? Well, go right ahead, darling. I'm sure a shot of brandy will work wonders for your balance."

"Ish worked wonders for mine!" crowed Irv.

"Give that man a business card," cried Woody as he sailed a card toward him ... and Osmond ... and Victor ... and—

Click-clack click-clack.

Eyes stilled. Heads cocked. Ears listened.

"What was that?" asked Cal.

"Shounds like the noise my knee makes when it pops outta joint," said Irv.

Click-clack click-clack.

"It's a cricket!" marveled Osmond.

"THERE'S BUGS IN HERE?" squealed Bernice, jerking her feet off the floor.

"Where's it coming from?" asked Osmond, hardly able to contain his excitement as he came to attention like a quail-sniffing bird dog.

Smiling precociously, Madeleine waved her hand in the air, revealing a flat, stubby gadget that was shaped like a pack of gum but measured no longer than a child's whistle. Holding it between her thumb and index finger, she depressed the snapping plate and clicked it again. "You are quite correct, Monsieur Osmond. You have heard of the crickets, yes?"

"I sure have. The army handed them out to the troops who parachuted into Normandy the night before the D-Day invasion. Clicking those things was the only way the landing force could tell if a fella was friend or foe in the dark. That one sure is shiny. What's it made of? Brass?"

"*Oui.* I found it in a meadow when I was a child, but others have found them in forests and apple orchards, graveyards and roadside ditches—anywhere they can use their expensive metal detectors." She pressed it to her chest. "It is my most prized possession ... and a reminder of the sacrifice that so many strangers made for my country. Parisians may be guilty of having short memories, but here in

Normandy, where the liberating forces fought such bloody battles, we will never forget."

"What about the French Resistance?" asked Tilly. "Was your family involved in the Underground efforts to sabotage the Nazi war machine? Or is that too personal a question to ask?"

"*Mais oui!*" Madeleine enthused. "My family played a crucial role in the liberation effort. My grandmother rode her bicycle through Nazi enclaves to deliver coded messages about the expected Allied invasion to other members of the Resistance. Her brother removed railroad ties, loosened spikes, and planted explosives to derail the trains that carried their munitions and fuel. My family placed itself in grave danger to defeat the Nazis, and for their efforts, they paid a very dear price."

The room grew so hushed, I could hear the mechanical whirr of individual seconds ticking by on an antique desk clock.

"It was a devastating time for my family," Madeleine confided in a pained voice. "When the BBC delivered the message that all of France had been waiting for—that the invasion was upon us—the Resistance took action. They blew up bridges, cut telegraph and phone lines, shut down nearly all communications between the occupation army and Berlin. Everyone knew their role. Several members of the Underground from our town made their way to the cliff at Pointe du Hoc, the coastal stronghold that the Germans had fortified with their most powerful artillery guns, which were aimed toward the Channel, ready to open fire on an invasion fleet."

"I'll say they were powerful," Osmond agreed. "They were hundred and fifty-five millimeter cannons."

Irv let out an off-key whistle. "That's not a cannon. Ish a Death Shtar."

"They hoped to create a distraction large enough to draw troops away from their bunkers and gun emplacements. The only way the German guns would be stilled was if no troops remained alive to fire them."

Virginia Martin clucked her disapproval. "Sounds like a recipe for suicide if you ask me."

"It was a great test of courage, my pet." Victor's tone was harsh with censure. "Something that few people know anything about."

"I hope enough folks went to get the job done," said Woody. "The Jerrys had a machine gun called the MG-42 that could mow a whole squad down in half a second." He punctuated his statement with an emphatic nod. "I oughta know. I spent a helluva lot of time diving out of their path in Italy."

"Five people undertook the mission to Pointe du Hoc," Madeleine continued. "They cut through barbed wire barriers. They booby-trapped potholes. They set off small explosions. At least, that had been their intent. We'll never know if they enjoyed even a small measure of success because they never returned from their mission."

Another silence descended, followed by Cal asking in a flat voice, "Were they captured?"

Madeleine shook her head. "Many days after the major battle ceased, the remains of my grandmother's brother and three others were found clustered in one spot on the cliff, as if they had been lined up and executed. One body was never found. We've come to believe that this missing person was a Nazi collaborator. A traitor within the Resistance movement. He warned the Germans of the mission and, for his cooperation was allowed to escape, while the others were killed."

Uff-da. My perception of World War II had been tempered by distance, time, and reruns of *Hogan's Heroes*, but to the local families who had lost loved ones on the front lines, there would never be anything even remotely humorous about it. "Was the family of the man who betrayed the mission ostracized by the people in your town?"

Madeleine hesitated, bitterness and regret darkening her eyes. "We never learned which person was the traitor."

I frowned. "Not even by process of elimination? If you found the remains of four bodies, wouldn't the traitor be the person whose body you didn't find?"

"In normal circumstances, yes. But in this instance, no. My grandmother identified her brother from the fragments of two gold incisors left in his skull. It was the only recognizable part of him. The other three victims were charred beyond recognition from the Allied bombardments on the morning of the invasion. There was nothing left to distinguish one from the other—no clothing, pocket watches, ammunition belts. But we considered it a blessing that their personal effects were incinerated in the bombing rather than end up as trophies of war in the hands of the men who slaughtered them."

Osmond looked suddenly distracted, as if he'd just recalled leaving a pot of water boiling on his stove before he left for vacation.

"What about the artillery guns?" Cal inquired. "Did the Allied bombing runs destroy them?"

"*Pssht.* Even I can answer that," said Bernice in a superior tone. "Didn't you ever see *The Longest Day*—that World War II flick starring every leading man in Hollywood? Robert Wagner scales the cliff with Tommy Sands, Paul Anka, and a bunch of unknown stuntmen. They're a special commando force, and their mission is to destroy the big guns. But after they clean out the Germans, they discover there *are* no guns. The bunkers are completely empty. I wanna tell you, even Fabian was ticked off to think he'd done all that climbing for nothing."

Cal looked perplexed. "So … where were the guns?"

"The Germans moved 'em to a safer location," said Osmond. "About half a mile inland. To an apple orchard. For all the good it did them. A couple of army rangers found 'em and placed incendiary grenades in the firing apparatus. When they detonated 'em, all the metal parts got welded together in a big molten clump. Those guns weren't worth a lick after that. A pea shooter woulda done more damage."

I stared at Osmond, thunderstruck at the depth of his knowledge. The guns, the clicker, the tides? How did he know all this stuff? And then it hit me.

Even though he *claimed* not to have cable TV, he could be pulling the wool over everyone's eyes simply to avoid having to host the gang's weekly get-togethers to watch reruns of *Family Feud* on the Game Show Channel. I shot him a suspicious look. He was watching the Military History Channel on the sly. He had to be.

"Grandmama!" Madeleine propelled herself out of her chair and hurried across the room to assist an elderly woman who appeared in the doorway. She was small-boned, arrow straight, and wore her white hair in a braid that formed a tidy coil around her head. Her cheekbones were high and angular, her complexion remarkably smooth. Her piercing blue eyes snapped with animation and good humor, and when she smiled, I caught a glimpse of the stunning beauty she must have been decades ago.

Madeleine cradled her arm around the woman's shoulders and planted a kiss on her head. "Mesdames and messieurs, this is a special treat. Allow me to introduce my grandmother, Solange Ducat."

Solange hugged her shawl more closely to her body and tipped her head. "*Bonjour tout le monde.*"

"*Bonjour,*" we offered in response, all except Osmond, whose breath suddenly caught in his throat like a fish bone. His eyes grew round, his face turned white. He swayed slightly forward, as if he were about to keel over.

Oh, my God! He was having a heart attack!

Propelling myself out of my chair, I clamped a steadying hand on his arm. "Easy does it. Stay calm. I just took a CPR refresher course, so I know exactly what to do. Someone help me get him on the floor!"

Irv swung his cane upward, poised it against Osmund's shoulder, and gave him a shove.

"What are you doing?" I shrieked.

"He*llll*p-ing him to the floor!"

Osmond batted the cane away and gaped at the woman. "Solange?" he choked out. "Solange Spenard?"

"*Oui.*" She regarded him with her impossibly blue eyes, her face registering surprise, followed by bewilderment. "I was once Madame Spenard."

Using my arm for support, Osmond boosted himself to his feet and stared across the room at her, his legs so wobbly, I thought they might collapse beneath him. "It's me." His voice shook with Richter scale intensity. "The chicken man G.I. with the broken leg."

A dozen emotions flitted across the woman's face before she pressed her hand to her mouth. "*Mere de Dieu*," she said in a breathless whisper. "Ozmund?"

Irv thumped his cane against the leg of the coffee table. "Hey, if this fella's not about to croak, could we get shome more Calvados over here?"

FOUR

"I was so frightened when I found an American soldier hiding in our barn, but I could see he was terribly hurt, so I ran back for my papa, and we sneaked him into zee house."

Solange Spenard Ducat sat on the living room sofa beside Osmond, her thigh touching his pant leg, her shoulder brushing his arm, her fingers intertwined with his in a kind of lovers knot configuration. "The silly boy had parachuted into a tree and broke his leg when he cut himself from his harness."

"That's because it was pitch black," teased Osmond. "I couldn't tell how tall the tree was."

Although Tilly and I had dragged our chairs close to the sofa so we wouldn't miss a word of the unfolding story, most of the other guests had tired of the reminiscing and were meandering around the room, snapping photos, shooting videos, and trying not to look bored. Madeleine was making a concerted effort to play hostess to her guests while being attentive to Osmond and her grandmother, but it was pretty much a lost cause since Bernice had commandeered her as her own personal photographer.

"We had to take evasive action once we hit the Normandy coast because of German flak," Osmond continued, "so we ended up making our jump miles away from the drop zone." He bowed his head and lowered his voice. "My whole squad got wiped out in that jump. All except me."

Solange patted his forearm with a familiar hand, seeming to ease his grief with the simple intimacy of her touch.

I looked from one to the other, then sat up ramrod straight in my chair. *Uff-da!* Was I bearing witness to more than the casual reunion of two old friends here? Because their body language was suggesting that back in 1944, they might have been a lot closer than mere friends. A *whole* lot closer.

"Did you get me posing in front of the sideboard yet?" Bernice's voice. Somewhere behind me. "The light's pretty good right here."

"*Oui*, madame," droned Madeleine. "I have you in front of the sideboard, the china cabinets, the sofa, the—"

"Well, take another one." The sandpaper rasp that was her voice morphed into a syrupy lilt. "Have I mentioned that I used to be a magazine model?"

Tilly leaned forward on her walking stick, curiosity oozing from every pore as she zeroed in on Osmond. "So you became entangled in a tree and broke your leg when you fell to the ground. However did you manage the hike to Solange's barn?"

"I rigged a crutch out of a broken tree limb, and then I headed away from the sound of artillery fire. Don't even know which direction it was because my compass got smashed in the jump. It's pretty embarrassin' for an Iowan to admit, but I was lost about as bad as the Israelites in the wilderness."

On a brighter note, at least it didn't take him forty years to find his way back to civilization.

He gave his head a disbelieving shake. "Eighteen thousand Allied troops parachuted into Normandy, but I never ran into another living soul that whole night. No Americans. No Germans. No one. Kinda felt like I'd arrived for the war all by myself."

"Osmond," I said gently, "does anyone in the gang have the slightest inkling that you participated in the actual D-Day invasion?"

"Nope. If I'd told 'em I'd been to war, the Dicks would've asked, 'Which one? Revolutionary or Civil?'"

"I'm not sure how you've kept it to yourself all these years," marveled Tilly.

Osmund shrugged. "If you'd seen the things I saw, you'da kept it to yourself, too."

"But you're a hero," I insisted.

He shook his head. "The fellas who jumped out of those planes and never lived to tell about it are the real heroes, Emily. Not me."

"That's not true, Ozmund. Have you not told your friends what you did for my family?"

His Adam's apple bobbed uncomfortably. "No need getting into that now. Far as I'm concerned, it's all water over the dam."

"*Non!* You tell them, Ozmund Chelsvig! If not for you, my mama and papa would have died at zee hands of zee Germans." Her voice grew sharp. "*I* would have died!"

"Hey, folks," Cal called out from the front window, "looks like the bus is here to pick us up."

"But I still have room on my memory card for five hundred and forty-four more pictures of myself," whined Bernice.

"If you do not tell them, Ozmund, *I* will," threatened Solange. She skewered him with a fierce look. "Well?"

He responded with a stubborn snort. "All right, all right."

My mom and dad had standoffs like this all the time, but it was usually over an issue that was even more vital to marriages than trust and fidelity: control of the TV remote.

"Solange's parents hid me in a secret room they'd built under their front staircase, but the day after I showed up, so did the Germans. Three of them came knocking, and it wasn't a social visit. They knew about the secret room and the family's involvement in the Underground, so they arrived to voice their objection." He thrust out his bottom lip and shrugged. "That's about it."

I frowned. "That can't be it. You can't end a story like that."

"Why not?"

Tilly rolled her eyes. "You've given us the exposition and the conflict, but you've left out the resolution. Without a resolution, we're dealing with random plot points that go nowhere. So you need an ending, accompanied by a satisfying denouement, if you can manage it."

"Confound it." Sucking in a lungful of air, he burst out with, "So the Germans barged into the house with their threats and guns, and I made sure they never left. Is that resolution enough for you?"

I looked at Tilly. Tilly looked at me. We both looked at Solange.

"Zee three men shot their way into Ozmund's room, but he was waiting for them, barricaded behind pillows, flat on his back, with his broken leg bound in splints. He returned fire, and when zee shooting stopped, it was Ozmund who proved to be zee better marksman. My brave little chee-ken man."

"Mesdames, messieurs, your tour director is waiting for you by the front gate." Madeleine strolled around the room, herding guests toward the doorway.

"Chicken man?" I stared at Osmond, baffled. "I—uh, I don't get it."

"He wore a chee-ken on his shoulder," said Solange. "A little screaming chee-ken."

"Chicken?" Tilly straightened her spine. "On a military badge? I seriously doubt it was a fowl. More likely it was an eagle. A screaming eagle...which just happens to be the emblem of the 101st Airborne Infantry." She regarded Osmond with a look bordering on awe. "You belonged to the 101st?"

He gave his head a nod. "Yup. I was one of the fellas who wore a screaming chee-ken on his shoulder sleeve." He smiled impishly and squeezed Solange's hand as he sidled a glance at her.

"When he's very naughty and pokes fun of my accent, I ignore him," she announced, nose in the air, head tilted at a coy angle, gaze averted, as if she were a young ingénue fending off a suitor whose advances she desperately wanted. And in that instant I could see them as they might have been decades ago, snatching moments of intimate pleasure from a secret look, a shared touch, in a world that had gone completely mad.

"The 101st Airborne was only the most celebrated, the most illustrious, the most battle-hardened division in the entire army," chattered Tilly. "They led the charge on D-Day. They held the line at the Battle of the Bulge. They—"

"Grandmama?" Madeleine came up behind Solange and placed a gentle hand on her shoulder. "Monsieur Osmond must leave us now. His coach is waiting outside."

"Leave? But he just arrived."

"Thank you for your hospitality." Virginia Martin bobbed her head at Madeleine as she guided her husband past the sofa. "I'm sure you did the best you could under the circumstances."

Victor halted his steps and jerked his hand away from his wife's arm, irritation causing his facial muscles to grow rigid. "My dear young woman"—he shuffled his feet slightly to face Madeleine—"I've heard rumors that my wife was once an engaging and gracious creature, but I've never had the good fortune of bearing witness to it myself. You are beautiful and kind, and I thank you for opening your home to us." He tipped his head politely and shifted his gaze to Solange. "And Mrs. Ducat, permit me to say that you are as lovely today as you were—"

He paused suddenly, as if his brain realized what was about to come out of his mouth and closed his windpipe to avoid disaster. He stiffened with panic for a brief second before he assumed a calmer demeanor, his brain and mouth apparently on the same page again. "You're as lovely today as I imagine you were when Mr. Chelsvig first met you." He inhaled a deep, wheezy breath. "Your eyes are quite haunting, my dear. A man could never forget a woman with your eyes."

Virginia elevated her hand to admire the jewels bedecking her fingers. "Do you know the only thing worse than a fool, Victor?"

"I expect you're about to tell me."

"An old fool."

He pivoted slowly toward her. His voice became gruff. "Help me out to the bus."

"Thanks for everything, Madeleine." Cal offered a brief valedictory wave. "I'm going to pick up some of that Calvados. Good stuff!"

Taking my cue from Cal, I stood up. "I guess we should be leaving, too. Don't want to keep the coach driver waiting."

"*Non.*" Solange clutched Osmond's hand. "Not yet. There's … there's much I should tell you."

Woody Jolly maneuvered around my chair to sketch a valiant, if arthritic, bow before the sofa. "Ladies, thank you for the conversation and refreshments. The obnoxious drunk I could have done without." He extended his hand, palm up, to Solange. "May I?"

After a moment's hesitation, Solange placed her palm atop his, smiling shyly when he pressed his lips to the back of her hand.

"I don't know if that's the way you French do it," he blurted out with enthusiasm, "but it sure works for me. I've wanted to do that all my life. 'Course, if I tried it with a woman in the States, I'd get my face slapped."

He released her hand but continued to linger, apparently not at all worried that his dawdling might earn him the dreaded status of last person on the bus. "You're such a beautiful woman, Solange, but like me and Osmond here, you're getting up there in age. Do you mind my asking if you've made advanced funeral plans yet? For a nominal fee, Jolly Funeral Home offers an online consulting service to help you decide exactly what arrangements will best suit your needs. And it doesn't matter that you live here and I live in the States. We're all connected now through the Internet, and we accept all major credit cards."

Solange stared at him, looking too speechless to respond.

"I brought a brochure with me. How about I leave it with you, and if you're interested, you can contact me through our website. You have a computer, don't you?" He slapped the numerous zippered pockets of his jacket in search of the missing document. "Can't remember which pocket I stuffed it in."

Madeleine waved him off. "Please, monsieur, it is not necessary. We—"

"Sure it's necessary. Folks in your grandmother's and my generation don't want to spend the afterlife cooped up in a jar the size of a flour canister. We want to be able to stretch out in a cheerful casket that's lined with tufted satin and rest our heads on a pillow made of one hundred percent breathable cotton. Aha! Paydirt." He unzipped a long, vertical pocket and slid his hand into—

"*Mon Dieu*," cried Solange, eyes wild, mouth contorted. "*MON DIEU!*"

Woody froze, brochure in hand. "Was it something I said?"

Solange hurled a barrage of rapid-fire French at him, her voice rising to a crescendo, the cords in her neck straining so violently against her flesh, they looked as if they might burst.

"What is it, *cherie*?" Madeleine darted around the sofa and sat down. "What is wrong?"

Solange's hands flew into the air. Her voice grew shrill. Her words spilled out of her mouth so quickly, even Madeleine looked baffled.

"Please, Grandmama. *Lentement*. I can't understand what you're saying."

Cal poked his head in the door. "Sorry to break up your farewells, folks, but I've just been told by the head honcho that if you're not on the bus in three minutes flat, our schedule is going to be seriously screwed up. You hear me, Dad?"

Osmond threw me a pleading look. "Emily, please, I can't leave Solange like this."

"Well, you can't stay here," said Tilly as she pulled him unceremoniously to his feet. "And you know you can't."

Woody backpedaled away from the sofa, a sheepish look on his face. "How about I leave the brochure here for you?" he suggested, dropping it on the coffee table in his hasty retreat. "Maybe you can check it out when you're in a better frame of mind."

Solange stabbed a damning finger at him as he rushed out the door. "*C'est toi!*" she scolded in a high-pitched shriek that bristled with venom. "*C'est toi!*"

The bus horn blared long and loudly, causing a wave of panic to ripple down my spine. "C'mon, Osmond." I grabbed his arm. "We've gotta go. I can guarantee you won't want to be anywhere around me if I have to walk back to the boat in five-inch wedges."

"Solange?" He reached out his knobby fingers to touch her, but she was collapsed in Madeleine's arms, seemingly inconsolable as she broke out in anguished tears, the sounds of her tormented wails filling the room. He took a step back, bowing his head with a remembered sadness. "She cried just like that the day she found her brother." He tried to catch Madeleine's eye, but she was so fixated on soothing her grandmother that she no longer seemed aware of the presence of other people in the room.

"I guess maybe we should go," he rasped, looking utterly bereft.

Once outside, we hurried down the front path in a footrace to the waiting coach.

"What was wrong with her?" Osmond puzzled. "What was she yelling at him? Does anyone know what *say twah* means?"

"It means, 'it's you,'" I said, dredging up a few remnants of my high school French. Solange had screamed *It's you* as if in that moment she had somehow recognized him.

FIVE

"MY SUGGESTION ABOUT THE makeup demonstration was such a hit." Jackie sat at the mirrored vanity in my cabin, applying gloss with a Mona Michelle lipstick wand. "If we could figure out a way to have more home visits, I'd make a killing. And you know what that would mean. *Hel-looo*, pink Porsche."

I slid into the strappy heels that elevated my little black dress to dinnerwear status. "Goes to show what I know. I take back what I said about your idea being tacky."

"You're forgiven. I don't expect someone who specializes in old people to know anything about product testing on upwardly mobile target groups."

Our boat was moored in a tidal estuary of the Seine, tied up alongside a granite quay in the river port of Honfleur, a picturesque town whose architectural design illustrated the passage of time from the Middle Ages—with its half-timber houses, cobbled lanes, and cramped alleyways—to the Renaissance, with its tall, slate-fronted tenements shouldered rooftop to rooftop around an inner harbor that had been "newly" excavated a brief four hundred years ago. My balcony faced Honfleur's main boulevard—a long stretch of road flanked by upscale wood and brick apartments on one side, a grassy esplanade on the other, and a noisy stream of horn-tooting traffic in between.

"So what products did you showcase in your demonstration?" I asked, surprised that the toothsome trio had given their blessing to anything Jackie had suggested.

"Everything! We did makeovers. Complete makeovers! When our hostess found out what the four of us did for a living, she begged us to share our expertise with her family, so we gave all the Roussel women miracle makeovers. Really, Emily, properly applied face powder can make *all* the difference in a woman's life."

It took me a moment to peel back the layers of what she'd just said to understand the gist of what had actually happened. "So the four of you didn't charge through the door with Mona Michelle concealer sticks in hand, all prepped to turn eager faces from ordinary to extraordinary? Your hostess had to sweet-talk you into it?"

She stared at my reflected image in the mirror, eyes thoughtful. "*Ewww*. Very nice. Turning a face from ordinary to extraordinary. Can I borrow that?"

"You can *have* it if you'll answer my question."

She swiveled around on her stool, looking a bit twitchy and awkward. "Okay. The girls threw major hissy fits that I was inviting them to actually *work* during our home visit, and they *hated* my idea about an international arm of Mona Michelle. They think domestic sales is where the action is. To quote Krystal, 'If it ain't broke, it's not broken.'"

Actually, considering the source, that was pretty profound.

"So they nixed my suggestion about makeup demonstrations for the host family, but after Mrs. Roussel came up with the very same idea, they were totally on board! I was so touched, Emily. Believe me, it takes a lot of character to execute a complete one-eighty in the space of an hour. Not everyone can do it with such style, but the girls are so anxious to please, they made it look easy."

She cast puppy dog eyes on me. "You're one of my best friends, Emily, so don't take this the wrong way, but Bobbi, Krystal, and Dawna? They're like ... the sisters I never had."

A chorus of digital *dings* chimed overhead before a man's voice floated out from the cabin intercom. "Ladies and gentleman, the restaurant doors are now open."

As if on cue, we heard a host of doors slam in the corridor. A low rumble of voices. High-pitched laughter.

Jackie capped her lipstick wand and sprang to her feet. "Hey, the boat's moving."

As she hurried onto my balcony to watch the boat ease away from the quay, I crossed the floor to check my hair and makeup in the vanity mirror. "So how many makeovers did you end up doing?"

"Three. Bobbi and Krystal grabbed the two Roussel daughters and Dawna took charge of Mrs. Roussel."

"So ... who did you work on?"

"I didn't have anyone to work on. I supervised."

"But ... if it was your idea to begin with, shouldn't you have gotten first dibs on which family member you wanted to remake?"

She stepped back into the cabin and closed the sliding glass door. "This may come as a shock to you, but I don't mind taking a back seat so others can assume their rightful spots in the limelight."

"Since when?"

She fisted her hand on her hip and drilled me with a fierce look. "You know, Emily, you don't really appreciate how selfless I am. But the girls have seen it firsthand. Laugh if you must, but I fully expect they'll be singing my praises to Victor so loudly, I'm going to be shame-faced with embarrassment."

I regarded her, deadpan. "Right." Grabbing my clutch, I turned off the overhead lights and motioned Jackie out the door in front of me.

At the far end of the corridor, guests were clogged together at the entrance of the restaurant like gumballs waiting to funnel through the mouth of a narrow-necked bottle. The *Renoir* carried only sixty passengers, housed in outside cabins on a single deck, but from the looks of things, every last one of them was in line ahead of us, pushing their way through the congestion to the dining room.

"Do we have assigned seating?" asked Jackie as we took our place at the back of the scrum.

"Nope. We get to sit wherever we want."

She cleared her throat and lowered her voice. "The girls will naturally want me to sit with them, so if there's only one seat at their table, you don't mind if I take it, do you?"

"Knock yourself out. I'm sure I'll find an open seat somewhere. There's lots of new people to meet."

"*Thank you!*" She flung her arms around me, crushing me against her as if I were a nut in need of cracking. "I'm *so* relieved. That's what I love about you Emily. You'd happily forgo an opportunity to shmooze with the big wigs at the Mona Michelle table in order to share a lackluster meal with a bunch of dotty strangers. You are *so* evolved."

Retrieving a mirrored compact from her pocketbook, she rechecked the gloss on her lips. "So, now that we have that out of the way ... did anything happen on your home visit that's worth mentioning?"

"*Uhh*—A guy in our group was hammered out of his head, we barely escaped having to buy advanced funeral plans, and Osmund was reunited with a woman who helped save his life during World War II."

She snapped her compact shut. "So, nothing out of the ordinary."

The bottleneck at the entrance to the dining room suddenly broke up, allowing guests to stampede through the doors like shoppers at a blowout sale. We exchanged "*Bon soirs*" with the official greeter at the door, sanitized our hands with a squirt of gel from the stationary dispenser, then angled off to our right, circling around the food station that occupied the center of the room.

Guests were loitering behind chairs, waving their arms to friends, flashing the number of seats still available, sitting down, standing up, bumping into the guests standing at the chairs behind them. Tables were set up to accommodate four, six, or eight guests, and each table abutted a sparkling clean, floor-to-ceiling window that overlooked the river and its traffic. What could be more thrilling than the prospect of oohing and ahhing over the spectacular views of the Seine while we dined?

Well, one thing might be more thrilling.

Finding an empty seat. Why were all the tables full?

"There they are ... with some bald guy I've never seen before. *Ew!* They've saved two seats. C'mon." Jackie seized my hand and sprinted toward a round table that occupied the far corner, arriving two steps behind an elderly couple who'd just claimed the chairs by pulling them out. "Excuse me," Jackie said in a voice breathy with apology, "but I believe those seats are taken."

"I know they are." The gentleman grinned. "By me and my wife." He tapped his name tag. "I'm Leo. This is Izetta."

"What I meant was, they're being saved for me and my friend."

"No they're not." Bobbi Benedict regarded Jackie from beneath the brim of her pale blue Western hat. "It's first come, first serve. No seat saving allowed." She glanced at her two blonde companions for confirmation. "Idn't that right?"

Alligator Boots, whose name tag identified her as Dawna Chestnut from Nacogdoches, Texas, inched her rosy lips into a smug smile. "Sure is," she drawled as she hiked her strapless bustier toward her chin.

Snakeskin Jeans dusted her cheek with the tail end of her long platinum hair, her eyes gleaming with satisfaction. "Ditto what Dawna said." I glanced at her name tag. Krystal Cake. Abilene, Texas.

I tugged on Jackie's dress. "There's an empty seat over there. I'm going to—"

"Mom? Dad?" A middle-aged woman in a clingy cocktail dress intercepted Leo and Izetta before they could sit. "We're saving seats for you on the other side of the room. You want to join us? I have your pill caddies." She flashed a smile at the Mona Michelle elite.

"Sorry." Grasping her parents by their elbows, she gently navigated them away from the table.

Jackie shot a puzzled look across the table at Bobbi. "I thought you said there was no seat saving."

"There isn't. And if that gal had read through the booklet they left in her cabin, she'd know it, too."

"I've failed to read any policy that prohibits guests from saving seats," rasped Victor as he motioned for Jackie and me to sit down. He was without his oxygen pack tonight, so his breathing sounded a little more forced.

"You have no credibility," scoffed Virginia. "You forgot to pack your reading glasses. You can't read anything." She turned in her chair to scan the room. "Where's the sommelier?"

"The *what*?" asked Woody, who had somehow ended up at our table rather than at his son Cal's.

"The *sum-el-yay*," she repeated in three drawn-out syllables. "The wine steward."

"Well, would you listen to those French words fallin' out of your mouth?" gushed Dawna. "You sound just like a native. Victor never mentioned you could speak *two* whole languages. I am *so* impressed."

"Don't be." Virginia fixed her with an imperious stare. "Sommelier isn't a French word; it's English. Perhaps instead of a new-and-improved retractable lip liner, you should think about buying yourself a thesaurus."

Confusion clouded Dawna's eyes, chased away by a sudden peal of laughter. "You are *such* a tease," she scolded. "Go buy myself a thesaurus. You know very well those creatures have been extinct for at least two thousand years."

Gee, Victor's wife might not be the easiest person to warm up to, but I was *really* beginning to like her.

Virginia angled a meaningful look at her husband. "However do you manage to keep the company afloat? Creative bookkeeping?"

"Leave her alone, my pet. The day Mona Michelle expands into the dictionary business will be the day I listen to your complaint."

Woody cast admiring looks around the table as he shook out his napkin. "I've lived a lot of years, ladies. More than I'll ever admit to. But I have to confess, I can't remember a time in my life when I've had the pleasure of being surrounded by so many beautiful women all at the same time. I feel like I've died and gone to heaven."

"Aw, aren't you just the sweetest man?" bubbled Krystal, rewarding him with a thousand-watt smile enhanced by flirtatious eye movements.

"And while I'm on the subject of dying, have any of you lovely ladies ever stopped to realize that your next meal might be your last?"

I dropped my head to my chest. *Not again.*

Dawna gasped. "The ship's run out of food?"

"No, no. I'm sure the ship's not going to run out of anything. But the question you should be asking yourselves is ... have *you* run out of time on our lovely planet? You need to be prepared for the end, ladies, and it's never too soon to start, which is why it's so important for you to think about advanced funeral planning."

Bobbi gaped at Woody, her mouth sagging open. "You're jokin', aren't you, sugah?"

"Advanced planning is no joke," cautioned Woody. "In fact, with the cost of living on the rise, it makes good financial sense to pre-pay your funeral in today's dollars rather than the inflated currency of tomorrow. We have payment plans to fit every budget, including a rather generous layaway plan where a client can—"

"Mr. Jolly," Victor interrupted, "I applaud your efforts to advertise your product. Being a businessman myself, I understand it behooves us to look at every situation as a marketing opportunity, but if you persist in hijacking the conversation to push your business model, I'll have you removed from this table. Do I make myself clear?"

Woody leaned back in his chair and folded his arms across his chest. "I'd like to see you try."

Unh-oh. I hoped this didn't escalate into a Mexican standoff. But at least there was no way it would turn into a pissing contest. Guys this old could barely provide urine samples.

Krystal gave Woody a playful swat on his arm. "Us girls don't wanna hear about no layaway plan at no funeral parlor, darlin'. Y'all need to target another age group." She scanned the other tables for possibilities. "Like … anyone else in the room."

"You must have missed a recent nightly news segment," I piped up, directing my comment at Krystal. "They posted the results of a decades' long medical study that showed that today's eighty- and ninety-year-olds are, by comparison, much healthier than the majority of today's thirty-year-olds. So there's a good possibility that most of the people in this room will end up living a lot longer than *you* will."

"I don't think so." She gave me a dismissive look. "Sounds like a bunch of liberal fiction to me."

Dawna furrowed her brow. "Is fiction the one that's real or make believe? I can never remember."

"Why don't you look it up in your thesaurus?" droned Virginia.

"*Ewww-weee!*" Krystal grabbed the edge of the table. "Can y'all feel that?" She suddenly looked a little woozy. "We're pickin' up speed. You know what that means?"

"We're going faster?" asked Jackie.

"It means I better pop a pill before I embarrass myself."

Too late for that.

"Krystal can get motion sick just standin' in one place," Bobbi explained, "so she's gotta take some honkin' big pills to help her walk without hurlin'. Don't ya, sugah?"

Krystal mined her pocketbook for a plastic pill container, flipped open the top, and popped a softgel the size of a dum dum bullet into her mouth, washing it down with a gulp of water.

"How come my motion sickness pills don't look like yours?" asked Woody. He removed a foil blister pack from his shirt pocket and slapped it on the table. "Mine look more like baby aspirin. Am I getting ripped off? I keep telling the druggist I need something stronger, but he keeps selling me the same damn pills. Airplane turbulence really does me in, even after I've chewed a couple of the things. And the older I get, the worse it gets. If the river gets choppy, I'll probably be holed up in my cabin 'til Paris."

"I buy all my drugs at the vitamin shop, hon, so I never have to deal with druggists giving me the wrong pills. I scan the shelves, read the labels, decide what I need, and buy it in economy-size, tamper-proof bottles. You wanna know the best thing for my kind of motion sickness? Ginger. In thousand-gram caplets."

"You don't consult your physician?" marveled Woody. "You just go out and buy it over the counter?"

"I never buy it over the counter, hon. I always use the self-checkout lane because it's usually a lot faster."

Virginia let out a pained groan accompanied by an impatient look around the room. "*Where* is the wine steward?" She stuck her bejeweled hand in the air and snapped her fingers. "You there!"

A man in black tie, tux, and red cummerbund hurried over to our table. "Mesdames, messieurs, I welcome you aboard the *Renoir*. I am Patrice, and it is my pleasure to serve you this evening. You will allow me to show you our wine list?"

"It's about time," huffed Virginia. "Yes, you can show me your wine list. But trust me, if this is an example of the poor service we can expect to receive for the rest of the trip, I guarantee you'll soon be looking for new employment."

"*Oui*, madame. *Pardonne*." He placed a long, narrow placard in her hands. "You would like to order for the table?"

She slid her rhinestone glasses onto her face. "I'm going to order for myself. The rest of them can take care of themselves. And I'm thinking that a fine Chateau Mouton Rothchild would do quite nicely this evening."

While Virginia dithered over vintage year and blend, Victor folded his hands on the table and smiled. "So, my lovelies, tell me about your home visit. Did you dazzle your host family?"

Dawna bounced gleefully in her chair, causing her bustier to plunge toward wardrobe malfunction territory. "We welcomed three new Mona Michelle converts into the fold! Bobbi and Krystal and me had sample products with us, so we—"

"—convinced our hostess that we could erase years from her face with our concealer gel and foundation," chirped Krystal.

"So we did freaking *amazing* makeovers for her and her two daughters," Bobbi enthused. "By the time we finished, they—"

"—were beggin' us to sell them our entire line of daywear products," gushed Dawna. "We left a few samples with them, Victor, but if you really want to make a killing, you gotta—"

"—create an international arm of Mona Michelle!" cried Bobbi.

Jackie came to attention beside me, shooting an adoring look at the blondes before preening like a starlet expecting to be named best actress in a foreign film.

Victor nodded his pleasure. "Personal initiative and enthusiasm for the product, ladies. *This* is why we lead the industry in sales. Your performance continues to exceed my expectations."

"Hey, Patricia." Woody waved his menu at the steward. "One of our entrees is listed here as 'Poison Grille.' I've got two questions for you. Number one: What kind of poison is it? And number two: How do I know it won't kill me?"

Patrice threw a nervous look in Woody's direction. "Poison, monsieur? No, no. That cannot be. *Excusé moi*, madame. Just for a moment."

"I haven't finished with you yet," snapped Virginia as Patrice circled the table to assist Woody.

Victor smiled at his bevy of beauties. "Don't be modest, ladies. I know great ideas need a spark to ignite them. Which one of you was the spark who envisioned the makeovers?"

"I did!" echoed the three blondes in near perfect unison.

Jackie stared at them aghast, her jaw falling with the speed of an excavator dropping its clam bucket.

"All three of you came up with the idea?" asked Victor.

They braved whiplash as they took sudden measure of each other. "We kinda … brainstormed," cooed Bobbi. "Idn't that right, girls?"

"Yes, ma'am," Dawna agreed. "When we were checkin' out that cute little seaside town, that's exactly what we were doin'. Brainstormin' and shoppin'."

Oh, sure. Like they could multitask at such an advanced level.

"And that's when it happened," declared Krystal. "*Zzzzt!* The three of us got zapped by the very same idea at the very same time. It was almost like ... like a religious experience."

A pilgrimage to Lourdes was a religious experience. What the girls were peddling as gospel was an outright lie. I kicked Jackie under the table.

"A printing error," *tsked* Patrice as he hovered over Woody's shoulder. "Not Poison Grille. *Poisson* Grille. Fish, not poison—a delicious pan-fried tilapia with reduced tomato and white wine sauce, presented on carrot mousseline and saffron rice." He poised his pencil over his order pad. "Is that your selection, monsieur?"

"Gimme a burger and fries, with extra ketchup. I'm a real ketchup guy."

Virginia glared at him, her eyes narrowing to slivers. "Exactly where do you think you are? The food court at your local mall?" She motioned to Patrice. "Would you kindly explain the purity of French cuisine to Mr. Jolly?"

"No burgers, monsieur. No fries. But we prepare seven mouthwatering flavors of tomato-based sauce to suit your individual taste." He ranged a look around the table. "Other questions? Yes? No?"

"I've got one." Woody twisted his head around to look up at Patrice. "What kind of end-of-life planning have you done, son? What are you? Thirty-five? Forty? You know, it's never too early to start making arrangements for that inevitable day when—"

"I have a question." Jackie leaned forward and braced her forearms on the table. Jaw hard and nostrils flared, she lasered a squinty look at the blondes. "Why am I remembering that the idea thingie happened a whole lot differently?"

Krystal flashed a coy smile. "You must be misrememberin', sugah."

"Am not."

"You *have* to be misrememberin'," Bobbi agreed. She crushed the brim of her hat and cocked it at a perkier angle. "As I recollect, you weren't even there."

"Was so!"

Dawna gasped. "Are you tryin' to take credit for *our* idea? Now that's just plain disappointin'. Are y'all as disappointed in Jackie as I am, girls?"

How did the saying go? If you can't dispute the facts, attack the messenger?

"Given that my own memory tends to be a bit faulty," Victor blurted out, "I think you ladies are being much too harsh on Jackie. None of us remember events in exactly the same way."

"I'm remembering that no one has taken my drink order yet," fussed Virginia.

"*Pardonne,* madame!" Patrice hurried back to her side, leaving Woody to puzzle over the menu himself.

"It doesn't matter who thought of the idea," conceded Victor. "Shall we call it a group effort? What interests me more are the results of the makeovers." He graced Jackie with an avuncular smile. "Why don't you tell me which products proved to be the most popular with your client."

"She didn't have a client," Krystal answered for her.

Victor frowned. "And why was that?"

"She was too busy taking pictures to bother," Bobbi spoke up.

Jackie let out an indignant breath. "That is *so* not true."

Victor calmed the waters with a palms-down gesture, a technique frequently employed by policemen when mediating domestic altercations, and travelers when expelling air from plastic zipper bags. His tone grew inquisitive. "So if you weren't performing a makeover, what *were* you doing?"

A whisper of uncertainty crept into Jackie's voice. "Well ... I was taking pictures, but—"

"Told y'all," mocked Bobbi.

"I wasn't taking them for myself. I was taking them for someone else. Another guest asked me to shoot some photos of her and her gentleman friend so she could post them in the Summer Getaway section of her Legion of Mary newsletter, so I was being a Good Samaritan."

Legion of Mary newsletter? *Unh-oh.* She was talking about Nana and George. I hoped the photos hadn't turned out too well because there was no way Nana would ever sneak pictures of George past the Legion's editorial board. The newsletter only published "Catholic" content, and for eight decades now George had been a flaming Lutheran. It was too bad Lutherans and Catholics couldn't find common ground that would allow them to celebrate their similarities rather than their differences, because other than the nagging issue of the Pope, I really wasn't sure what separated the two. Well, other than five hundred years of bloody religious strife and dissention.

"And furthermore," Jackie ranted on, "if the three of you hadn't hogged all the females in the host family, no one would have asked me to snap photos for a religious publication that's read by no one other than a handful of saintly octogenarians with pre-dementia and degenerative eye disease!"

Dawna's lips twitched with amusement. "I hate to tell ya, darlin', but whinin' is really unbecomin' to a lady. Idn't that right, girls?"

If this was the blondes' idea of "singing Jackie's praises" to Victor, Jackie might have to rethink the whole sister thing.

Victor sighed. "Could we set the drama aside for the moment, ladies? I've come to a decision that I'd like to share with you."

The girls exchanged breathless looks with each other, but it was apparent from their expressions that they didn't know if they were going to be on the receiving end of a compliment or a reprimand.

"I'm very impressed with the initiative you showed today, no matter whose idea it was originally, so as a token of my appreciation, I'm going to add a small bonus to the perks we've already provided you. Shall we say, a cash award?"

Virginia whipped her head around, her eyes skewering him. "Exactly what do you think you're up to?"

"I'm being spontaneous."

"No, what you're *being* is ridiculous. The board hasn't authorized you to hand out cash awards at your own whim."

"They don't need to. I brought my checkbook."

"Excuse me?" An angry vein popped out on her forehead. "You're making plans to write out checks to your prima donnas from *our* personal account?"

"Yes. That's exactly what I'm planning to do."

"I absolutely forbid it."

"It's going to happen, my pet, so I advise you to spare me the histrionics. Excellence should be rewarded, and I happen to be in a position where I can reward it as much as I like."

"Not with *my* money, you can't."

He fixed her with the same look dragons sport before they incinerate fairytale villages. "*Whose* money?"

Her bravado cracked beneath his gaze, causing her to shrink like a genie being sucked back into her bottle. Lips compressed in an angry slash, chest heaving, she jutted her chin in the air and snapped her head away from him.

"Now, what was I saying?" He grinned, looking immensely proud of himself. "Ah, yes. Does twenty-five thousand dollars sound like a fair amount, ladies?"

Shrieks. Squeals. Hands clapping.

"This is absurd," sniped Virginia. Rising to her feet, she crumpled her napkin into a ball and threw it on the table. "I'm leaving." As Patrice scrambled to pull her chair out, she delivered her parting shot to her husband's face. "I hope it fills you with great pleasure to know you ruin everything you touch, Victor."

"Shall I have a tray delivered to your cabin, madame?" Patrice called after her.

"No! I've lost my appetite."

"Pay no attention to Virginia," Victor soothed in an amused tone. "I don't."

"Can you get back to the part about the money?" urged Krystal. "Are you givin' out twenty-five thousand dollars apiece?"

Victor shook his head. "I plan to make out only one check."

"*Aww.*" Bobbi shot him a hangdog look. "You're gonna make us share?"

"Not at all. The check will go to only one of you."

"Which one?" coaxed Dawna.

"I want to be fair, so I'm not going to rely on partiality or guess-work. The four of you have the highest sales of our entire workforce, but only one of you is at the top of the sales ladder. I'll be presenting the check to that individual."

"C'mon, Victor," Krystal whined in a singsong voice. "Which one of us is it?"

"Frankly, my dears, I don't know. I'll need to make a call to the home office to find out the specific figures, and then I'll be able to make my presentation."

"You're gonna make us wait?" pouted Dawna.

"Waiting a few days for the results will help the four of you build anticipation. You can start a buzz. It should be quite exciting."

Or utterly disastrous. The three blondes and Jackie locked in com-petition for a generous cash prize? Oh, sure. Like that was going to happen without sticks, stones, and at least one major hair-pulling event.

Patrice waved his order pad. "I have no wish to rush you, but if I fail to place your orders soon, the kitchen may run out of your cho-sen entrée. So"— he loomed over Victor's chair—"may I take your order, monsieur?"

"Twenty-five-thousand dollars," mused Krystal in a dreamy voice. "Y'all know what I could do with twenty-five grand? I could remodel my guest bathroom into an automatic weapons room!"

"Or you could buy yourself a pair of jeans that aren't made of snakeskin," cracked Dawna with a honeyed smile on her face. The notion of impending personal wealth had obviously emboldened Dawna into replacing the "All for one and one for all" routine with the ever more popular "Every man for himself."

Krystal's beautiful face shifted slightly out of kilter. "In case you hadn't noticed, hon, I rock my jeans."

Dawna shrugged. "If you say so."

"Snakeskin jeans are my signature."

"They wouldn't be if you could see what you look like from the back."

Krystal's eyes and mouth rounded like bubbles about to burst. "Well, idn't that rich. The person paradin' around in alligator boots is criticizin' *my* snakeskin jeans."

Dawna sneered prettily. "In my corner of Texas, alligator boots are a bigger status symbol than three-tier, window-mounted gun racks."

"Sure they are," retaliated Krystal. "If you're six years old."

"Will the two of you hush up before someone mistakes you for Yankees?" chided Bobbi.

"Blow it out your ear," Krystal sniped at her.

"Yeah," Dawna agreed. "Stop actin' like you're runnin' the show, because you're not. I am *so* sick of you givin' orders like you're God or something."

Bobbi gasped in shock. "If you think I'm going to sit here calmly while you take the name of the Lord in vain, Miss Dawna, you have another thing comin' to you."

"You don't like it?" asked Dawna. "Leave."

"You're both bein' *so* snotty," accused Krystal. "Don't you think they're bein' snotty, Victor?"

Wow. They were shedding their façades faster than a retriever sheds water. I could think of only two words to describe the phenomenon: Game on!

"And you, monsieur?" Patrice momentarily bypassed the warring blondes to take Woody's order. "What is your pleasure this evening?"

"Hell, I can't read this damn menu. It's all gibberish. Just give me a burger and fries, and throw in some extra ketchup."

SIX

WE WERE JUST FINISHING dessert when we arrived at Caudebec-en-Caux, our first port of call. Not that any of my dinner companions noticed. Jackie had withdrawn into hurt silence for most of the meal, the girls were officially in "moods," Woody was filling the void with nonstop tales of his war exploits in Italy, and Victor was slouched in his chair, chin on his chest, sound asleep. Wanting to view the new town from someplace other than the confines of the dining room, I decided this was the perfect time to part company with the group.

"Well, this has been fun," I lied as I placed my folded napkin on the table and stood up. "We'll have to do it again sometime."

Victor snorted explosively and gasped awake, his eyes ranging around the table as if trying to figure out who we were and why he was with us.

"Can I escort you back to your room?" I asked him, goaded by a niggling sense of duty. With Virginia gone, *someone* had to help him out.

"Why … thank you," he rasped. "That's very kind of you to offer."

"Say, Vic." Woody shot him a curious look. "Where'd you see action in the war anyway? European or Pacific theater?"

Victor's eyes grew suddenly wary. "That should be of no concern to you."

"Why the hell not? You had to fight someplace. Guys our age *all* had to fight someplace."

Victor ignored him as he struggled to his feet.

"You *did* fight. Didn't you?"

I shoved Victor's chair out of the way and grabbed his arm. "I'll say this one last time," he repeated. "My war experience is none of your affair, so don't ask me again."

"So what kept you out?" Woody persisted. "Flat feet? Bad hearing?"

"Do you guys need another arm?" asked Jackie, crawling out of her lethargy long enough to see that I might need a little help.

I shot her a grateful look that prompted her to pop out of her chair and circle her hand around Victor's forearm in a grip that nearly lifted him off his feet. Waving away my help, she struck out down the aisle and fought to keep him on course as he veered to left and right like the proverbial grocery cart with the wobbly wheels. "What's your cabin number?" I asked when we finally exited the dining room.

"It's right here." He nodded toward a door. "First one on the left. Although I don't imagine it's going to be too pleasant inside. Virginia will no doubt want to extract a pound of my flesh for embarrassing her. Unfortunately, we're often condemned to live our lives in the personal hells we unknowingly create for ourselves." He looked down at the plastic sheath hanging from the lanyard around his neck. "My key is tucked behind my name tag, Emily. Would you be good enough to dig it out?"

I removed his keycard, inserted it into the proper slot, and opened his cabin door. "Can we help you inside?" I asked as I returned his key to its sheath.

"You dare brave the lion's den?" He laughed. "Thank you for the offer, but I believe I can manage from here. Until tomorrow, ladies."

Using the door handle for support, he shuffled into his cabin and closed the door behind him.

"*Sooo*...do you want to stop by my cabin to discuss what happened at dinner?" I asked Jackie as we continued down the corridor.

She shook her head. "I don't want to talk about it. I don't *ever* want to talk about it."

"Okay."

She sniffed pathetically as she proceeded to talk about it. "The girls don't like me, Emily. I bet they got a big charge out of giving me the wrong phone numbers. They were in cahoots with each other the whole time, weren't they? They didn't want me bugging them in Arromanches, and they don't want me bugging them anyplace else."

"Really, Jack, it's their loss."

"They lied about who came up with the makeover idea, and they tried to make me look like a slacker in front of Victor."

We stopped in front of her cabin door. "Do you know what a guy would do if something like this happened to him?"

"What?"

"Nothing! You know why? Because guys don't *do* stuff like this to each other! If a dude doesn't like you, he might let the air out of your tires or beat you to a pulp, but he'd never do anything really mean."

In a bizarre way, this actually made sense. Jackie could never claim to be a philosophical genius, but her sudden pronouncement struck me as being both powerful and insightful. "Are you implying that...the physical bruises that men inflict on each other heal a lot faster than the psychological ones inflicted by women on other women?"

She stared into space for a long, contemplative moment before shaking her head. "Nah." Reaching into her shoulder bag, she removed her keycard. "Anyway, I apologize for abandoning you, but I'm going to lock myself in my cabin, crawl under the covers, curl up in a fetal ball"—she flashed a grim smile that reached all the way to her eyes— "and plan my revenge."

Unh-oh. This wasn't good. "C'mon, Jack. Let it go. Getting even with them is beneath you."

"What? And let all the synthetic hormones I've knocked back all these years go to waste? *Au contraire.* I'm one of you now, Emily, and by God, I'm going to act like it."

Yup. This is exactly what the tour was missing—a six-foot transsexual skulking around the boat like Sylvester Stallone in an old Rambo movie. *Oh, God.* I hoped she'd have a change of heart, but even more importantly, I hoped she hadn't packed any wigs.

I walked to the end of the corridor, which opened up into an area like a hotel lobby. After waving to the perky female purser who manned the information desk, I exited the automatic sliding glass doors to starboard and climbed the metal stairs to the sundeck.

For those guests who preferred to experience the sundeck minus UV rays, small groupings of patio tables and chairs were arranged beneath a canopy around midship, kind of like a circus tent without the sides. For guests who preferred their sun with all the trimmings, a double row of chaise lounge chairs sat back to back in the center of the deck, lined up in military order. Pockets of guests were scattered near the rails, drinks in hand, talking, laughing, and gazing toward the town of Caudebec, whose main street paralleled the quay where we were moored.

As I crossed the deck to the port rail, I was surprised by how modern Caudebec looked with its three-story hotels, wrought-iron balconies, flower-filled window boxes, and profusion of satellite dishes. No half-timber houses and cramped alleyways here, just a steady stream of compact cars cruising the waterfront like lowriders cruising Hollywood and Vine.

"I got pictures, dear. You wanna see?"

Nana charged toward me at the head of the pack, elbows thrust outward in blocking mode, fist manacled around her iPhone, outpacing her nearest competitor by a whole half-step.

"Mine are better," urged Bernice as she muscled past Nana's right elbow to shove her camara in my face. "That Saint-Sauveur woman got some great closeups of me. I dare any of you to look at this picture and tell me my camera isn't making love to my face."

"I hope the camera was wearing protection," howled Dick Stolee in a fit of laughter. "You wouldn't want any surprises nine months down the road."

George scratched his head. "I thought the gestation period for women in Bernice's age bracket was longer than that."

"You're thinking of elephants," said Tilly.

"In case you didn't know this already, Bernice," Margi warned in her official capacity as a Windsor City nurse practitioner, "bearing children can have serious health risks for women our age. Varicose veins. Hypertension. Diabetes mellitus. Death."

"Hey, I'm suffering from the veins, the hypertension, and type 2 diabetes already," crowed Dick Stolee, "and I'm not dead yet."

"You will be if you keep ogling those three blondes who're traveling with us," cautioned his wife.

"I'm sorry, Bernice," I said as I squinted at her camera, "but can you move your hand? Your fingers are hiding the screen."

"Lemme see." Dick Teig snatched the device from her hand and took a peek at the onscreen image. The wisecrack he'd cued up suddenly withered and died on his lips. "Holy mackerel. This photo is amazing. Who is it?"

"It's me, you moron," sniped Bernice.

"Is not."

"Is so."

"You don't look anything *like* this."

"I look *exactly* like that."

"Do not."

"Do so!"

Everyone paused, breathless with anticipation. Heads turned. Eyes shifted.

Five seconds …

Ten seconds …

"Shouldn't we be votin' by now?" Nana piped up.

"See?" balked Dick Stolee. "What'd I tell you. The whole system's broken."

"Where *is* Osmond anyway?" asked Tilly.

Heads swiveled. Feet shuffled.

"There he is," said George, pointing toward a secluded spot in the canopied area where Osmond sat slouched in a patio chair, head bent, eyes downcast, looking as if he'd just learned that, in an effort to stimulate the economy, all three C-Span channels were being replaced by Home Shopping Networks.

"Gee," whispered Lucille. "What's wrong with him? He seemed okay at supper."

"He's probably brooding over our home visit," said Bernice. "He reconnected with some woman he met in the war, and it's probably just hit him that neither one of them will live long enough to ever see each other again. So, poof! There he sits. The face of tragedy."

"Osmond fought in a war?" quipped Dick Stolee.

"Which one?" snickered Dick Teig. "Revolutionary or Civil?"

Helen swatted her husband's arm with the back of her hand. "That's not funny."

"Yes, it is."

"No. It's not."

Ten seconds...

Fifteen seconds...

"Shouldn't we take a vote?" asked Alice.

"We can't," George lamented in a low voice. "It's not official unless Osmond calls for a show of hands and does the tallying."

Eleven sets of eyes fired unblinking stares across the deck at him.

"He's ruining everything," whispered Grace. "It's so unfair. What are we going to do?"

"Should we switch political parties?" asked Margi.

George pondered the suggestion. "It'd be pretty easy. All we'd have to do is reject health care reform and buy a few guns."

Noses wrinkling. Heads shaking.

They stared at Osmond more intently.

"*Unh-oh*," Nana whispered after a few moments. "Poor fella's worse off than he's puttin' on. He's not answerin' his phone."

Gasps. Shock. More gasps.

"I wish my hearing were as acute as yours," Tilly marveled. "I'm embarrassed to admit this, Marion, but I can't hear his phone ringing."

"That's on account of it's not. I just sent him a text."

"Saying what?" I asked.

"Sayin' 'How did the Norwegian break his leg while he was rakin' leaves?' Them Norske jokes always get a rise outta him."

"Marion's on the right track," said George. "We gotta do something to cheer him up."

"I could transfer a million dollars into his bank account," enthused Nana. "When I done that for the Senior Center, a whole bunch of folks got real giddy."

"Oh, sure," whined Bernice. "Make yourself look good with a grand gesture that sticks Osmond with a mountain of tax headaches. How generous is that?"

"Hey, Marion, if you make the transfer to *my* account, I'll be happy to burden myself with the tax implications," razzed Dick Teig.

"Brown-nose." Bernice plucked her camera out of his hand. "You morons don't know anything about men and their libidos." She jabbed a button several times until she arrived at the desired image. "I, on the other hand, know exactly what'll get Osmond's blood flowing again." She smiled seductively at the screen. "One hundred and forty-seven glamour shots of Bernice Zwerg—up close, personal, and untouched by Photoshop."

Boos. Hissing.

"Okay, people, I'll take it from here," I announced as the hissing continued. "I have an idea, so just back off until I see if it works."

"Whatcha gonna do, dear?" asked Nana.

I knew what I *wasn't* going to do. I wasn't going to show him one hundred and forty-seven glamour shots of Bernice Zwerg. "I'm going to talk to him."

"You want to take my camera with you?" asked Bernice. "I'll start the slide show, and Osmond can look at the pictures in between pretending he's listening to you."

"Ladies and gentlemen," a heavily accented bass voice announced over the loud speaker, "please join us in the lounge for this evening's entertainment of live jazzy music with Elodie and Jean-Charles. Tonight's specialty cocktail is a Rob Roy at a 15 percent discount. The festivities begin in ten minutes."

"Hot damn!" cheered Dick Teig as he pumped his fist. "We're outta here."

"Marion?" Margi sidled up to her. "Out of curiosity, how *did* the Norwegian break his leg while he was raking leaves?"

Nana smiled. "He fell outta the tree."

I crossed the deck to where Osmond sat and pulled up a chair beside him. "You've had quite a day," I said in a gentle tone.

He nodded glumly. "She's the only woman I've ever loved, Emily."

"Would you like to tell me a little about her? I've got all night."

He nodded again, his gaze riveted on the deck. "The night she found me, I noticed she was wearing a wedding band, so I thought she was married. But she wasn't. She was a widow. Barely a bride, and then a widow. The Germans had hauled her husband off to prison a month after her wedding, and she never saw him again. But it wasn't until the spring of '44 that the Germans bothered to tell her he'd died in captivity. When I showed up in her barn, her emotions were still pretty raw, so maybe I made a difference in her life when she needed it. I hope so."

"How long were you together?"

"Less than three weeks. I tried to find a way to get to the evacuation beach so I could be shipped back to England for rehab, but the fighting was so fierce on the ground after the invasion that I had to lay low until things let up. I didn't want to be declared MIA or AWOL, so with the help of a hay wagon and a half-starved horse, the family finally got me back to where I needed to be."

"And that's the last time you saw her?"

He nodded.

"Did you contact her after the war ended?"

"I wrote her a couple of times, but the letters came back all marked up with official stamps saying they were undeliverable."

"Did you try phoning?"

"Yup. You had to go through special overseas operators back then, but they could never find a number for her."

"She never wrote to you?"

"She might have, but I never received anything." He shrugged. "All of Europe was a mess back then, so mail service was pretty much a disaster."

The corners of his mouth curled upward as he studied his misshapen fingers. "She's still a beauty, isn't she, Emily?"

"She is indeed."

He heaved a sigh. "Do you think I'm pathetic for moping over what might've been?"

"Certainly not! But when you're through moping, you might want to look at the bright side."

"There's a bright side?"

"There's *always* a bright side." Unless your name was Bernice Zwerg. "Look, Osmond, what's past is past. It's like water under the bridge or over the dam. You can't change what's already happened."

He nodded dejectedly. "Will you let me know when you get to the part that's supposed to make me feel better?"

"What I'm trying to say is, you might have lost track of Solange once, but that was decades ago. The world has shrunk. You never have to lose touch with her again through the miracle of iPhones, iPads, laptops, email, Twitter, Facebook, Skype."

"I don't know how to Skype."

"Nana can help you figure it out. You'll be able to talk to each other face to face whenever you want. It'll almost be as good as being in the same room together."

"What if she doesn't have a computer?"

"Madeleine will have a computer."

He inched his chin off his chest, looking desperate to believe me.

"But I still don't know how to get in touch with her. We left before I got a chance to exchange any contact information."

"Have you Googled the French white pages?"

"Yup. I entered Solange's name and village, but I didn't get any hits. I didn't get any for Madeleine either." His voice grew thready with anxiety. "What if the family has gone wireless? How will I find her if they only use mobile phones? There's no white pages for cell phone numbers."

I reached for his hand and squeezed hard. "That's true, but... Madeleine is an employee of the tour company, so she *has* to communicate with them somehow. Why don't I try to convince the person in charge of that stuff to share her contact information with us."

His rheumy old eyes lit up like the grand finale in a fireworks display. "Really? Are they allowed to do that? Even with all the privacy laws?"

I offered him a reassuring smile. "You know me. I can be very convincing." And if that didn't work, I had my usual ace in the hole: Nana could hack into anything.

"Golly." He propped himself higher in his chair. "All of a sudden, I feel a whole lot better."

"Of course you do! You've just caught a whiff of the world's most natural mood-elevating elixir." I smiled. "Hope."

Blinking away tears, he leaned sideways and threw his bony arms around me. "I'm going to invite Solange and her whole extended family to Iowa," he vowed, sniffling into the crook of my neck. "Her last name isn't Spenard anymore, so I reckon she got married again, but that doesn't matter. I'll reserve a whole floor of that new hotel opposite the waterpark. And she can bring her kids and grandkids and great-grandkids if she has any."

"You'd better ask about a senior citizen discount," I teased as he released me. "You might need it."

He swiped moisture from his cheeks as his newfound generosity introduced itself to his Iowa practicality. He gave his jaw a self-conscious scratch. "Not that it matters, Emily, but do you suppose Solange had a whole brood of kids?"

"Well, she had at least one—Madeleine's mother. That's about all we know for now . . . other than your name is apparently a popular one in the family."

"Isn't that something? I've never known another Osmond in all my life, and here Madeleine says there's a whole bunch on her family tree. I wonder what the deal is? Why Osmond?"

"I'm sure Solange will be happy to take you through the family genealogy the next time you talk to—" The words leaving my mouth suddenly jogged something in my brain, prompting me to consider a possible twist in the family genealogy. Was the name Osmond popular because it had been carried down through the centuries? Or was it popular for another reason entirely? One that had me staring at Osmond, gobsmacked.

"Osmond? This is none of my business, so please don't feel obligated to reply, but during the war, did you and..." I gave my head an awkward bob, suddenly tongue-tied. I cleared my throat and tried again. "What I'm trying to say is, were you and Solange... you know ...an 'item' while you were together in France?"

A faraway look crept into his eyes, chased away by a hint of a smile that slowly slid into an incredulous grin. "Holy smokes. I could be a father."

SEVEN

THE FOLLOWING MORNING, IN an attempt to avoid a repeat performance of last night's dinner, I showed up at the restaurant ten minutes after it opened and staked out a quiet table for four. It stood in an intimate corner, was happily unoccupied, and best of all, sat in the direct path of the morning sun, which splashed across the table in a warm flood of blinding light. Anyone foolish enough to sit with me would face the risk of having their retinas incinerated.

I'd stopped at the reception desk before returning to my cabin last night to inquire about the possibility of obtaining Madeleine Saint-Sauveur's contact information and was thrilled when the purser told me she'd be happy to share the information if Mrs. Saint-Sauveur agreed. "I'll send her a message, Mrs. Miceli," she told me in her clipped British accent. "I don't foresee any problem. Guests are usually so enamored with Mrs. Saint-Sauveur that they often ask for an email address so they might continue to correspond with her."

Yes!

I felt giddy with anticipation as I slid my oversized designer sunglasses onto my face and opened the breakfast menu. Would my efforts pave the way for Osmond and Solange to reunite permanently? Would the star-crossed lovers decided to tie the knot after all these years? Would Osmond learn he really *was* a father? Oh, my God. The poor guy probably wouldn't know what to send out first: wedding invitations or birth announcements.

"Mrs. Miceli? Why do you sit here in the sun with all these other tables to choose from?" Patrice appeared out of nowhere, wielding a beverage carafe in each hand. "Come. I move you."

"Not necessary." I tapped my sunglasses. "I've adapted."

"But the sun. You find it annoying, yes?"

"Not half as annoying as I hope some other guests will find it."

He squinted at me, clearly uncomprehending.

"If one of those carafes contains tea, I'd love for you to pour me a cup, and I'm going to skip the buffet this morning in favor of the breakfast special."

"Ah. *L'omlette de jambon et de legume avec le raifort a infuse la sauce.* An excellent choice." After pouring my tea, he set the carafes down and made a notation on his order pad. "*Très bien.*"

"Don't go anywhere, Patricia!" Woody's voice boomed out behind me. "Not before you pour me some coffee."

I sagged in my chair. *There was no God ... There was no God ...*

He rapped his knuckles on my table as he drew abreast. "This seat taken?"

"The sun, monsieur," fussed Patrice. "Would you not prefer to sit—"

"Hell, I invaded North Africa in '42. Don't talk to me about sun." He pulled out the chair opposite me and sat down.

"You're all alone this morning?" I asked in what I hoped would pass as a normal tone. "No Cal?"

He offered up his cup for Patrice to fill. "The boy is slower than molasses. He was still in the shower when I left the cabin. Not sure how his wife puts up with it. Someone needs to light a stick of dynamite under him. You can't get ahead in life if you spend all your time pulling up the rear."

"Maybe Cal has a different idea about what getting ahead in life actually means."

He rolled his eyes as he took a sip of coffee. "I'm passing on the family business to a man who's the proverbial guppy in the shark tank. Great-grampa Jolly, who was one of the first lions in the funeral industry, is probably rolling over in his grave. But look, I don't want to talk about Cal. I want to talk about Victor." He downed another mouthful before setting his cup on its saucer. "Is it just me, or is there something fishy about that fella?"

"Fishy...how?"

"He talks funny. If he's a Texan, how come he doesn't talk like one? There's a story there. And you heard him last night. No way was he going to tell me where he fought in the war. Don't you find that strange?"

"From what little I know of the men who fought in World War II, the experience was so horrific that a good majority of them chose *never* to talk about it. Maybe Victor falls into that category."

He shook his head. "There's more to it than that. I've got a good nose for sniffing out funny business, and I say Victor's hiding something. All that rubbish about Solange and how haunting he found her eyes. Guys use that as a pickup line when they're in their twenties, not when they're the age of that old duffer. And *never* in front of the wife. What the hell was he thinking?"

"Speaking of Solange," I said, taking advantage of the opening, "do you have any idea why she reacted to you the way she—"

"Mornin', y'all! I'm thinkin' that little chair next to the window has my name on it. Y'all mind if I make your twosome a threesome?"

I debated banging my forehead on the table until I knocked myself out, but I was pretty sure I couldn't do it before Krystal seated herself, so what was the point?

"Come sit yourself down," Woody boomed as he stepped into the aisle to let her by. "Would you look at me? Having breakfast with two beautiful women? They never mentioned this in the cruise brochure, but it's a great selling point if they want to attract old codgers like me."

"You gotta promise though," Krystal insisted as she settled next to him. "None of that depressin' talk about funeral plannin', or I promise I'll leave y'all and sit somewhere else."

Pleeeease revert to your default setting... Pleeeease revert to your default setting...

"Where's your girlfriends anyway?" Woody asked as he glanced around the dining room.

"They're not my girlfriends," she corrected in a tight voice. "Not after what they said last night." She gathered her platinum locks in one hand and draped the long tail over her shoulder as if it were a giant python preparing to mate with her overly tight snakeskin top. "They know I'm a shoe-in for Victor's bonus, so they're miffed. And all's they're provin' is what poor losers they are. No one has ever outsold me at Mona Michelle. I know it for a fact, and so do they."

"Have you seen a spreadsheet comparing the actual sales figures?" I asked.

"I don't need to see the figures, hon. I just know."

Right. Kinda like the politicians who didn't actually need to *see* the WMD to know they were there.

"Why're you wearin' sunglasses indoors?" She wrinkled her adorably upturned nose at me. "That's kind of affected, idn't it? Are you hopin' someone'll mistake you for a celebrity?" She giggled. "Big disappointment there!"

I took solace in the fact that breakfast was the quickest meal of the day. "The sun," I said calmly as I pointed skyward. "It's in my eyes."

"Have you got sensitive eyes, darlin'?" She slapped her palm on the table. "Do I have a deal for you. Mona Michelle sells clump-free mascara for sensitive eyes, and if you apply enough coats, your lashes will get so voluminously long and stiff, you'll never have to worry about seeing the sun ever again! I swear by the stuff. See?" She blinked several times to demonstrate the usefulness of stiff, overly long lashes. "You want I should write you up an order? It's only $49.95, excluding postage and handling fees."

"FOR MASCARA?"

"It's not just *any* mascara, darlin'. This mascara is transformational. Men will be dazzled. Your boss will beg to give you a raise. I guarantee you'll feel more sexy, empowered, confident, influential—"

"—ripped off. Don't you sell anything for like … $8.99?"

She lowered her brows dramatically. "For $8.99 I can sell you a travel-size bottle of alcohol-free mouthwash." Her voice dipped to a whisper. "The alcohol thing can be a *huge* deal breaker in the Bible Belt."

"You sell any products for guys my age?" asked Woody.

"Is the Pope the Pope?" she teased.

I guess it wasn't relevant if he were Catholic or not.

Lifting Woody's hand off the table, she examined his fingers with dollars signs spinning in her eyes. "You would *love* the seaweed based cuticle treatment we sell, hon. And from the condition of these nails, I'd say, the sooner you buy it, the better. In one quick treatment, I can guarantee you healthier nails polished to a liquid shine... or your money back. Three-way buffer and nail file not included."

"How much'll that set me back?"

"The oil is only $49.95, excluding postage and handling fees," she tittered. "And the three-way buffer and file are on special, so I can let you have them both for an inclusive charge of $49.95, excluding postage and handling fees. I'll thank you for noticin' that I'm practically givin' 'em away."

Even through the film of UV protection coating my lenses, I could see every ounce of blood drain from Woody's face. "You got anything else?"

Focusing on his hand with renewed interest, she patted his finger. "Well, idn't this just the cutest ring. What's this doohickey on the top here? Some kind of flower?"

"Yup. It's either a lily or an iris, stylized up the wazoo. The French call it a fleur-de-lis. We're supposed to see them everywhere over here—on flags, coats of arms, postage stamps. I think at one time it was the symbol for the French monarchy."

"How come one of the petals is broken?"

Woody shrugged. "Beats me. But that's what makes it special. It's not perfect. The jeweler put a daring spin on an old theme."

"Look at it, Emily." She twisted his hand around to show me. "Idn't it just the purdiest thing?"

I nodded. "Very eye-catching."

"Fourteen carat?" asked Krystal.

"Gold? Not on your life. It's solid brass." He rapped it on the edge of the table. "Gold is for sissies. Real men wear brass."

"Is it a family heirloom or somethin'?"

"Yup. Been in my family as long as I can remember. I'll hand it down to Cal when I'm gone."

Patrice arrived with my breakfast before Krystal could attempt another sales pitch.

"That looks pretty tasty," Woody commented as he eyed my plate. "What is it?"

"*L'omlette de jambon et de legume avec le raifort a infuse la sauce,*" said Patrice as he freshened Woody's coffee and poured a cup for Krystal.

Woody nodded. "What is it in English?"

"Ham and vegetable omelet with horseradish-infused sauce," Patrice translated.

"Sounds good. That's what I'll have. I could do with a good ole American breakfast."

"Make that two," said Krystal as she perused the sumptuously fluffy creation before me.

"*D'accord.*" Patrice scribbled the orders on his pad before whisking himself off to the kitchen again.

"I can't handle the buffet this morning," Krystal complained. "Too many men waiting to ogle me."

93

"Could be the mascara," I said as I poured a ramekin of what looked like ketchup over my omelet. "Maybe you should try something less transformational."

"So, where's the bus taking us this morning?" asked Woody as I savored the flavorful herbs of the most appetizing omelet that had ever occupied my mouth.

"Someplace that begins with an E," said Krystal. "Which reminds me." She dug a whole bottle of jumbo softgels out of her totebag and plunked it on the table. "You wanna try one of my supplements, hon?" She unscrewed the cap and offered one to Woody. "I guarantee it'll work better than those little weenie pills you got with you."

"Hell. Why not?" He plopped it into his mouth and downed it with a gulp of coffee.

"I don't imagine you'll be needin' one, Emily. Yankee women aren't known for their delicate constitutions." She downed one herself before tossing her hair back over her shoulder and fanning her face. "This mornin' sun is an absolute killer. I'm about to burn up."

I waved my fork in several directions. "Lots of empty tables in the shade," I said hopefully.

"Change places with me," urged Woody as he got to his feet. "Shoot, I haven't been hot since the North African campaign in '42."

Krystal grabbed her tote and slid over onto his chair. "So ... what was happenin' in '42 that sent you to Africa, hon?"

She'd obviously bypassed the war museum in Arromanches.

"Were you huntin' big game? *Euw*! Did you get to shoot one of those elephant guns? I would *kill* to pull the trigger on one of those puppies."

The dining room started filling up as Woody launched into a detailed history of Axis invasions, Allied strategies, and the best World

War II movies available on Netflix. As I devoured my omelet, an army of waiters flew past our table, some wielding beverage carafes and order pads, others carrying chafing dishes of hot food to the central serving station. The noise level increased. The wait staff quickened their steps. By the time a young waiter arrived at our table, Krystal's attention span was so maxed out with world history, I figured she might even be desperate enough to discuss advanced funeral planning. Specifically, Woody's.

"Two breakfast specials." The waiter slid the plates onto the table and paused a bit breathlessly to ogle Krystal. "*Bon appétit.*"

"Did y'all see the way he looked at me?" she whispered when he'd departed. "I get those looks *all* the time. It's so annoying."

I dabbed my mouth with my napkin and pushed away from the table.

"Of course you get those looks," Woody allowed. "I mean, a fella would have to be blind not to stare. Isn't that right, Emily?"

"Absolutely." I stood up. "I'm off. See you guys on the bus. And a word of warning to the faint of tongue: go easy on the horseradish sauce. It's got a kick."

"The hotter the better!" boomed Woody as I grabbed my shoulder bag. "So tell me, little lady," he asked Krystal, "where was I in my narrative? Had I reached V-E Day yet?"

As I made my escape, I heard Krystal's voice cut through the rising din. "Can we save that for another time, darlin'? I'm just dyin' for y'all to tell me what kind of advanced funeral plannin' you've done for yourself."

EIGHT

"THOSE OF YOU WHO are art enthusiasts will notice something very familiar about our next destination."

We'd been riding in the bus for about an hour, paralleling the Seine on a river road that ran arrow straight through a broad flood plain. Barges and small cargo vessels plied the waters to our left, while to our right, a forest of young hardwoods marched to the base of a ridge of limestone cliffs. As we veered inland, the landscape grew wilder and more lush, the roads narrower and more corkscrewed, turning the trip into a sightseer's dream, but a carsick sufferer's nightmare. I wasn't sure where Krystal and Woody were sitting, but I sure hoped Krystal's supplements were working, because unlike cruise ships or airplanes, buses furnished no motion sickness bags in their seat-back pockets.

We drove through tiny French villages where the houses were completely flush with the road, save for a narrow strip of pavement that wasn't even wide enough to wheel a pram. We passed fields that were leaf-green with ripening crops, meadows whose grass rippled toward gently rolling hills, ramshackle barns whose crooked clap-boards were held together with spit and bailing wire, and formidable embankments that were surmounted by an impenetrable tangle of hedgerows and trees. Country lanes boasted no shoulders, but on more traveled roads, fences abounded—stubby posts with chicken wire between, split-rail fences that looked hand-hewn, fieldstone fences with decorative gates, industrial steel guardrails, white picket fences, livestock fences, and high stone walls overhung with a riot of shrubbery and foliage that closed in on the road like the walls of a tunnel.

Norway had fjords.

Holland had canals.

France had fences.

"What if art's not our thing?" Dick Teig called out. "Are we still gonna notice something familiar about this place…whatever it's called?"

"Étretat," replied our tour director, a slightly built, middle-aged expatriate from Idaho whose name was Rob. "If you can't figure out what the main attraction is, you'll find information plaques on the promenade that'll give you a hint. But I'll provide you with your first clue: beware of elephants."

"Where's the promenade?" asked Dick Stolee.

"It fronts the beach. Just follow the signposts that say *La Mer* and they'll lead you right to it. For those of you who enjoy invigorating hikes, I recommend you follow the paths at either end of the beach. Have your cameras ready, because the views from the hiking trails are spectacular. There's a good reason why the French call this the Alabaster Coast. We'll be here for three hours, which should give you plenty of time to shop, eat, hike, or try your luck at the casino, which you'll find by following the signposts that say Casino d'Étretat."

Nana's iPhone began *dinging* like a hyperactive pinball machine. I sidled a glance at her as she scrolled through her new messages. "Do you ever get tired of being bombarded with all that texting stuff?"

"Nope. I love hearin' them dings. It means I don't gotta run out and buy no hearin' aid yet."

"So what's the scoop?"

"We're gonna skip the shoppin', eatin', and hikin' and head directly for the casino. Osmond says he's feelin' lucky."

"Can't fault him there." I smiled a secret smile. "He might be on the biggest lucky streak of his life."

She looked up at me, curiosity in her little wrinkled eyes. "What'd you say to him last night anyway, dear? I never seen no one go from sad to glad so fast. He was a whole different fella when he caught up to us in the lounge."

"Got his batteries recharged, did he?"

"I'll say. He was so fired up, he staked out a spot on the dance floor and done the chicken dance until the musicians packed it in."

"Osmond did the chicken dance ... to jazz?"

"He didn't know what kinda music he was dancin' to on account of he turned off his hearin' aids." She sighed. "Wish I coulda done that. Them polyrhythms kept throwin' me way off beat."

I gave her an incredulous look. "You were doing the chicken dance with him?"

"We all was, dear. It was the only way we could escape havin' to look at them photos of Bernice's."

The bus pulled into a parking lot in the center of town, and the minute our driver cut the engine, we grabbed our belongings and poured into the aisle.

"See you back here in three hours," Rob reminded us. "If you need the comfort station, it's at the opposite end of the parking lot, so you'll pass it on your way to the beach. And one word of caution. Do not, I repeat, DO NOT remove any stones from the beach. There's a statute forbidding it, so have fun, but leave the rocks where they are."

"You wanna tag along with us to the casino?" Nana asked me as we exited down the stairs.

"I hate to pass up a chance to lose all my money in a slot machine, but I'm off to the beach to find out why this place is supposed to look familiar."

"You want I should Google it for you?"

"Nope. I want to be surprised."

I escorted her to the random spot where the gang was assembling, my eyes widening in alarm when I saw Osmond. "Why is Osmond wearing a cervical collar?"

"It's on account of one of them fancy spin moves he done last night, dear. It accidentally got away from him, so he's got a crick in his neck this mornin.'"

"Did he seek medical attention?"

"Yup."

I called up a mental picture of the *Renoir's* floor plan. "Do we have an infirmary on board?"

"Nope."

"So where did he go?"

99

"Margi's cabin. She give his head a crank both ways, said, 'Aha!' and slapped the collar on 'im.'" She gave a little suck on her uppers. "She always leaves plenty of space in her grip for medical supplies."

I shook my head. Yup. That's exactly what we needed. Unauthorized medical personnel diagnosing and treating potentially serious geriatric ailments.

"Have all of you pulled up the map of Étretat on your phones?" Tilly called out as we joined everyone on the sidewalk.

Nods. Yups.

"And you've located the casino?"

More nods and yups. Excited foot shuffling.

"All right then. Time's a wastin'. Forwarrrrd … march!"

"Don't forget," I cautioned Nana. "If you don't understand what the locals are saying, just smile. Smiles are a universal language."

"You bet. But we don't gotta worry too much about no language barrier. Margi took a French language course at the Senior Center what's s'posed to help all of us muddle our way through the country."

"Wow. Good for Margi." I was embarrassed to admit that my main preparation for the trip had been to have a French manicure.

"She can ask directions and introduce folks real good. I'm dyin' for her to ask someone where the public potty is, but she can't do it right now on account of I can see it from here."

I could see it, too—a light brick building with a decorative roof extending over the two entry doors. A dozen women were already lined up outside the ladies' room door, but what caught my attention were the four at the head of the queue.

Jackie and the three blondes? What in the world were *they* doing together? Well, other than yanking tissues out of their shoulder bags, fussing over Krystal's snakeskin top, and schmoozing with each other as if they were the best of friends again. They'd obviously undergone some serious attitude adjustment since breakfast, but if this had been Jackie's idea, one thing was painfully clear.

She didn't know squat about revenge.

"Did you get the number, Emily?" Osmond was suddenly standing in front of me, his little head perched on his cervical collar like a six-minute egg on an egg cup.

"I've set the wheels in motion, so the minute I hear something, I'll let you know. Okay?"

He flashed a goofy smile, looking deliriously happy despite being unable to bend, nod, or swivel.

"Osmond, do you need to see a doctor?"

"For what?"

I flicked my finger toward his collar. "Your neck?"

"This?" He chuckled as he patted the Velcro strips that secured the heavy foam brace. "Shoot, I don't need this thing. It's just decorative. But I didn't wanna see the look on Margi's face if I told her I didn't wanna wear it. She would've been crushed." He shrugged. "I'm kinda hoping I twist my ankle sometime though, 'cuz I wouldn't mind trying out the collapsible crutches she brought with her."

Oh, God. "Just a suggestion, but could you possibly take them for a test run *without* twisting your ankle first?"

He rubbed his forehead in thought. "Why would I need to take them for a test run if there's nothing wrong with my ankle?"

"Okey-dokey. You have me there." I'd come to realize that arguing logic with a post-octogenarian was about as effective as trying to eat Jell-O with chopsticks. "But promise me if you're still having problems tomorrow, you'll let me know so we can get you in to see a professional."

"You bet." He dashed off as fast as his spindly legs would take him, catching up to the gang as they trooped down a street that was posted with a red and white one-way sign. I paused a moment to get my bearings, found the *La Mer* sign, and followed my nose toward the smell of salt water and french fries.

Étretat appeared to be a typical seaside resort town that catered to tourists with an appetite for two-star hotels, T-shirts, postcards, outdoor cafés, novelty flags, and pizza. Shops were densely packed together and boasted three stories, dormered roofs, window boxes, and striped canopies overhanging sidewalk displays of must-have souvenirs. Half-timbered structures hunkered between brick buildings that flaunted a cake frosting façade of cream-colored stone embedded with flint. Cafés overran the sidewalks and spilled into the street where they were cordoned off like jury boxes behind wooden barriers and flower pots. Neon signs glowed in red and blue, advertising the specialties of the house: *Crêperie. Bar. Brasserie. Moule Frites. Pizzeria. Kebabs.*

"Emily! Hey, wait up!"

I turned around to find Cal Jolly barreling past a spinner of postcards to catch up with me.

"Are you heading for the beach?" He stopped beside me, cheeks flushed from his little jog.

"Sure am. I'm a sucker for a good mystery."

"So you don't know why Étretat is supposed to look familiar either?"

"Don't have a clue. I confess complete ignorance on the subject of French coastal towns and their significance."

"Oh, good. I thought I was the only one. Would you mind if I tag along with you?"

"Heck, no. I'm happy for the company." I pointed north. "I guess we just keep walking thataway. So where's your dad?" I asked as we got underway again. "I've eaten my last two meals with him, so I think we're becoming something of an item."

"Actually, it's my dad I wanted to talk to you about. You were in the room yesterday when Madeleine's grandmother suffered her melt-down, weren't you?"

"Oh, Lord. It was heart wrenching."

"Do you have any idea what set her off? I caught the tail end when I poked my head back in the door to hurry you guys up, but I missed the main event, and Dad has clammed up completely. Refuses to talk about it. And he's been avoiding me ever since, which is probably why he's pestering you at meals. I apologize if he's been harassing you and your tablemates about funeral arrangements. I'm afraid he sees every chance encounter as a marketing opportunity."

"Victor threatened him with eviction from the table last night, and one of the Mona Michelle blondes muzzled him at breakfast, so there's no need for apologies. The poor guy isn't making much headway. As to the incident with Madeleine's grandmother, I'm still baffled. Your dad went into his spiel about his website and online funeral planning services, and when he tried to hand Solange a brochure, all hell broke loose. She kept crying, 'My God, my God,' in French, and then she started screaming a whole barrage of stuff at him, which is about the time you stuck your head in the room. I think it shook him up pretty badly. He dropped the brochure on a table and hightailed it out the door. Madeleine did what she could to calm Solange, but at that point, the poor woman almost seemed beyond help."

We veered into the street to avoid running into a sidewalk display of Hello Kitty balloons, Étretat placemats, and key chains. Cal grumbled something inaudible and threw an angry hand into the air.

"You know, I keep harping about the fact that some people don't like to talk about end-of-life issues. The death and dying stuff really frightens them, so you have to softpedal your approach. But Dad just blows me off. I don't understand how he's had as much success as he's had in the business."

"Lack of competition?"

"Yeah, there's that. He was the only show in town for decades. Say, can I treat you to an ice cream?" He paused before the Le Glacier d'Étretat shop, with its glass counter offering frontal views of treats so enticing, I doubted the ability of any tourist to pass by without indulging. "I won't feel so guilty about splurging if I can tempt you, too."

"I'm afraid you don't have to twist my arm. But the next one's on me, okay?"

After a fun twenty minutes spent taste-testing every flavor in the shop, Cal purchased a *Pomme Verte* cone for me and a dish of *Fleur d'Oranger* for himself. As we continued our trek to the beach, he picked up the thread of our conversation exactly where we'd left off.

"So did you happen to understand any of the barrage of stuff that Solange was yelling at my dad?"

"You mean, besides *mon Dieu*?" I rotated my cone, licking up all the drips. "She yelled, '*C'est toi*' at him as he ran out the door. You probably heard that part. She said it a couple of times. Pretty vehemently."

"And that means what?"

"'It's you.'"

"Right." He heaved a sigh. "I'm open for insights if you have any."

"Well, my initial thought was that she recognized him from somewhere, and not in a good way. But that's probably a stretch. I know your dad fought in the war, but he said he was in North Africa and then Italy, so he wasn't anywhere near France, was he?"

"Not that I'm aware. As far as I know, this is his first foray onto French soil. But he sure doesn't want to be questioned about what happened with Solange, which is really unlike Dad. He's so talkative, my main problem is usually trying to find a way to shut him up. I guess it goes with the territory. If you can talk a person's ear off about the benefits of writing his own obituary, you can talk his ear off about anything."

"Maybe your dad is finding it difficult to admit that, given the circumstances, his hard sell was politically incorrect."

"Dad has never in his life admitted he's wrong, so... who knows? Maybe you're right. But I'll tell you one thing. Profits at the Jolly Funeral Home would skyrocket if Dad wasn't so pig-headed and stubborn. In fact, that's the main reason we signed up for this tour. The idea was that a relaxed atmosphere in a neutral setting would promote calm and allow us to iron out some grave matters. Pun intended."

"I didn't realize the funeral industry had matters *to* iron out."

"That's because you've obviously had no need to employ our services yet. But there's a real battle going on between the cremationists and the terra-firmists, and as baby boomers age, it's only going to get worse."

I shoved the remainder of my sugar cone in my mouth and flicked crumbs off my top as I finished chewing. "Sounds like you're talking science fiction."

"I'm talking profit and loss. I'll give you the Cliffs Notes version. The cremationists, like me, are pushing for affordable crematory services and low-cost mausoleums. The terra-firmists, like Dad, stand behind traditional services like in-ground interment and coffins that can withstand nuclear attack, and they're petitioning for additional cemeteries to accommodate the future onslaught of boomer clients. Our morticians association has just hired an expensive lobbyist to push our agenda through the state legislature, but none of us can agree *whose* agenda is going to be advanced, the cremationists or the terra-firmists. Hence, our desperate attempt to arrive at some type of unanimity before we fly home."

"Any breakthroughs yet?"

"Nope. There's a dozen of us on the trip, equally split between opposing camps, and no one's willing to give an inch yet. But there's a meeting scheduled tonight in the lounge, so if everyone gets liquored up, maybe we'll see some movement. The old-timers are just too mired in tradition to realize that shifting religious attitudes, tax revenues, and commercial land development are changing the industry. They've clung to their 'business as usual' motto for decades, but if they continue, the only thing they'll have to show for it will be a fistful of bankruptcy notices. Quite a legacy for the family members who are hoping to inherit the business, hunh?"

While Cal scouted out a trash bin for his plastic dish and spoon, I waited at a noisy intersection opposite the public parking lot, intrigued by the one-story building on the opposite corner. It occupied a large slab of real estate, was half-timbered in a pre-fab kind of way, sported no windows, and was mostly roof. The name attached above the front entrance read *casino*.

"That's where my group is," I told Cal when he returned.

"Are they lucky with the slots?"

"Not particularly. I think the only reason they like casinos is because they're addicted to the noise."

He lifted his eyebrows. "They get off on all that digital racket? *Yow*. Makes my head pound."

"Not them. It reminds them of texting."

Herring gulls soared overhead as we climbed the stairs to the promenade, their screeches quickly drowned out by the primitive roar of sea greeting shore. For a long moment I stood at the rail, stunned into silence, for there was almost too much to comprehend. A white stone beach nestled between chalk-white cliffs. Hang gliders sailing over the channel like predatory birds. A great gaping hole punched clear through the western cliff, creating an elegant natural arch. Children dashing into the surf armed with pails and shovels. A steepled church perched high atop the eastern cliff. Rental boats piggybacked atop each other above the high tide line like a string of turtle shells. White-capped rollers rumbling onto the beach with a deep-throated *boom* that vibrated through my feet into my gut. Beach stones shifting in the tide. Spinning. Floating. Clacking.

"Wow," was all I could think to say. And although the sight was awe inspiring, it wasn't at all familiar.

"I know this place," Cal marveled. "Dad has a painting of that arch hanging up in his den. The arch. The beach. A little fleet of boats heading out to sea. Well, I'll be damned. I never realized it was an actual place. But ... here it is."

"Is the painting an original?"

"Beats me. I think he picked it up at an estate sale years ago. Rob said something about information plaques." He ranged a long look down the promenade and swept his hand toward the cliff. "Shall we?"

As we strolled, I noticed more intimate details. Layers of horizontal striations that shot through the cliff face like the sugar filling in vanilla wafers. Jagged peaks and angles. Caves eating their way through the soft limestone base. Moss-green algae carpeting the exposed rocks beneath the cliff. A lush swath of grass atop the cliff. Well-worn footpaths crisscrossing the plunging slope. A few adventurous hikers milling around the very lip of the precipice. A set of impossibly steep stairs rising from the promenade to provide access to the hiking trails above.

"Here we go." Cal planted himself in front of a plaque that was attached to the rail. "I'll be damned again. This is Dad's picture."

The plaque was a weatherproofed reproduction entitled, *Étretat, la porte d'Aval, bateaux sortant du port,* and the artist was— "Claude Monet," I read aloud. "Eighteen-eighty-five."

"Hunh. So Monet didn't spend all his time fixated on his lily pond. He traveled to the seacoast to paint ocean scenes. Who knew? You have any idea what the title says?"

"Well, *la porte* means door, and *bateaux* is boats, so my best guess would be something like, the door of d'Aval, boats leaving from the port. The arch must be called the door of d'Aval, but where's the elephant that Rob was talking about?"

I spun in a slow circle, thinking I'd missed something obvious. Cal snickered as he tapped my shoulder. "We're both blind. Stand here and look at the arch from this angle."

And there it was—the chiseled crooks and curves of the arch morphing into the illusory vision of an elephant dipping its trunk into the sea.

That's when I heard a scream, accompanied by the sight of a body tumbling off the cliff in a horrifying freefall to the rocks below.

NINE

WE WERE LATE GETTING back to Caudebec.

"I wasn't anywhere near her when she fell." Jackie drained her second discounted cocktail in the ship's lounge. "But I'm getting the willies just thinking about it. I mean, it could have been me."

Since the commune of Étretat supported no police or emergency medical services of its own, assistance had to be summoned from a town ten miles away. Once the authorities arrived, they swarmed over the cliff, reconstructing the scene and taking statements from witnesses who spoke no French and needed the help of a translator. The more grisly work was left to a handful of medics who braved the hazardous terrain at the foot of the precipice to remove Krystal's body before the incoming tide washed it away.

"I'm thankful it wasn't you. When I close my eyes, I can still see her body falling through the air." I folded my arms close to my body to ward off a chill. "You're lucky you didn't see it. I wish I hadn't. It was horrible."

She clutched my forearm and drilled me with a terrified look. "You're not catching my drift, Emily. It really *could* have been me. It probably *would* have been if the three of them had been able to keep up with me."

I paused. "Please tell me you're not suggesting what I think you're suggesting."

"They want to kill me, Emily. I know they do."

I hung my head, eyes shut, shoulders slumped. I'd vowed this trip would be different from all the others. No dead bodies. No sleuthing. No lame-brained accusations. Unfortunately, two days into the trip, we were already dealing with a dead body. But there was no evidence suggesting anything suspicious about the death. According to what the gendarmes had told Rob, Krystal had ventured too close to the edge of the cliff, lost her footing, and fallen off—a tragedy they attributed to lack of guard rails on the part of the French and inappropriate footwear on the part of the victim.

Fortifying myself with a deep breath, I looked up. "Okay, Jack, why do the girls want to kill you?"

"Well, duh? I already told you. They don't *like* me."

"No one likes Bernice either, but they're not lining up to kill her."

"Yet. You've gotta believe me, Em. The minute I saw that cliff, I knew I was a goner."

I checked both ways to see who was within earshot and lowered my voice to a whisper. "If the girls wanted to kill *you*, how come Krystal ended up dead?"

"*That* was an accident. You heard the police report. She wandered too close to the edge in the wrong shoes. You can't hike in five-inch platform slides. Even I know that. Three-inch maybe. But with five-inch you're just asking for trouble."

111

"So if you suspected they wanted to kill you, *why* did you go hiking with them? You couldn't have declined the invitation?"

She shifted her gaze self-consciously. "*Uh*—It was my suggestion."

"*Your* suggestion?"

"Actually, it was Victor's suggestion. Look, he had a 'Come to Jesus' meeting with us this morning before we boarded the bus, and he threatened to fire all four of us if our demeanors didn't become more reflective of the Mona Michelle corporate image. Translation: get along or else. I guess Virginia had some pretty harsh things to say about the tenor of our conversation last night. She thought the girls were extremely unkind ganging up on me the way they did, so she forced Victor's hand. I wish you could have seen the look in their eyes when they were being dressed down, Emily." She looked off into space, cringing with the memory. "It was bone chilling. That's when I knew I was in trouble. The three of them are so gorgeous, they've probably never felt the sting of a rebuke before."

"So you thought hiking a cliff with three would-be killers would be a good way to fend off imminent death?"

"I didn't *know* it was a cliff. I thought it was just some ordinary hiking trail along the beach. And the only reason I suggested hiking was because I figured it's the thing they'd *least* want to do. I mean, why ruin your pedicure if you have other options? But surprise, surprise, they *love* to hike." She let out a dismissive snort. "Sure they do. And I'm Luke Skywalker."

"What made you think they were lying? They're in great shape. How do you know they haven't hiked all over Texas?"

"They asked if the vending machines along the trail would be offering Coke or Pepsi products."

I shook my head with doubt. "I don't know, Jack. I think you're off base with this one."

"Easy for you to say. You haven't been skewered with their spiteful stares. I tell you, Emily, my head's on the chopping block. I'm not imagining it. They have it in for me. Blonde hair, black hearts. I need to figure out a plan to stay alive before they figure out I'm onto them."

Thankfully, her new plan sounded a lot less self-destructive than the one she promised to devise last night while curled up in a fetal ball in her cabin. But still. "I hope this means you're going to forget about your vow to get even with them."

"Why should I?" Her eyes lit up with supreme satisfaction. "In fact, you might be interested to know that I've already set my plan in motion." She ticked off an imaginary item in the air. "Step one. Check."

I gasped so loudly, my ears popped. "You said you had nothing to do with Krystal's death!"

"I didn't! When my feet hit the hiking trail, I fired the afterburners and put as much distance between me and them as possible. When the accident happened, I was actually standing on a footbridge talking to a lovely couple from England." She pulled her camera out of her shoulder bag. "Clive and Fiona. I took pictures. You wanna see?"

"Please tell me the police cleared you."

"They didn't even bother to question me. I told you! I was too far away to be of use to their investigation."

I gave her the evil eye as I blew out a calming breath. "If you were intending to give me the fright of my lifetime, Jack, it worked."

"Sorry." She bowed her head in contrition for a whole half-second. "So...do you want to see my photos? They're really good. The perspective is amazing from three hundred feet up."

A commotion at the opposite end of the lounge announced the arrival of Nana and the rest of the gang. I shot my hand into the air to get their attention, then watched them descend on us like a swarm of hungry locusts.

"I got news," Nana choked out as she reached a nearby chair a full body length ahead of Helen Teig.

Helen crossed her arms beneath her ample bosom and tapped her foot with impunity. "I was here first, Marion."

"Then how come I'm the one what's sittin' down?"

"DICK! GET ME A CHAIR."

As the gang rearranged the loveseats and chairs into a "circle-the-wagons" grouping around us, the barmaid hovered at the perimeter, waiting to take drink orders.

"I'll have a Shirley Temple," said Nana. "Hold the ice. Double the grenadine. As many cherries as you can spare."

"I'll have the discounted special," said Dick Stolee. "Don't care what it is as long as it's cheap."

"I'll have a fuzzy navel," said Dick Teig.

"You already have a fuzzy navel," sniped Helen. "Bring him a diet pop. He's trying to lose weight. Or better yet, a glass of water. None of that fancy brand-name stuff either. Tap is good."

Nana scooted to the edge of her chair, all aflutter. "We just over-heard Rob talkin' to that fella what's got the oxygen strapped to his back, dear. They're doin' an autopsy on that poor girl what fell off the cliff, and as soon as the results come back, Rob'll make an an-nouncement." She clucked woefully. "Here she's gone, and I don't even recollect if I ever seen her yet. Anyone know what she looked like?"

"Long, platinum blonde hair," offered Dick Teig in a dreamy voice. "Blue eyes. Full lips. Creamy skin. Jeans so tight—" He stopped abruptly.

"Anything else?" Helen asked with a calm that was far more frightening than her ire.

"I was just repeating what Stolee told me. Honest to God, Helen. I have no idea what those three blondes look like."

Dick Stolee's jaw dropped like a faulty erector set. "I did *not* tell him anything! Don't listen to him, Grace. The only blonde I've seen on this trip is Lucille."

"My hair is *not* blonde," balked Lucille. She primped the stylish layers. "It's called Seashell."

"Looks pink," said George.

"Cancel that order of tap water!" Helen called out to the barmaid.

"I think the pink is quite becoming," Alice enthused. "It suits your complexion much better than the old color."

"What was the old color?" asked Osmond.

"I would have called it melon," said Tilly.

"Honeydew or musk?" asked Dick Teig.

"My hair was *never* melon," huffed Lucille. "It was peach." She elevated her chin at a jaunty angle. "Peach Margarita to be exact."

"It was apricot," groused Bernice. "You looked like a toy poodle." Boos. Hissing. Razzberries.

"Yah, yah, you people need to upgrade your shtick." Bernice pooh-poohed the furor with a wave of her hand. "And I don't know what the rest of you jokers have been looking at, but there's no way you could have missed the gal who stepped off the cliff. Peroxide blonde? Hair extensions? Fake eyelashes? Fake cheekbones? Fake tan? Does any of this ring a bell? Capped teeth? Double-D implants? Blood-stained top? Saddlebags? Fat ankl—"

"Hold it!" I held up my hand. "Blood-stained top?"

She shook her head in disgust. "Considering how much you morons miss, I don't know why you even bother going on vacation. When we got off the bus in Étretat, she had fresh blood all the way down that dopey-looking top of hers." She pulled her iPhone out of her pocketbook and tapped the screen. "See?" She flashed a picture of a headless torso in a clingy snakeskin top that was smudged with blood.

I blinked in surprise. She certainly hadn't been blood-stained at breakfast, but if she'd been sloppy…I narrowed my gaze. "Are you sure that's blood and not tomato-based horseradish sauce?"

"It was blood," droned Jackie. "She had a nosebleed on the way to Étretat. You didn't hear her? Lucky you. I was sitting behind her, so I couldn't escape. She made such a fuss, I'm surprised all of upper Normandy didn't hear her."

Margi perked up in her chair, brightening like a light on a timer. "Was she prone to nosebleeds?"

"She was prone to whining about them," said Jackie.

"Did she suffer from sinusitis or allergies?"

Jackie stuck out her lower lip and gave a palms-up shrug. "Beats me."

"She suffered from acute motion sickness," I spoke up. "She took some big honking herbal supplement for it."

"I take some big honking supplements that Grace saw advertised on TV," complained Dick Stolee. "What'd you say they're for, Grace?"

"Shut up, Dick," she said out the corner of her mouth.

Margi continued her litany. "Do you know if the victim had a deviated septum, nasal polyps, hypertension, or idiopathic thrombocytopenic purpura?"

Jackie stared at her. "What?"

"I can get a bloody nose if the air's too dry," said George.

"Dick used to have nosebleeds all the time," Helen piped up. "But I found a cure."

"Really?" Margi slid to the edge of her seat, looking breathlessly excited at the thought of a new medical breakthrough. "What'd you do?"

"I taped the entertainment section of *The Des Moines Register* to the glass door that overlooks the deck to remind him to slide the thing open instead of walking into it."

"Would anyone like to be wowed by my photos?" Bernice waved her camera like a scalper waving concert tickets. "I'll let you see them for free. If you wait 'til we get home, you might have to fork out $11.95 to see them in an upcoming issue of *Iowa Hog and Travel*. C'mon, people. I'm offering them to you at a bargain basement price."

"*Ew,*" Jackie cooed. "I love a bargain." She waved her camera at Bernice. "I'll look at yours if you'll look at mine."

The corners of Bernice's mouth curved into a slow droop. "Let me get this straight. You want me to waste my valuable vacation time poring over pictures that I didn't take myself?" She let out a disdainful snort. "I don't think so."

The barmaid returned with the drink orders. As she navigated through our maze of chairs, Osmond stood up and caught my eye, then indicated with a bob of his head that he'd like to speak to me privately. "Be back in a jiff," I said as I popped up.

"I don't mean to make a pest of myself, Emily," he said when we'd rounded the bar into a more secluded area, "but have you received any contact information for Solange yet?"

"I set the wheels in motion last night, but I forgot to check at the front desk when we got back, so why don't I do that right now?"

"I'd sure appreciate it." He wrung his bony hands. "Truth is, I've been on a rollercoaster ever since last night. What'll I do if I *am* a father, Emily? What'll I say? How should I act? What if Solange's family doesn't accept me? What if I'm a disappointment to them? It gives me acid indigestion just thinking about it." He sighed. "But then I look at the other side of the coin, and I think, what happens if I've got it all wrong, and I'm not a father? Then I'll look like a pathetic old fool." He dropped his head. "A disappointed old fool. I'm kinda looking forward to the thrill of it now. I bet there's not too many fellas who become first-time fathers at my age."

Nope. Only the filthy rich ones.

I wrapped my arm around his shoulders. "I'm sorry you're stuck on the rollercoaster, Osmond, but the last thing you should be obsessing about is whether Solange's family will accept you or not. Of *course* they will! And you can quote me on that. Everyone who knows you, loves you. Bernice can't even manage to say anything ornery about you." I gave his shoulder a reassuring squeeze. "There's nothing better that could happen to *any* family than to have you in it."

I laced the fingers of my free hand through his and held tight for a long, consoling moment. "You were a blessing to Solange, Osmond," I said in a quiet voice. "But you weren't her screaming chicken. You were her angel."

He bobbed his head as if dismissing the idea, which is when I noticed what I hadn't noticed before. "You're not wearing your cervical collar anymore!"

"Nope. Pulling the lever on that one-armed bandit all afternoon did my neck more good than a month's worth of physical therapy. Pain's all gone. See?" He swiveled his head left, right, forward, back. "Good as new." He winced as he rubbed his arm. "Now the only pain I've got is in my elbow."

"So how'd you do at the casino? Were you as lucky as you felt?"

"Nah. Margi was the only big winner."

"No kidding? The church raffle, now this? Good for Margi!"

He lowered his brows and tucked in his lips. "We're not so sure it's good."

"Why not?"

"I don't wanna be spreading rumors, so the only thing I'll say about the matter is—unexpected windfalls aren't always what they're cracked up to be."

"Oh, c'mon, Osmond. You can't leave me dangling like this."

He locked his lips with an imaginary key. "Talk to your grandmother. She'll fill you in."

Both baffled and alarmed by his statement, I made my way toward the lobby, taking note of other guests who had wandered into the lounge for conversation and discounted drinks. Woody was holding court in the center of the room, surrounded by distinguished-looking white-haired and bald gentlemen with sober demeanors and serious eyes. Cal was deep in discussion with a group of men his own age, occupying the settees and chairs next to the port windows. I wondered if the two opposing parties had conducted their business meeting yet, because if they had, it didn't look as if they'd resolved anything. As I neared the exit, I passed good old Irv, slouched in an armchair, cane braced against the cushion, dark glasses still hugging his face, highball glass nestled in his lap, with three empties sitting on the table in front of him. I gave him a little finger wave as I passed, but when he didn't wave back, I figured he was either dozing behind his shades or too impaired to lift his hand. Either way, it looked as if Irv was planning to indulge in a liquid diet this evening rather than the four courses the rest of us would be served.

"I'm so sorry, Mrs. Miceli," the purser commiserated when I made my inquiry at the front desk. "Mrs. Saint-Sauveur hasn't responded to your request yet, but I promise to let you know the moment something comes in. It shouldn't be long. She's ever so good about answering her email."

We both winced as feedback blared out over the speaker system. *KREEE… KREEEOOO! "Bon soir, mesdames et messieurs."* Heavy breathing. More feedback. "Good evening, ladies and gentlemen. For your dining pleasure, the restaurant doors are now open."

Knowing what would come next, I idled at the front desk in an effort to avoid the stampede from the lounge, but to my amazement, there was no stampede. A few of Cal's cremationists trickled out from the lounge, but they were well-mannered and orderly, and proceeded down the corridor without throwing one elbow, cutting anyone off, or accidentally tripping each other on purpose. They were so civil, it nearly brought tears to my eyes.

"Anything wrong, Mrs. Miceli?" asked the purser. "You look so… forlorn."

"I'm just surprised that my group is being so laid back this evening. They usually fight their way to the front of the line when the dinner bell rings."

"In the lounge, are they?"

I nodded.

"Enjoying Happy Hour?"

"Yup."

"Brilliant." Bending toward me over the counter, she remarked in a confidential tone, "The discounted drink specials always cause a bit of a lag in response time." Her expression turned solicitous as she looked beyond me. "Blimey," she whispered. "Poor Mr. and Mrs. Martin. The dishy girl who fell off the cliff was in their party. I can't imagine how dreadful they must feel about the accident."

I turned around nonchalantly to observe Victor being ushered from the reading library by Bobbi and Dawna, who'd each grabbed an arm and were assisting him across the lobby. Virginia trailed behind, stone-faced and aloof, her makeup untouched by tears, appearing ill-tempered and bored.

"He looks devastated," the purser rasped.

And so did the girls. They were both red-eyed and weepy and didn't look as if they'd bothered to retouch their lip gloss or comb their hair, which said a lot about their mental state. They actually looked crippled by grief, which kinda surprised me because, based on their performance last night, I wasn't convinced they were capable of being affected by someone else's misfortune.

Did they regret acting so snotty to each other at their last meal together? Victor's proposed bonus had really brought out the worst in them. But if Krystal's assessment of her sales record had been correct, and Bobbi and Dawna *knew* she was the undisputed top dog, why had they gone out of their way to insult her? I mean, why waste your breath if you already know who's going to win?

As the foursome entered the main corridor, I realized that Krystal's death had changed the entire dynamic of the Mona Michelle group. The prize would now be awarded to one of the other contenders because, as of this afternoon, the "sure thing" was out of the picture.

A frisson of unease pricked my spine as I watched the girls disappear.

Gee. How convenient.

TEN

FOUR HOURS UPRIVER FROM Caudebec-en-Caux sits the capital of Upper Normandy—a medieval port famous for having the highest church spire in France and infamous for having burned a nineteen-year-old peasant girl at the stake. It's called Rouen, and when we moored alongside its north bank after breakfast the following morning, the sky was clad with angry storm clouds that were drenching the city in a torrential downpour.

From behind my balcony doors I looked out at the rain lashing the pavement and tried to decide which pair of favorite sandals I'd be forced to ruin on our port walk.

Knock, knock, knock.

"We voted to skip the walkin' tour," said Nana when I answered the door. "The final tally was eleven yeas, one nay, and one abstention."

"Eleven and two? Isn't that ... thirteen votes?"

"Yup."

I regarded her narrowly. "You only have twelve people in your group."

"We got thirteen now. We're makin' Jackie an honorary member on account of them two blondes are tryin' to kill her, so we're puttin' her under our protection."

Oh, God. I pulled her into my room. "No one is trying to kill Jackie."

"We figure it's better bein' safe than sorry."

I sat her on the bed. "Her conspiracy theory is imaginary. She's inserting herself where she doesn't belong because she doesn't know how *not* to make everything about herself. I know. I was married to her. Him. Her."

"She says if she'd been anywhere near them girls on the top of that cliff yesterday, she woulda been the one what fell."

"Did she tell you what prompted her to think her fellow reps are trying to kill her?"

"She says they was lookin' at her funny."

"How does that signal murderous intent?"

"She explained it to us real good, dear, but I can't recall what she said now. We was all on the edge of our seats though. She really got our hearts poundin'."

Alarm bells went off in my head. "No good is going to come of this, Nana. Trust me. I can feel it in my bones."

"Maybe what you're feelin' is a touch of rheumatism, dear. The rain can bring it on real bad."

"How do you propose to guard a six-foot transsexual?"

She regarded me over the tops of her wirerims. "We was plannin' on wingin' it."

I rolled my eyes. "So in a concerted attempt to keep Jackie safe, you all voted to skip the port walk and miss exploring one of the oldest towns in Normandy?"

"We're stayin' on the boat on account of it's rainin.' Folks don't wanna risk ruinin' their orthotic inserts, 'cuz once you get 'em wet, they're not worth beans no more, and Medicare don't pay for no more than one set a year."

"Oh." Viewed in that light, they'd actually made a very calculated, reasonable choice. Wow. What was up with that? "So have you given any thought as to how you're going to entertain yourselves if you stay aboard ship all day?"

"There's a whiteboard in the lobby what lists all the onboard activities what's happenin' in the lounge all day long, dear. Food tastin'. Lectures. Demonstrations. Art lessons. And a couple of time slots sayin' 'surprise session.' George says it sounds a lot like boot camp, only without the guns or latrine duty." She peeked at her watch. "I hate to cut this short, dear, but Tilly's savin' a seat for me in the front row, so I gotta run." She hopped off the bed.

I held up a finger to detain her. "Two things before you go. I was going to ask you to make a special effort to keep Osmond's spirits up, but if he was feeling engaged enough to conduct a vote this morning, he must be feeling more like his old self, right?"

"Osmond didn't conduct no vote, dear. It was Osmond what abstained. He's so twitchy right now, he got a notion to give up his official duties until he's not feelin' so 'mentally distracted.'"

"So who did the honors?"

"The Dicks. One of 'em called for the vote while the other one done the tally." She gave her head a woeful shake. "Them two's gonna make a real sham of the democratic process. The one don't know how to state the proposition and the other don't know how to add. It took 'em five rounds to get the tally right on account of Bernice decided to tweet her vote, so the final count never jived. She never would of pulled no stunt like that with Osmond 'cuz he woulda disqualified her for votin' irregularities. He don't tolerate no funny business with the electoral process. So's all I'm gonna say is, if the Dicks have to fill in for Osmond for more than a day or two, it'll be the end of the group as we know it. Them Dicks don't got a half a brain between 'em." She regarded me with pleading eyes. "You got any idea how much longer Osmond's gonna be mentally distracted?"

I offered her a reassuring smile. "Not much longer, I hope. Which brings me to my second point. What's the scoop with Margi? Osmond suggested that her winning streak at the casino was more curse than blessing. He said you'd clue me in."

She shuffled back to the bed and sat down. She exhaled a deep sigh. "I hate to break it to you, dear, but Margi's turned into one of them folks what does the same thing over and over again."

I gasped. "She's been diagnosed with obsessive compulsive disorder?"

"Nope. She's one of them addicts."

"MARGI?"

"I never thought it could happen to one of my own friends. Stuff like this is only s'posed to happen to movie stars recoverin' from back ailments."

"Oh my God. Is it work related? She has such easy access to drugs at the clinic. What's she addicted to? Oxycontin? Vicodin? Percocet?"

"The BBWS Network."

I waited a beat. "What?"

"The Big Beautiful Woman's Shoppin' Network. It's on account of that shoppin' spree what the church raffled off. Ever since she won, she can't do nuthin' but buy, buy, buy. We're thinkin' she needs an intervention."

Unh-oh. Sounded like she got zapped. I knew such things happened to people—that a person's life could change in the blink of an eye. But I thought the transformation typically revolved around an experience that was more deeply religious than a church raffle. "You're telling me that Margi had such an awesome time at Farm and Fleet when she selected her new wardrobe, that she somehow activated a latent buying gene that's turned her into a flaming shopaholic?"

Nana looked puzzled. "She didn't buy no new wardrobe at Farm and Fleet."

"Then how did she come by all her spiffy new clothes?"

"I just told you. The Big Beautiful Woman's Shoppin' Network."

I eyed her narrowly. "If she didn't buy clothes with her five-thousand-dollar gift certificate, what *did* she buy?"

"Flat screen TVs. One for every room in her house. She didn't have no high-definition megapixel set before, so now that she can see what all them shoppin' items really look like, she's buyin' everythin' in sight, from every room in the house, twenty-four hours a day." She lowered her voice to a library whisper. "Even from the potty. She's got her sleep cycle so topsy-turvy, she's been real bound up."

"So ... if I'm understanding this correctly, none of you are happy she was the big winner at the casino yesterday because ... you're afraid she'll blow it on things that make her look chic and elegant?"

"Them winnin's are just gonna feed her addiction, Emily. We couldn't hardly pry her away from them TVs of hers before. Now that she's got cash to burn, she's gonna go straight to the dogs. We'll never get to see her no more." She glanced down at her hands dejectedly. "We'll probably have to start buyin' our own hand sanitizer."

"How much money did she win?"

"Ten thousand Euros."

"WHAT?" I tried to do a quick currency conversion in my head but got hung up on all the zeroes. "How much is that in US dol—"

"Thirteen thousand forty-eight dollars. And eighty cents. She just kept movin' around the room, hittin' the jackpot on everythin' she touched. The management finally asked her to leave on account of they was runnin' out of money to refill the machines. I never seen nuthin' like it. But I'm glad we left early 'cuz that give us a chance to see the beach."

"Oh my God! How come she wasn't shouting the news from the rafters last night?"

"She was too busy carryin' on about nosebleeds. You seen her. No one on earth gets more of a buzz talkin' about blood than Margi."

"So is she planning to spend some of her winnings in Paris? Think of the shopping spree she can have, Nana. Yves Saint Laurent. Chanel. Christian Dior. Givenchy."

"She don't plan to try on no clothes in Paris."

"Why not?"

"'Cuz gettin' in and outta clothes is a pain. The fun part for Margi is pickin' up the phone and makin' that call. The one-on-one contact with the gal what takes her order makes her feel like she's gettin' real old-fashioned customer service."

She checked her watch again and leaped to her feet, panic in her eyes. "Dang. Tilly's probably havin' to use her cane to fend off folks what's fightin' for my chair. I gotta run."

I hurried ahead of her to open the door.

"Are you goin' on the walkin' tour?" she asked as she rushed into the corridor.

"You bet."

"Would you take a picture of the site where them fellas burned St. Joan of Arc? I promised the gals at the Legion of Mary that I'd bring back authentic photos, so they'll revoke my membership if I show up empty-handed."

"I'm sure they won't penalize you for weather-related issues beyond your control."

"They might. I forced 'em to brush up on the life of St. Joan by makin' 'em sit through that 1948 tearjerker movie with Ingrid Bergman. At the end of two and a half hours, Lena Eggebraaten was so worn out from cryin', her eyes swelled shut behind her trifocals."

"She didn't realize St. Joan was going to die?"

"She didn't realize the dang movie was gonna be so borin'. There wasn't no special effects. Not a one. Lena takes her grandkids to see them *Transformer* flicks, so she was missin' the thrill of watchin' the screen explode in digital 3-D and Dolby surround sound."

The corridor started getting congested as passengers ventured out of their cabins toting raingear and umbrellas.

KREEEOOOO! Bzzzzt . . . Bzzzzzt. "Good morning, ladies and gentlemen, and welcome to Rouen. A reminder to those of you who'll be participating in our port walk this morning. Please stop by the front desk to pick up your port passes, headphones, and receivers. The tour is set to commence in fifteen minutes. Thank you."

I hurried back into my cabin, riffled through my shoes, jammed my feet into my least favorite pair of wedges, threw on my raincoat, stuffed my umbrella into my shoulder bag, and joined the crowd that was surging toward the lobby.

Mayhem surrounded the front desk. Hands yanking pre-packaged earbuds out of bins. Cellophane wrappers being ripped. Port passes flying out of mailbox slots. Receivers being slapped into waiting hands. Names being yelled to the purser and her assistant over the counter. I'd intended to inquire about the status of our email request before leaving the boat, but the situation was so chaotic, I figured I'd have better luck when I got back.

I announced my name to the assistant purser, picked up my port pass, hung a receiver around my neck, pulled a package of earbuds from the bin, snugged my hood over my head, and headed down the gangway to join the guests clustered beneath their umbrellas along the embankment. Happily, the pelting rain had dwindled to a light but steady shower, so my feet weren't getting as wet as I thought they would. Rob stood off to the side, studying a clipboard beneath his oversized tour director's umbrella. I hastened over to him.

"Any word back on Krystal's autopsy report yet?"

He regarded me blankly, as if trying to figure out who I was.

"Emily Miceli? I'm on the tour?"

"Oh, sure. Emily. Sorry. Names and faces are my downfall, but I'm working on it."

A tour director who was bad with names and faces was a bit like an accountant who was bad with adding and subtracting, but hey, what did I know? "You're not alone," I sympathized. "I think a majority of people are bad with names and faces." But fortunately, they were wise enough to enter professions where remembering names and faces *wasn't the most essential part of their work.*

"Yeah. It's hell. No sooner do a few guests start looking familiar than they leave, and you have to start all over again with a different group."

"I guess that's why you encourage us to wear our name tags."

"It'd be a lot more convenient if we could print guest names on baseball caps. That way we wouldn't always be staring at people's chests. The company gets a lot of complaints from the ladies about that." He paused. "I'm sorry. What was your question?"

"Krystal's autopsy?"

"Right. I received a call just before I left my cabin but haven't had a chance to tell anyone other than Mr. and Mrs. Martin. She apparently died from a brain hemorrhage."

My mouth fell open. *Uff-da.* I hadn't seen *that* coming.

"The report states that the hemorrhage was so massive, she probably died instantly, so she was most likely dead even before she fell off the cliff. In fact, the police might have to amend their initial report to state that it was her sudden death that caused her fall rather than her poor choice of footwear."

"Oh, my God. I don't know what to say." Other than I was relieved foul play hadn't been a factor in her death, and I was sorry I'd looked at Bobbi and Dawna last night with mounting suspicion.

Krystal had died from natural causes.

There were no killers in our midst, which meant Jackie was in the protective custody of the gang for no reason at all and would therefore be treated to the full brunt of Bernice's tirades all day.

I had to restrain my feet from breaking out in a happy dance. *Yes!*

"They can't release the body until they run a few more labs. Unknown what's going to happen after that. I've never had a guest die on me before, so this is all uncharted territory."

A remembered image of Krystal's snakeskin top photo flashed in my mind. "She suffered a nosebleed on the bus yesterday. Were you aware of that?"

"I thought everyone on the bus was aware of it. Where were you sitting that you missed it? The way she was carrying on, you'd have thought she was about to die." He hesitated, reassessing his words. "Of course, she *did* die, but—"

"Is it possible that her nosebleed was the first indication that something was going terribly wrong inside her brain?"

Rob lifted his shoulders. "You got me. I'm not a doctor. I provided her with extra tissue. That's about all I'm authorized to do."

Feeling a sudden presence at my right shoulder, I turned my head slowly.

"What's the purpose of all this extra crap anyway?" whined Bernice as she waved her receiver and earbuds at me. "Isn't it bad enough that we have to schlep umbrellas because of this crappy weather?"

I stared at her, deadpan. *There was no God. There was no God.*

Rob noted the time. "Would you excuse me?" He ranged a look around the area where the guests had assembled. "I need to make a phone call to see what's happened with our local guide. She's running late."

"So, Bernice—" I ducked quickly to avoid getting my eye poked out by her umbrella. "I was under the impression you'd voted to skip the port walk."

"You never get it right, do you? The *wusses* voted to ditch the walk. *I* voted to take it."

"You're not worried about ruining your orthotics?"

"What orthotics? My feet are perfect ... thanks to two over-priced bunionectomies and Medicare parts A, B, C, and D. So what am I supposed to do with all this junk they crammed down my throat at the front desk?"

"This is your receiver." I plucked the bar soap-sized gizmo from her hand and looped the attached lanyard around her neck. "When you plug your earbuds into it, you're supposed to be able to hear whatever the person on the transmitting end is saying."

"Who's gonna be on the transmitting end?"

"The local guide, I assume."

She stared down at the added clutter on her chest. "It's covering up my name tag."

"Why don't we join the crowd so we can get further operating instructions?"

"Slackers. What's wrong with the guides in France that they can't scream the information at us like all the other guides do?"

We skirted the perimeter of the group until we reached what I deduced might become the front of the pack since it was closest to the stairs that linked the river promenade to the street above. Faces were obscured within hoods and beneath umbrellas, but I was able to pick out Woody and some of the men he'd been sitting with last night. Cal huddled with a few of his buddies in the opposite direction of where Woody was standing. Victor was here with Virginia, which surprised me. I thought he might be too devastated to venture off the boat today, but perhaps a long walk in the rain would help soothe his emotional upheaval. I didn't see Bobbi or Dawna until I caught sight of their blonde hair in the middle of the group, surrounded by a phalanx of doe-eyed males.

"Could I have your attention, please?" Rob hopped up on a bench with his yellow umbrella. "Our local guide is running a few minutes late, so this is a good time to introduce you to our mobile speaker system. Have you all hung your receivers around your necks?"

Nods. Mumbles.

"Locate the dial on top of your receiver and turn it to channel four."

Studied silence. Heavy breathing.

"My receiver doesn't have a dial," complained an older male voice.

"Move your thumb," suggested another guest. "It's underneath."

"Is everyone on channel four?" asked Rob.

"What's on the other channels?" someone called out.

"We're only interested in channel four. Now, plug your headphones into the port on the side of your receiver."

"I didn't get any headphones," protested a female guest.

Rob held up the cellophane package containing our audio equipment. "Headphones, earphones. Whatever. Plug the prong into your receiver."

A woman standing nearby sniggered to her friend as she ripped open the pouch containing a coil of spaghetti wire that resembled string licorice. "I'm glad he explained what's inside here. I thought it was a mid-morning snack."

"Is everyone plugged in?"

Murmurs. Head bobbing.

"Now, insert your earphones into your ears in a comfortable position."

I stuck a bud in each ear and winced. Hard plastic. Odd shape. Uncomfortable fit. This should go over well. I sidled a glance at Bernice who was so entangled in audio wire, she looked like the poster child for self-strangulation. As I helped her sort through the jumble of cords, Rob's voice suddenly erupted inside my head. "TESTING... ONE, TWO—"

YOW!

I hit my volume control and dialed it back to a level that wouldn't cause my brain to explode.

"Are we supposed to be hearing something?" Woody called out.

Rob's breath hissed softly in my ears. "Can you hear me now?"

"Why can't I hear anything?" asked Woody.

"I hear a philharmonic orchestra," enthused a nearby guest.

"*Ride of the Valkyries?*" asked her friend.

"You hear it, too?"

"It's my cell phone."

Cal sprinted over to his dad. "Have you turned your volume up?"

"How do I do that?"

Cal made the adjustment.

"Testing... one, two, three," said Rob.

"*YOW!*" cried Woody.

"Do these receivers put us at risk of being electrocuted?" a woman fretted.

"Only if you're struck by lightning while you're wearing one," teased Rob.

"Is that a yes or a no?" she huffed.

"Sorry," Rob apologized. "To clarify, you cannot be electrocuted by your receivers. You can stand waist deep in water, and nothing, I repeat, nothing will happen other than you'll get really wet."

"Why do they look like garage door openers?" questioned a man in the back. "Will they actually open garage doors?"

"What about reproductive health?" asked one of Woody's cohorts. "Can wearing one of these things decrease our sperm count?"

"*Uhhhh…*"

"Is medical research going to find out years from now that these receivers cause cancer?" queried a man near the front.

"How come these things don't have touchscreens?"

"Can we take photos with them?"

I smiled broadly, tickled I wasn't the one having to field their questions.

"My receiver's a dud," bellowed Bernice.

"Are you tuned in to channel four?" asked Rob.

"Yup."

"Is your volume turned up?"

"Yup."

"And you can't hear my voice?"

"Not through your stupid earphones, I can't."

I looked over her equipment, finding the problem immediately. "Okay, Bernice. Here's the thing. In order to hear anything through your earphones, you actually have to insert them in your ears."

She pushed her features into a scowl. "Go ahead, genius." She shoved her hair out of the way and angled her ear toward me. "Make my day."

I shifted my gaze from her earphones to her ear. *Oops.* I cupped my hands around my mouth and called out to Rob, "Is there a way to insert earbuds around hearing aids?"

"*Uhhhh…*"

"Do these things carry the ESPN sports channel?" asked a man standing by Woody. "I want to find out how the Cubbies did against the Brewers."

"Your receivers aren't broadband radios," barked Rob. "They can't open garage doors. They won't take pictures. They *will* allow you to hear what our local guide is saying, and that's *all* they'll do. If you're unable to insert your earphones comfortably into your ears"— he bobbed his head as if considering the options—"then stand close enough to our guide so you'll be able to hear her without them. Any questions?"

"What'll I do if my receiver short circuits my pacemaker?"

Oh, God.

I heard a *splat, splat, splat* of footsteps rushing in our direction and turned to see a woman with a canary-yellow umbrella scurry past me toward Rob.

"And here she is now," Rob announced in a voice that was thick with relief. "Our local guide. Come on up here so people can have a look at you."

She hopped onto the bench beside Rob and tilted her umbrella back, favoring us with a wave and a bright smile.

Oh my God! Madeleine Saint-Sauveur!

ELEVEN

"IN 1348, THE CITY of Rouen suffered the worst outbreak of bubonic plague in its history."

Madeleine's voice crackled in my ears as we gathered around her in a courtyard surrounded by ancient two- and three-story buildings.

"History has given the catastrophe many names: the Great Plague, the Great Pestilence, the Black Death. By the time it had run its course in Rouen, three-quarters of the city's population lay dead, which presented a gruesome problem for the living: With parish cemeteries having run out of burial space, where could so many bodies be interred?"

A large rectangle of grass occupied the center of the square, and in the middle of this, nearly camouflaged within the leafy canopy of a dozen hardwoods, rose a crucifix that was both tall and painfully slender.

"The task of burying the victims fell upon parish priests who understood they needed to dispose of the bodies quickly to prevent more disease from spreading. So they decided to do so in a most unfortunate manner." Madeleine made a sweeping gesture that included the entire courtyard. "They buried them in a mass grave. Here. At Aitre de St. Maclou."

Gasps, followed by uneasy silence. Eyes slowly drifted to the pavers beneath our feet. "You mean, we're standing on them?" asked Woody.

Madeleine nodded. "*Oui*, monsieur."

Woody shook his head. "Damn. That's just wrong."

"By the time another plague struck two hundred years later, the cemetery could no longer provide in-ground burial, so facilities were expanded above ground to the buildings around us. Three of the galleries were completed in 1533, and for nearly two centuries, they were used to store the bones of Rouen's dead, stacking them from floor to ceiling on every floor and in the attic space. To this day, few people walking along Rue de Martainville, with its upscale artisan shops and sidewalk cafés, realize that the antiquated wooden doors at number 186 are the unlikely entrance to the site of an ancient charnel house."

"Us folks in the profession never say charnel house," Woody spoke up, an air of authority in his voice. "We call it an ossuary, a place that holds the bones of the dead."

"How come I've never heard that word before?" asked Bobbi Benedict.

Virginia Martin regarded her without mirth. "Perhaps you should expand your friendships to include people who can use words longer than one syllable."

Unh-oh. Truce over.

"So if an ossuary holds bones," said the woman who'd been going to eat her earbuds as a morning snack, "what's the purpose of a mausoleum?"

"A mausoleum is a grander structure," offered one of Woody's buddies. "It's a free-standing monument that encloses the body of the deceased. Like the Taj Mahal."

"I thought a crypt enclosed the body of the deceased," argued another woman.

"It does," said Woody. "There's a lot of terminology connected with—"

"But if a crypt encloses the dead body, what does a vault do?" asked a man wearing a wide-brimmed bucket hat.

"I think a vault is the same thing as a tomb," said the woman standing next to him.

"So if the Taj Mahal is a mausoleum," questioned a man who was standing near Bernice, "what does that make the pyramids? Mausoleums, vaults, crypts, or tombs?"

"It makes them overrated tourist attractions," crabbed Bernice. "Like this place."

Dawna folded her arms across her chest and stomped her booted feet on the ground to ward off the chilly moistness in the air. "I don't know about the rest of y'all, but I'm gonna be cremated when I die. And I don't want to end up in any musty old mausoleum for all eternity, so I'm gonna have my ashes scattered in a place that's near and dear to my heart."

Bernice smiled dourly. "Where? The cosmetic aisle at Wal-Mart?"

Dawna sucked in her breath, looking almost too horrified to form words. "The National Firearms Museum in Fairfax, Virginia, which just happens to be the world headquarters for the National

Rifle Association. I'm gonna spend eternity with the folks who're gonna defend my freedoms against the excesses of a tyrannical government."

"Dream on," mocked Bernice. "If your ashes get scattered on the floor of some fancy museum, you'll be spending eternity at the bottom of an industrial strength vacuum cleaner bag in a landfill on the outskirts of DC."

"You'll need documentation to have your cremains transported legally," asserted Woody. Unzipping the side pocket of his jacket, he removed a small leather case. "My card," he said as he handed her his business card. "Don't hesitate to contact me if you have any questions, although I can say with absolute certainty that cremation should be your choice of last resort." He waved the case in the air. "Anyone else want one?"

Oh, God.

The rain had stopped about ten minutes ago, allowing us to collapse our umbrellas, but dark clouds still loomed overhead, threatening to drench us at any moment.

"Do these buildings serve any purpose now?" asked Victor.

"*Mais oui,*" chimed Madeleine. "The galleries have become the home of Rouen's Fine Art Academy."

"What became of the bones?" asked Cal.

"In the eighteenth century, the buildings were earmarked to become a school for poor boys, so the bones were removed to—"

BONG*bong*BONG*bongbongbong*BONG!*DING*bong*ding* BONG!

"…outside the…" *BONGBONGBONG!*

I gazed at the church spire towering above the rooftop of the galleries and realized that even though Rouen was a city of medieval houses, winding passageways, and sidewalk cafés, it was mostly a city of church bells that rang out with riotous abandon at any odd minute on the hour. Even earbuds and receivers were no defense against the cacophonous clang.

"Could you repeat that?" Cal yelled out to Madeleine. He waved his hand toward the distant spire. "The bells."

She nodded happily. "In the eighteenth…" *bong… bong…* BONG BONG… "poor boys…" *ding…* DING… DING… *dingding…*

Yup. This was going well. I unplugged my earbuds, which were wedged in my ear canal as comfortably as a couple of peach pits, and wandered away from the group to shoot a few photographs.

The four buildings that boxed in the square were an architectural mixture of half-timbered masonry panels, long banks of framed windows, and decorative wooden columns carved in chilling, graphic relief. Spooky skulls grinned down at me with empty eye sockets embedded with eight hundred years of soot and grime. A ghoulish chain of crossed bones marched above the window frames, vying for space with coffins, burial shrouds, gravediggers' shovels, and the Grim Reaper's scythe. Aitre de St. Maclou might have appeared less gloomy in full sunshine, but with its macabre history and the overcast sky, it seemed as if a veil of gray haze had descended upon the entire complex, tarnishing the view.

"Do you want to have your picture taken with the mummified cat?" asked Cal as he headed toward me.

I zoomed in on a skull and snapped my camera shutter before turning to him. "Excuse me?"

"The mummified cat. Full-grown, I might add." He pointed toward the entrance. "They discovered it in the wall when they were doing some repair work, but instead of removing it, or walling over it again, they slapped a glass panel over it so it can be on display for the tourist crowd. I'm a dog guy myself, but that doesn't mean I can't feel for future hordes of grossed-out cat lovers."

"How did a full-grown cat get inside the wall?"

Cal shrugged. "It has an Edgar Allen Poe feel about it, doesn't it? Madeleine says certain felines were thought to embody the devil. Black cats, mostly, so some overly superstitious zealot probably entombed the thing to help ward off evil spirits. And, yes, rumor has it that this particular creature was black."

BONG... BONG... BONG... BONG... BONG...

Cal rolled his eyes. "You think it's like this every day, or only on Sundays?"

"Are you taking pictures?" Woody called out as he hustled toward us.

"Of what?" asked Cal.

"The mass grave! What? Too obvious for you?" Woody eyed the courtyard in the same way P. T. Barnum might have eyed the Feejee Mermaid. "There's money to be made here."

"Geez, Dad, will you give it a rest?"

"You know what your problem is, Cal?" scolded Woody. "You don't think like a funeral director. You think like an accountant. We're standing on a mass grave. Think of the presentation we could put together comparing the barbaric burial customs of our ancestors to the humane practices offered by funeral homes today. Give it historical context, stir in some subtle marketing, add a pinch of a discount, top it off with a followup call after potential clients have let our offer bake in their brains for a week. We could be looking at the windfall of a lifetime."

Cal skewered his dad with a sour look. "Always pushing the envelope, aren't you?"

"Someone has to. Leaving the marketing decisions to you will probably throw us into bankruptcy."

BONGbong*bong*BONGBONG*bongbongbong*BONG...BONG...

"I'm not going to use a human disaster of this magnitude to fatten our pockets," Cal shouted over the symphony of ringing bells. "Using this place for your personal advertising is not only crass and in bad taste, it's sacrilegious! So if you want pictures, get Walt or Ed to take them." He shot a curious look around the courtyard. "Where are they anyway?"

A hint of alarm flickered in Woody's eyes before he brushed off the question. "None of your business where they are."

"Did they stay on the boat?"

"Last I knew, you weren't their keeper, so they can damn well do what they want to do."

"What are you trying to hide? They must be doing something you don't want me to know about, else you wouldn't have a problem..." Cal narrowed his eyes with sudden perception. "You arranged something, didn't you?"

Woody hardened his jaw and stuck out his bottom lip. "What's it to you?"

"Did you con the purser into letting Walt and Ed give some kind of powerpoint presentation about pre-packaged funeral plans? There were a whole bunch of learning sessions being offered on the boat today. Did you manage to weasel your way onto the schedule?"

Woody's face turned florid, his voice acerbic. "We all make mistakes in life, Cal. Apparently my biggest was bringing you into the business. I should have recruited your sister instead. *She* gets it, which is more than I can say for you."

"You want to can me, Dad? Go ahead. Turn my share of the business over to Jody. I'll give you a month before you come crawling back to me with your tail between your legs."

"Don't hold your breath."

Cal snorted derisively. "If that's supposed to scare me, it doesn't."

"It should." Woody hitched up his belt and fixed Cal with a sharp look. "I own you, son. You're just too dumb to realize it. Remember, wills can be changed."

"Go ahead," Cal spat. "I dare you."

"Is Madeleine trying to round us up?" I asked in an attempt to redirect their attention. "Looks like she's counting heads. Shall we join the crowd?"

"Why not?" quipped Woody. "The damage here is already done." He caught my eye. "Sorry you had to witness that little scene, Emily. What can I say? My son spends a lot of time acting like the hind end of a horse."

He strutted off to join the crowd as light rain began drizzling down on us again. I opened my umbrella and, not knowing what else to say, let fly the first thing that came into my head. "Your sister's name is Jody Jolly?"

Cal laughed despite his obvious irritation. "Yah. She's never forgiven them for that particular act of sadism."

"She's not part of the family business?"

"Nope. She had no intention of spending her life living under Dad's thumb, so she got out while the going was good. Studied languages in college and became a translator at the UN. She doesn't get home much, so I don't see her too often. Dad's temper isn't a big drawing card, and the older he gets, the less control he seems to have over it."

"He'd never actually get angry enough to make good on his threat, would he? I mean, I've eaten a couple of meals with him. I've seen him in action. He's more bark than bite. Isn't he?"

"If you're asking if he'd ever really cut me out of his will, the answer is, when it comes to the business, he'll do whatever it takes to make a dime. And if that includes shutting me out and finding a new partner, he'd do that, too. But I've paid my dues for more years than I want to admit, so if he decides to give me the shaft, he'll do it over my dead body."

I shivered as the drizzle grew into a light shower, but I wasn't sure if the chill in my bones was a reaction to the dampness in the air, or the venom I heard oozing from Cal Jolly's voice.

———

We followed Madeleine down a pedestrian walkway that threaded between a monstrous church on the left and a series of businesses on the right whose storefronts were locked behind sliding metal grates. The church looked older than the Great Flood, its stone façade blackened with soot, its lacy spikes and spires and arches resembling the buttercream frosting piped out of a pastry tube. We passed restaurants and bistros with immediate outside seating for customers who dared to brave the weather and sip their cafés au lait with a heavy dose of rainwater. We detoured into a narrow alley between two unassuming buildings and wandered into an Alice in Wonderland-like rabbit hole that opened up into a trove of unexpected treasures: a garden of pink hydrangeas tucked behind a wrought-iron fence. A half-timbered house painted the scarlet red and white of a Christmas candy cane. Arcane wooden doors built into a solid brick wall that was half-hidden beneath overhanging vines. By the time we circled around toward the ginormous cathedral whose steeple reached halfway to the stratosphere, it was raining so hard, we ran for cover beneath the columned portico of a furniture shop that stood opposite the church. Huddling together, we collapsed our umbrellas, flicked water off our raingear, and detached our earbuds so we could enjoy the symphonic effect of rain pounding eight-hundred-year-old pavers.

"If I'd known the weather was going to be this foul, I wouldn't have come," Virginia Martin complained to Madeleine. "You should cancel these walking tours when storms are predicted. Everyone is miserable. Why don't you just take us back to the boat and be done with it?"

Madeleine shrugged, palms skyward. "The rain starts, and then it stops. If you go back, there is so much you will miss."

"How many people demand to be taken back to the boat?" asked Virginia. "Show of hands."

"Hey, she's not authorized to do that," protested Bernice, apparently incensed on Osmond's behalf.

"You're overstepping your authority, my pet," Victor warned in a tight voice.

Virginia shot a defiant hand into the air. "Anyone else?"

"According to the weather radar, this thing should blow over in about five minutes." A man standing near Cal held up his cell phone. "Did anyone else download a local weather app?"

"Five minutes is not so long, yes?" said Madeleine. "I will tell you about the Cathédrale of Notre-Dame while we wait." She gestured toward the behemoth across the walkway. "The first cathedral on this site was consecrated in 1063, but a fire in 1200—"

"I thought Notre Dame was in Paris," a woman called out.

"The very famous Notre Dame cathedral, with its storied gargoyles and hunchback, *is* in Paris," said Madeleine, "but throughout France, there are many, many churches dedicated to Our Lady, and they are all called Notre Dame. Rouen's cathedral was rebuilt after the fire and completed in 1250, but it underwent an expansion that lasted for three centuries, and even now—"

BONG*bongbongbongbong*BONGBONG*bongbong*BONG-BONGBONG!

Madeleine spoke more loudly into her transmitter, channeling her voice with absolute clarity into the uncomfortable earbuds that everyone had removed from their ears. I caught a few informative phrases blasting through the wires dangling around my neck, but mostly, I heard the unrelenting clash and clang of bells.

...*bongbongbong*..."...painted by Monet..." BONGBONG... "...tomb of Richard the Lionheart..." *bong* BONG BONG*bong*... "heavily damaged in World War II..." *BONG BONGBONG*...

"This is a good time for you to look at my pictures," said Bernice as she sidled up to me.

"But—" I pointed in Madeleine's direction and leaned close to Bernice's ear. "I'm trying to listen."

"Oh, yeah? How's that working out for you?" She hit the power button on her camera and stuck the screen in front of my face. "Here I am in front of the china cabinet while Osmond was reminiscing with that old broad on our home visit."

I blinked to refocus my eyes. "Bernice, how would you feel if someone referred to *you* as an old—"

"Here I am by the sofa. Osmond's head completely ruins the shot, but I should be able to Photoshop him out of the picture."

She looked absolutely dazzling in the screen image, her smile engaging, her complexion youthful. Even her wiry tangle of hair looked sleek and elegant. How did she *do* that?

"The lighting was great by the east window, so this one really showcases my high cheekbones and expressive eyes. Cindy Crawford used to look like this before she went to seed."

"I don't think Cindy Crawford has to worry about going to seed for a very long ti—"

"Here I am in the doorway"—*zzzzzt*—"beside a floor lamp"—*zzzzzt*—"under one of the ugly paintings they had on the wall"—*zzzzzt*—"in front of the sideboard with the gazillion picture frames." She frowned at the image. "That clutter is really distracting." She pressed a lever that caused the camera to *whir* and the picture to supersize her face. "There. More of my bone structure and less of the other stuff. I won't even have to zap the background." She pursed her lips. "Other than this thing that looks like a cookie sheet growing out of my head."

I eyed the "thing" to discover that it was neither kitchenware nor photo, but an intricate piece of needlepoint displayed in a small, ornate frame. The zoom function had blown it up to a size where the details were clearly visible, but the realization of what I was looking at left me a bit baffled. Was I seeing it correctly?

"Can you tell what's in the picture frame?" I asked Bernice.

"Looks like some ratty piece of embroidery."

"Of what?"

She studied the image. "Looks like a funny-shaped iris with a broken petal. Or maybe a lily."

Or a fleur-de-lis, imperfect and stylized—just like the one that graced the ring on Woody Jolly's finger.

TWELVE

Why would Woody be wearing a piece of jewelry whose embroidered likeness occupied a place of honor on Madeleine Saint-Sauveur's sideboard?

The question kept floating through my head as we soldiered on toward the site where St. Joan of Arc had been burned at the stake.

The rain had stopped abruptly, allowing us to scoot back onto the walkway without our umbrellas raised. We followed a shortcut through a walled courtyard on the side of the cathedral and arrived at a broad plaza fronting the west façade, where we discovered that the pinnacled doorways and colonnades once immortalized by Claude Monet were now obscured by an Eiffel Tower of metal staging.

"What a scam!" Bernice griped. "What are we supposed to take pictures of? The scaffolding?"

"You will find some very nice souvenir shops along the Rue de Gros Horloge," Madeleine announced, waggling her umbrella toward the pedestrian mall in front of us. "If you would like to see the cathedral without the scaffolding, you should purchase a postcard that shows what it looked like before the war. There are many selections to choose from."

"Oh, sure," whined Bernice. "And I suppose there are no kickbacks involved in that little deal. You can bet someone's going to be reading about this on your evaluation."

Madeleine shrugged. "*D'accord.*"

As we trekked down the cobblestoned mall, I wove my way forward through the group until I caught up with Woody.

"You'll never guess what I just saw," I exclaimed as I quickened my pace to keep up with his unexpectedly long stride.

He let out a burst of laughter. "Cal handing out business cards?"

"*Uhhh*—No."

"Of course not. That was a trick question. Cal never hands out business cards. That would be too much like advertising."

Talk about dog with bone. "I saw a picture of your fleur-de-lis ring."

"Did you now?"

"In fact, you might have seen it, too. At Madeleine's house on our home visit. On her sideboard. It was a needlepoint piece in a frame. Same fleur-de-lis. Same broken petal."

"Never saw it."

"Bernice has a picture of it among her photos. Isn't that weird that the Saint-Sauveurs would have an embroidery of your ring?"

"Why is it weird? Look around. Everything over here has some kind of fleur-de-lis on it."

"But they don't have broken petals, which is what makes your ring and her embroidery rather unique."

"So … what's your point?"

"Well, I was thinking that if you're curious about your ring's history, Madeleine might have some insight into both the embroidery *and* the ring. Wouldn't it be interesting to learn the story behind—"

"Why would I care?" His voice bristled with irritation. "I told you. It's always been in the family, so why would I need to know its history? It's mine. End of story."

"I...I just thought—"

He fluttered his hand in annoyance, as if shooing me away. "No disrespect, Emily, but when I want your help, I'll ask for it. Okay? Hell, you seem to be taking up where Cal left off, and I *don't* appreciate it."

I slowed my steps, allowing him to forge ahead of me. *Euw.* Cal was right. Woody's temper really *was* kind of volatile. I just hoped his cantankerous outbursts turned out to be a passing phase and not an indication of a more serious mental health problem.

Halfway down the mall, we stopped before an ornately sculpted stone arch that acted like an entrance tunnel to the street beyond. A tower in the style of a French chateau sat atop the arch, and in the center of this was a giant clock face, housed in a frame of gold scrolls and fretwork, with a wreath of blue frills circling it like a medieval ruff. It was far more grand than Big Ben, but Big Ben probably kept better time, given that this clock only boasted one hand. As Madeleine began her spiel, we inched around her in tight formation, partially to be less of an obstruction to foot traffic, but mostly because we'd all ditched our earbuds, so we were hoping to improve our chances of hearing her.

"The Great Clock, known as Le Gros Horloge, was placed in its present location in 1527," she told us, "but its inner mechanism dates from the 1300s, when it was first lodged in the belfry of the attached building."

Feeling a raindrop splat on my nose, I looked up to see an ominous bank of storm clouds rolling over us ... again.

"I hope you're not fixin' that we should set our watches by that thing," Bobbi fretted. "I hate to be the one to point out the obvious, but it's only got one hand."

"It's more of an astronomical clock than an actual timepiece," said Madeleine. "The ball above the clock indicates the phase of the moon, and the inset below the Roman numeral VI specifies the day of the week. And even though the single hand only indicates the hour of the day and not the minute, two thirteenth-century bells inside the tower ring out the hour, half hour, and quarter—"

The clouds burst above us like water surging from a pitcher pump. Down came the rain. Up went our umbrellas. Out came the boo birds.

"I've HAD it!" snarled Bernice.

"Me, too!" spat Virginia.

Madeleine herded us beneath the shelter of the arch, where a flock of sheep grazed in magnificent stone relief above us.

"Take us back to the boat," Bernice demanded.

"I am required to stay with the guests who want to continue the tour," Madeleine explained in an even tone, "but if you would like to return to the boat, I will give you directions."

"You brought us here, so you should take us back," insisted Virginia.

"*Non, non.* I am not contracted to escort you back, but it is very simple. Walk back to the cathedral, turn right onto the Rue Grand Pont, and continue straight until you reach the river. The *Renoir* will be moored along the embankment."

"Which cathedral are you talking about?" asked Woody. "The first one or the second one?"

"The one you can see from here," said Madeleine. She gestured back down the mall toward Notre-Dame. "Turn right onto that boulevard."

"But how do we find our way back to the boat?" fussed another woman.

"The boulevard to the right of Notre-Dame will lead you straight back to the boat."

"How are we supposed to find Notre-Dame?" pressed Bernice.

Madeleine pursed her lips, her eyes shooting tiny sparks. "It is right *there*. At the end of the mall. Can you not see it?"

"I'm not sure how you expect us to find our way back by ourselves," groused Virginia. "It's outrageous that you're just going to abandon us. The next time I take a tour, you can be sure it won't be with any slipshod company like this one." She flung a disgusted look at Victor. "This is all your fault. River cruise. I didn't want to take a river cruise."

"How many of you would like to leave the tour now?" asked Madeleine.

Bernice and Virginia shot their hands into the air immediately. Other hands drifted up more slowly. Bobbi. Dawna. Woody and his contingent.

"But I've got a question," said Dawna, as she kicked rainwater off her alligator boots. "How do we get back to the boat?"

Oh, God.

"I'll take them," offered Cal. "Or at least get them on the right road. I've got a map."

"*Merci beaucoup,*" Madeleine gushed, her voice dripping with gratitude.

"Not so fast, pretty boy," taunted Bernice. "I'm not going anywhere until it stops raining."

"Neither am I," declared Virginia. "I'm staying put until the storm lets up."

"Whatever," said Cal. "Just don't go wandering off. When we head out, we head out together."

"But if the rain doesn't stop in the next thirty seconds, I'm gonna shoot across to that shoe store to browse," warned Bernice. "Pick me up when you head back."

"*Ewww!*" cried Dawna as she followed Bernice's gaze. "You can pick me up there, too. They've got boots on sale." She hesitated. "Does *Vente* mean sale?"

"It means the place is air-conditioned," said Bernice.

"It does not," countered Virginia. "If the store were air-conditioned, why would they throw the front doors wide open?"

"It doesn't seem to bother you at home," Victor commented with some snark. "I thought you rather enjoyed cooling off the neighborhood with our central air unit. I can't think of a better way for you to waste my money. Can you?"

"I'll work on it." She leveled a menacing look at him, eyes narrow and splintered with ice.

While the deserters waited out the storm, the rest of us ventured out into the pelting rain, splashing past centuries-old buildings that were timbered in pink and red and inset with tiers of arched windows. We passed an optician, a tobacconist, jewelers, clothiers, shoe shops, and a confection shop whose specialty chocolates and pastel macaroons were stacked in sumptuous pyramids in the display window, filling the air with the aromatic scent of cocoa beans. Just beyond Foot Locker and the Swatch store, the mall opened up to a huge square that bore the look of an Old World market with its fresh flower stalls and farm produce. Sidewalk cafés sat cheek to jowl on the cobblestones, their boundaries blurred by their sheer numbers, their menus chalked onto freestanding blackboards, their tables empty in the rain. A children's carousel stood deserted, while directly behind it, a structure shaped like the curved sidewall of a skateboard arena rose above a trio of shade trees. In a city where the architecture was as delicate as spun sugar, this piece, whatever it might be, looked as out of place as hiking boots at a prom.

As we traipsed behind Madeleine, past the square's many cafés, I realized that the odd structure was actually a roof that looked like Darth Vader's imperial flagship landing atop a squat concrete building that was being slowly crushed beneath its prodigious weight. After skirting an area in front of the building, where the ruins of an ancient stone foundation poked up from the ground, we detoured right, heading for cover beneath the extended roof of the building's portico. As the handful of us who remained collapsed our umbrellas, Madeleine resumed her spiel.

"This is the Church of St. Joan of Arc and it sits atop the place where she was burned at the stake in 1431. Six hundred years ago, this lovely square was the site for public executions, so where tourists dine today, the people of Rouen once gathered to watch justice meted out to convicted criminals. The actual spot where St. Joan died is marked by a plaque just there." She pointed to a fenced garden just beyond the church where a notably austere cross towered skyward. "I would recommend that you visit the spot and take a picture once it stops raining."

"Is this church very old?" I asked, guessing the answer before Madeleine gave it.

"It was built in 1979, so by Rouen standards, it is brand new. The roof, with all its unusually placed points and peaks, is supposed to represent the flames that consumed St. Joan, but most people say it looks like the underside of an overturned boat, or, if you ask my twelve-year-old son, Darth Vader's imperial flagship."

I guess that clinched it. I had the imagination of a twelve-year-old boy. I was obviously spending way too much time with my five nephews.

"You can step inside the church to see the interior if you like. The inside is much more impressive than the outside. Do you have any questions before I turn you loose?"

"I have one," said the woman beside me. "How do we get back to the boat?"

While Madeleine explained, yet again, which route to follow back, I dug out a gratuity and waited for the remaining guests to leave before I approached her. "Do you remember me?" I asked as I pressed a five Euro note into her hand.

"Of course! Osmond's friend. But, Emily, you are much too generous." She nodded to the fiver.

"No, no. You deserve a much bigger tip simply for your patience. How do you remain so even tempered when guests keep asking you the same question that you've answered a dozen times already?"

"My temper is *not* even. I want to strangle some of these people with my bare hands, but I don't. I celebrate their departure with a drink instead." She smiled impishly. "Do you know why the French have become such great connoisseurs of wine?"

"Superb vineyards?"

"American tourists."

Which prompted an idea. "If you have the time, could I buy you a glass of wine? The ship's purser has been trying to contact you by email for us, but talking to you in person would be so much nicer."

"My computer service." She made a face. "It's up. It's down. It's on. It's off. But, yes, you and I must have a drink. My grandmother has asked for Osmond's address and perhaps you are the person to give it to me. *Oui*?"

"*Oui*!" I was so thrilled by this unexpected twist of luck, I hugged her.

———

"My grandmama thumbs her nose at my computer. She calls it 'that silly box.' But if I tell her 'that silly box' will allow her to send an instant message to Osmond and receive a reply within minutes rather than weeks, I guarantee she will insist on learning."

We'd found a table in a bistro that overlooked the church, and even before our wine arrived, we'd exchanged contact information.

"Please tell Solange that Osmond can even receive email on his IPhone, so no matter what time of day or night she writes to him, when the alert dings, he'll reply."

"He will reply to her in the middle of the night?"

"Yeah. He probably takes the thing to bed with him." I sighed. "They all do."

"But then I will have to explain the iPhone to her." Madeleine lifted her brow and puffed out her lips in a comic expression. "Better I tell her it happens by magic. In grandmama's world, magic is much more believable."

I took a sip of wine, steeling myself to broach a subject that Madeleine Saint-Sauveur might think I had no business broaching. "Seeing her with Osmond at your house... They had their own magic going on in the war, didn't they?"

"The war threw them together for less than three weeks, but during that time, they kept each other alive. He needed her to help him survive physically. She needed him to help her survive emotionally. When they found each other—" She smiled. "You saw them together. There is probably not one detail of their encounter that they have forgotten."

"Osmond told me she's the only woman he's ever loved. He apparently wrote to her after the war ended, but his letters were returned as undeliverable, and when he tried phoning, the operator couldn't find a number. I think he eventually just gave up. It seems so unfair that two people who were so deeply in love ended up spending their lives apart. Do you think your grandmother ever tried to contact him? Do you suppose she ran into the same problem?"

"*Non*. I'm sure my grandmother *never* tried to contact him."

Her certainty surprised me. "Why not?"

"Because her husband would not have approved."

"*Ahh*. So she married again shortly after Osmond left?"

"Again? I do not know what you mean by 'again.' She was married to my Grandfather Spenard for over fifty years."

"But... her name is no longer Spenard, is it? You introduced her by another name."

"*Oui*. Ducat. Three years after my grandfather died, she married a man who had been a widower for many years, but they were only married a brief time before he passed away, too."

"Okay, but Osmond told me that when he met her, she was a widow. That her husband had died in a German prison. 'Barely a bride, and then a widow' is the way he stated it."

"*Oui.* My grandfather was arrested for engaging in subversive acts against German soldiers, so he was thrown into Amiens Prison. You have heard of Amiens, yes?"

I shook my head.

"It was a brutal place. No prisoner ever walked out of Amiens alive. It was where the Wehrmacht sent Resistance fighters to die. My grandfather was imprisoned for three years. He was never allowed to send a letter home, receive packages, communicate with *anyone* outside the prison. When my grandmother finally petitioned the German authorities to allow her to visit, they told her that my grandfather was dead and his body disposed of." She sat back in her chair and took a slow sip of wine. "But they were lying."

The down at the back of my neck stood on end. "He was still alive?"

She nodded. "He most likely *would* have died, if not for a British bombing raid four months before the D-Day invasion. Two hundred and fifty-eight prisoners escaped through a breach in the prison wall, my grandfather among them. Barely alive, but determined to survive. They searched for him with their dogs, but my grandpapa was too clever for them. He hid in the woods. In caves. He foraged for food. He crossed over into Belgium, in a direction completely opposite where Grandmama was. He knew the Germans would be looking for him at home, so he stayed away. Only after the Allied invasion did he think it safe to find his way back to his bride. And as you might imagine, after June 6, 1944, German troops found

161

themselves battling American tanks and infantry, so they had more pressing problems to address than the escapees from Amiens Prison."

"Oh, my God. What must your grandmother have thought when he showed up at her door?"

"She tells me that for the first and only time in her life, she fainted. Her husband come back to life? *Non*. Such miracles did not happen in occupied France."

I couldn't imagine the elation Solange must have felt when she regained consciousness to find the husband she'd presumed dead standing over her. There was probably no word in the English language that could adequately describe it. But this turn of events certainly cast doubt on the notion of Osmond's fatherhood. It might all boil down to a question of timing.

I knocked back a swig of my wine. "Did you say what your grandfather's name was?"

"Henri. Henri Spenard."

"How long did it take him to work his way back to Normandy? Weeks? Months?"

"He was traveling on foot, so it took many weeks. And he was further delayed by the fighting in Caen. The Allies met strong German resistance there after the invasion. The town was virtually leveled. But when the Americans finally broke through, he was able to return home."

"So when was that ... exactly?"

"The Battle of Caen ended on July twentieth. Grandpapa managed to make it home four days later."

About three weeks after Osmond had shipped back to England to recuperate. Boy, I wouldn't even dare to hazard a guess about—

"It was a glorious homecoming, and so much celebrating that, as you might expect, late the following winter, my grandfather was presented with the son he never thought he would live to sire. Grandpapa wanted to name him Eisenhower, in honor of the American general who liberated France, but Grandmama insisted on naming him for the man who singlehandedly saved her and her family from the Germans. So she named him Osmond."

"Aw, that's so sweet." But I couldn't help wonder if that was the only reason she named him Osmond.

Madeleine laughed. "The next baby they named Eisenhower. And my mama was called Betsy after the woman who sewed your first American flag. The Spenards became known as the most American family in the village. Should I bore you with a photo?"

"Please! I'd love to be bored." If there was a resemblance between Osmond Spenard and Osmond Chelsvig, maybe I'd be able to spot it.

Madeleine pulled her wallet from her purse and removed a small photo from a plastic sleeve. "It was taken in the early sixties when all seven children were in their teens. They were like little stepping stones." She laid the photo in front of me and recited the names as she glided her finger over the faces. "From youngest to oldest— Amelia, Eleanor, Lincoln, Roosevelt, Betsy, Eisenhower, and Osmond. All still living, and with large families of their own, many of whom are named after my Uncle Osmond."

Yup. Did I call that, or what? Osmond was definitely going to need the senior discount if he invited the entire brood to Iowa.

I studied the handsome face of the teenaged Osmond Spenard with his angular face, narrow nose, expressive eyes, and mop of wavy black hair. Yes! There was a resemblance. But not to Osmond.

To Solange.

Osmond Spenard was the spitting image of his mother.

I sighed my disappointment. "It's a wonderful photo." I plucked it off the table and handed it back to her. "Your grandmother experienced the emotional rollercoaster of her life during the war, didn't she? Henri pronounced dead. An American literally falling out of the sky to save her from a German assault. Henri returning from the dead like the risen Lazarus, and fathering seven children in quick succession."

Madeleine smiled coyly. "But of course! He was French."

"Did ... did Solange ever confide to you how close she and Osmond became during those short three weeks?"

She averted her gaze as she slid the photo back into its sleeve. When she looked up again, the warmth in her eyes had disappeared. "My grandmother has never made a secret about the part an American soldier played in her life during the war. It's a story she has told and retold for decades. But there is nothing more to the story than what she has shared. She lived through one of the most brutal periods in the history of the world, and for that she deserves our admiration and respect. *Whatever* my grandmother did to survive is entirely her business. Our family has never questioned *any* of her decisions or motivations, and we don't expect anyone else to either. Ever." She drilled me with a fierce look. "Do you understand?"

I did indeed. Whatever happened between Osmond and Solange had the family's blessing and was to remain private. No speculation allowed. Violators would be refused future access. So if Osmond Chelsvig had fathered Solange's first child, the family didn't want to know.

I nodded. "I understand."

"And you will help Mr. Chelsvig to understand?"

I nodded again. "I'll, *uh* . . . I'll see that he abides by your family's wishes."

"*Merci.* It would not be right to introduce scandal into my grandmother's life after all these years, even if there is truth in it."

But how would I break the news to Osmond that it seemed unlikely he was a father? And even if he were, the Spenards didn't want to hear about it.

"You will be able to walk back to the boat without your umbrella," said Madeleine as she nodded toward the street. "You see? The sun is coming out." She marked the time. "And I must be leaving. I promised to bring Grandmama a decadent confection from Les Larmes de Joan d'Arc, so she'll be wondering where I am."

"Is she feeling better? I'm sorry Mr. Jolly upset her so much the other day. Apparently, a funeral director can't always gauge how someone's going to react to his marketing pitch, but when the potential customer starts screaming, you'd think he'd know enough to stop. Poor Mr. Jolly is proving to have something of a tin ear."

"Grandmama refused to tell me what provoked her outburst, but for the past two nights, she has wanted to sleep with the light on. *Pourquoi?* I do not know. All she will say is that she no longer has the energy to poke the hornet's nest."

"What does that mean?"

Madeleine shrugged. "Perhaps she mistook him for someone, yes? Someone she once knew? Someone she feared? You heard her. '*C'est toi, c'est toi.* It's you, it's you.' And then the anger and tears. But to me, she will say nothing."

Which, in a roundabout way, reminded me of another enigma. "Out of curiosity, could you tell me the significance of the framed embroidery piece that sits on your sideboard? The one with the chopped-off petal on the fleur-de-lis? I didn't notice it initially, but it got included in one of the thousands of photos Bernice Zwerg strong-armed you into taking of her when we visited your house."

She frowned Etretat as if trying to recall the thing. "Grandmama brought so many pictures with her when she moved in with us. They've become invisible to me. But I know the piece you describe. Grandmama embroidered it when she was a new bride. It's so old, I fear the pressure of the frame may be the only thing holding the threads together."

"Is there a story attached to it? I mean, do you know why Solange embroidered a fleur-de-lis with a broken petal?"

"*Mais oui.* Grandmama's village boasted a metalsmith who created the broken-petaled fleur-de-lis as his trademark. He made lovely jewelry—broaches, pendants, bracelets. But since Grandmama could afford to buy none of it, she embroidered the design instead. She was known to boast it was a fair likeness to the original trademark, and it cost her far fewer francs. The only problem was, she couldn't wear it."

"Did the metalsmith ever design a line of rings?"

"There was only one ring. He never made another."

A chill feathered up my spin. "Do you know why?"

"He apparently complained that rings were too complicated and too heavy on a man's finger, so he was going to stop at one. Perhaps if he'd chosen another precious metal for his designs, he would have made more. But he worked exclusively in brass."

The chill crawled down my arms and spread to my fingertips. "Do you know if he ever sold the ring?"

"He wore it himself, and the only reason I know that is because when he visited my grandmother after grandpapa was imprisoned, he cracked her best china with that ring, so she was always short one teacup. She still curses his name every time we set the table with her china. 'Damn Pierre Lefevre.'" She regarded me oddly. "You look so shocked. The elderly in America do not curse?"

"What would you say if I told you that Woody Jolly is wearing a brass ring designed with a broken-petaled fleur-de-lis that looks exactly like Solange's embroidery?"

"I would say it was impossible."

"Why impossible?"

"Because the other reason the metalsmith fabricated only one ring was because the war greatly foreshortened his career. He died on the morning of the D-Day invasion. He was part of the five-man team who went to Pointe du Hoc and never came back."

———

Dodging puddles the size of kiddie pools, I retraced my steps back to the Church of St. Joan of Arc to take a picture of the commemorative plaque for Nana's Legion of Mary meeting, then set a course back to the boat by way of the cobblestoned mall with the giant clock.

Madeleine had been right. With the skies clearing, I didn't need my umbrella anymore, but the sun was doing little to cast light on the mystery of how Woody Jolly could be in possession of a one-of-a-kind ring worn by a Resistance fighter whose body had been incinerated in the Allied bombing of Pointe du Hoc on the morning of the D-Day invasion. Had Pierre Lefevre removed the ring before undertaking his mission? That would have made sense. A shiny object like a brass ring might have given away their position. But how would the ring have then found its way to America to become an heirloom in the Jolly family? Had it become one of the spoils of war, pocketed by an Allied soldier as a souvenir? Yet Woody had said the ring had been in his family for as long as he could remember, so that didn't square.

Well, some cryptic chain of events had allowed the ring to survive the war, because Woody was wearing it.

Turning the corner onto the Rue Grand Pont, I slowed my steps as another explanation suddenly occurred to me.

Nah, that wasn't possible, was it? But if it were … *Good God.*

"Are you on your way back to the boat?"

I avoided colliding with the man by mere inches. Startled, I did a double-take, laughing with relief when I saw his face. "Patrice! Fancy running into you here. I mean, literally running into you. Sorry."

"You recognize me out of uniform?"

"Any reason why I wouldn't?"

"Most guests don't."

"It seems to be a universal problem. Don't take it personally. Free afternoon?"

"*Oui.* One afternoon and one morning a week. Rouen is a good port. Many sales along the Gros Horloge." He smiled, looking a little embarrassed. "Cycling shoes. A man can never have enough."

"You're a cyclist?"

"I ride a bicycle. There is a difference. But the Tour de France passes through much of the countryside nearby, so I avail myself of the same roads. Do you need directions back to the boat?"

I chuckled. "Nope. They've been involuntarily imprinted on my brain. I couldn't forget them even if I wanted to."

"The police cars will probably still be there when you arrive."

Unh-oh. "Police cars?"

"*Oui.* Something to do with the woman who suffered the fatal accident in Étretat yesterday." He lowered his voice. "One of the staff overheard the conversation the police were having with the captain, so there's a rumor flying around the ship now."

"What kind of rumor?"

"Apparently, what was initially thought to be an accident was no accident at all."

THIRTEEN

"Drug overdose," said Nana.

My jaw hit the floor. "You're kidding."

"They run one of them toxicology panels. Got it firsthand. Straight from the horse's mouth. That Irv fella what sits in the lounge in a stupor all day? He told us. He can be pretty chatty between cocktails."

"How did Irv find out?"

"He heard it from the bartender, what heard it from the purser, what heard it from the waiter what was servin' some snacks to the gendarmes when they was talkin' to the captain in the dinin' room."

I grinned. "Yup. It doesn't get any more firsthand than that."

I'd found most of the gang on the top deck, sitting beneath the canopy, fondling their iPhones and sipping drinks that sported little parasols, swords, and pink flamingo swizzle sticks. Their eyes were glassy. Their mouths were curved into silly grins. They looked a little punch-drunk, as if they'd just been forced to sit through eight hours of nonstop campaign speeches—and something else was different about them, but I couldn't quite put my finger on it.

"Did Irv know what kind of drug she overdosed on?"

"Not yet," said Tilly. "But his plan was to continue tippling in the lounge until the end of the day, so he's well positioned to hear further information. He told us to check back with him later."

Stunned, I pulled out a chair and flopped down at the table with them, my thoughts heading off in eight different directions. "A drug overdose? Does that mean she didn't die from a brain hemorrhage?"

"The toxicology report doesn't change the results of the postmortem," said Tilly. "But what it might indicate is that the overdose *caused* the brain hemorrhage. The police were in her cabin earlier. No doubt searching for the drug in question. If they find it, I believe they might suspect an accidental overdose. If they don't, I assume they may reclassify her death as a homicide."

Nuts! We were home free. A natural death. No suspicions. No flags. I sighed. *Here we go again.*

"If the police don't find the drug in her cabin, what are the chances they'll search for it elsewhere aboard ship?" asked Dick Stolee, trying unsuccessfully to hide a nervous tremor in his voice. "You think they'll search all the guest cabins?"

"What do you care?" questioned Grace, eyeing him suspiciously. She gasped. "Oh, my Lord! ARE YOU HIDING ILLEGAL CONTRABAND IN OUR CABIN?"

"*Shhhh!*" He shot a furtive look to left and right.

Tilly raised her forefinger. "If you'll allow me to make a grammatical correction, Grace. Contraband is always unlawful, so the expression 'illegal contraband' is redundant ... much in the same way as 'close proximity' or 'false pretense' or 'foreign import,' or my absolute favorite, 'two twin beds.'"

Grace drew her lips back over her teeth in an unflattering sneer. "What about 'buzz off'? Is that redundant?"

"I thought 'two twin beds' was one a them oxymorons," said Nana.

Tilly shook her head. "An oxymoron is an expression that seems to contradict itself, like 'jumbo shrimp,' or—"

"Isn't 'two twin beds' hotel lingo for a double?" asked George.

Dick Teig snickered. "'Oxymorons' are what Bernice calls us when we're all in the same room together. You know. More than one moron." He squinted in thought. "'Oxy' means 'more than one', doesn't it?"

"Quiet!" snapped Grace, her gaze boring into her husband like a drill bit into butter. "Out with it, Dick. What are you trying to hide from the police?"

He slouched in his chair, shoulders slumped and head bent, looking as if he were about to confess to leaving the toilet seat up for fifty years on purpose. "Rocks," he mumbled.

"Did he say, 'rocks'?" questioned Alice.

"You're hiding diamonds?" shrieked Grace.

He shot up higher in his chair. "Diamonds? Where would I get diamonds?"

"Where would you get rocks?" demanded Grace.

I leveled a look at him. "Oh, my God. You took stones off Étretat Beach."

Dick Stolee hung his head with guilt. Dick Teig froze in place. "What's wrong with that?" he asked in a tentative voice.

"Didn't you hear Rob before we got off the bus? He warned us that it's expressly forbidden to remove stones from the beach."

"I didn't hear him say that," swore Dick Teig.

"We weren't supposed to remove stones from the beach?" asked Alice. "Why didn't anyone tell us?"

Oh, God.

Dick Teig stood up. "How many people heard Rob tell us that we—"

"No voting!" I stabbed my finger at Dick Stolee. "How many did you take?"

"Two," he said in an undertone.

I waited a beat. "Only two?"

"And they're smaller than my thumbnail. Pebbles! Nobody's gonna miss them, Emily. I bet no one even knew they were there. I'm no thief. Honest. They were just so unusual, I couldn't resist." He heaved a sigh. "Should I turn myself in to the police?"

"No!" cried Grace. "What if they throw you into a jail cell and let you rot there for the rest of your life? You're not going anywhere long term until you clean out the garage."

"He's *not* going to be thrown in jail." At least, I hoped not. I softened my gaze, relenting. "Okay, Dick, the beach might be able to spare two of its pebbles, but the next time Rob informs us that a town has ordinances that must be respected, you'd better—"

"Two stones," snorted Dick Teig. "Hell, I took a whole handful."

"I took at least a dozen," confessed Alice. "They're so smooth and white, I plan to make a paperweight out of them."

I tossed my head back and groaned. "Guys!"

"I only took one," said George.

"Yeah," Nana piped up, "but it's as big as your head."

"Had to be." He smiled. "I'm gonna use it as a doorstop."

I shot them a disgusted look. "Anyone else want to own up to petty thievery?" I eyed Tilly and Nana expectantly.

"Don't look at me," clucked Nana. "I was busy talkin' to the Frenchie in the neon thong, so I didn't have time to steal no rocks."

George's mouth popped open. "Marion! You were flirting with the fella in that ... that"—he swept his hand from his neck to his groin—"in that green rubber band that barely covered his privates? He looked like he was wearing a slingshot!"

"It's not a slingshot. It's called a mankini, and you can buy 'em over the Internet. He says all the hotties are wearin' 'em." She waggled her eyebrows at George, eyes glowing with anticipation. "And they come in jumbo."

"So what are we supposed to do if the police search our cabin and find the goods?" persisted Grace. "Plead the Fifth, throw ourselves on the mercy of the court, or send them down to Alice's cabin? She swiped a lot more than my Dick."

Alice gasped. She threw me a desperate look. "They can't arrest me, can they, Emily? It would be so unfair. I've never even had a parking ticket."

"Don't listen to Grace," I soothed. "She was just pulling your leg."

"No I wasn't," quipped Grace.

Dick studied his wife's face, thunderstruck. "Grace Stolee, I can't believe my ears. After all you and Alice have meant to each other through the years? The friendship, and church groups, and book clubs, and fundraisers? What kind of heartless creature are you? Can you actually sit there and tell me you'd be willing to throw Alice under the bus to save me?"

"Damned straight."

He threw his shoulders back, his chest swelling with pride, his eyes a little dewy. "Aw, shucks, honeybun. That's the nicest thing you've said to me in decades."

"Okay, that settles it." Alice dusted off her hands. "I'm throwing my stash over the balcony rail. Sentence commuted." She arched a self-satisfied brow at the Stolees before turning back to me. "If the police don't know I *have* the rocks, they can't haul me away for destroying evidence, can they?"

My eyelid began twitching like a Mexican jumping bean doing the Macarena.

Tilly thumped her walking stick on the deck. "I'm not so sure I'd count on the police conducting a cabin-to-cabin search. If Krystal ingested an over-the-counter drug, like aspirin, ibuprofen, or acetaminophen, a search would be entirely futile. All of us probably carry the big three. But if she overdosed on an exotic prescription drug, now that's a different matter."

"If I killed someone with meds I brung with me," said Nana, "I'm chuckin' 'em over the side with Alice's rocks. No way I'm lettin' anyone find 'em in my pill caddy."

"Are you sure it was pills?" asked George. "What if the killer used something more common, like a cleaning compound or hair product or ... or hand sanitizer?"

Alice sucked in her breath. "You think Margi did it? Oh, my stars. Why would she kill someone after buying all those new clothes? They'll never let her wear them in prison."

"Margi Swanson *did not* kill anyone," I stated firmly. "And furthermore, we don't have any information about when Krystal ingested the drug, so no one's going to know anything until someone figures that out."

"Emily's right," Tilly agreed. "If the drug was fast acting, the implication would be that someone on the tour might have slipped it to her. But if it was slower acting, then she could have ingested it even before she boarded the plane. Is it possible that someone back home wanted her dead?"

Uff-da. I hadn't thought of that. Bobbi and Dawna had reason to want her out of the picture, but had someone back in Texas beaten them to it? "I've just realized that I don't know anything about Krystal other than she was blonde, beautiful, turned heads, had a fondness for snakeskin, and was probably the top sales rep for her cosmetic company." I regarded the gang expectantly. "Anyone want to volunteer to dig up more background on her?" This was the nifty part of traveling with seniors with major iPhone addictions. They were always looking for an excuse to surf the Web.

Breathing stopped. Heads froze. Eyes shifted. Phones remained idle in their hands.

Hunh. What was wrong with this picture? They should have been gunning to see who could access Google first by now. I frowned. *Ohhh*, I got it. "Cell signal down?"

"WHAT?" Alice cried.

They whipped their phones up to their faces, exhaling a collective sigh of relief when their devices lit up in their hands. "False alarm," sang out Dick Teig.

I searched their faces in disbelief. "No volunteers? Not even one?"

Nervous glances. Guilty expressions.

"Okay, what's going on?"

The Dicks looked at Tilly. Tilly looked at George. George looked at Nana. "It's like this, dear," she hedged. "The crew's keepin' us so booked up with lessons and lectures and demonstrations, we don't got no time to dig up no dirt on no dead girl, so we're gonna have to pass."

I stared at them, gobsmacked. "You're passing up a chance to be glued to your iPhones?"

Tilly shook her head. "There's a bit of overkill involved in our schedule, Emily. I think we're all suffering from mental exhaustion brought on by overstimulation. But it's absolutely inspiring."

"We're so hyped up, we're pooped," said Grace.

"But if we take time away to dish up the dirt on that girl, we're afraid we'll lose our momentum," explained Alice.

"Sorry," said the Dicks.

I waved off their apologies, feeling as if I'd just been jilted by my longtime steady. "No, really, it's okay. I'm perfectly capable of doing this myself. It's just that...you're so much better at it than I am."

"Malarkey alert! Malarkey alert!" warned Dick Teig. "She's using flattery to change our minds."

"I am not. You *are* better with Internet searches. You...you're like a bunch of ten-year-olds."

"Aw," gushed Nana, "that's an awful nice thing for you to say, dear."

I realized this might be one of the few instances where being compared to a group of juveniles was actually a compliment. "So what have you learned from your lectures and demonstrations that's left you so inspired?"

They all began talking at once.

"…woozy from all the wines we tasted from the different regions of—"

"The more I sampled of the *brie* cheese, the less it tasted like old dirt, but the *Pont l'Eveque*—"

"…said I excelled at fields of flowers, but she thought I might be even better with nudes. We just need a model."

"…tasted like a moldy sock even *with* the garlic cracker."

"…started snoring through the slide presentation and…"

"…so surprised when she offered five-minute makeovers with sample-size products that she actually let us keep. My eyes look so much bigger with—"

"…been set on cremation since I paid your Grampa Sippel's funeral expenses, but them Walt and Ed fellas was so convincin' that I'm gettin' a notion to order the Fisherman's Retreat casket what's got the eight-inch memory foam mattress on the inside and the authentic fiberglass fish scales on the outside. It's an exact replica of the spotted bass what your grampa mounted forty years ago."

As their chatter grew faster and louder, I let fly my signature ear-piercing whistle to restore order.

Ear-muffling ensued, followed by cussing and collective wincing.

"Thank you. Sounds like you've had a whirlwind day. Just one question." My voice cracked as I choked out the word. "Nudes?"

"You're all still here!" Jackie bounded onto the deck. "Fabulous! Now I don't have to run around looking for you." Pausing by the rail, she clapped her hands to cheer on the people who were trooping up the stairs behind her. "Quick like bunnies," she encouraged as Margi, Osmond, Lucille, Helen, and Bernice popped into view and joined her.

There was only one thing wrong.

"Oh, my God! Why are they wearing cervical collars?"

I watched in horror as Osmond, Lucille, and Helen shuffled toward the canopy, backs stiff, chins elevated, heads immobilized. Springing to my feet, I grabbed several chairs from other tables and motioned the Dicks to help Lucille and Helen while I assisted Osmond. Seizing his elbow, I ushered him to the nearest chair and sat him down. "How did this happen? Did you reinjure your neck? Are you in pain?" A possible explanation struck me. "Please don't tell me you were in the lounge doing the chicken dance again."

"It's on account of what happened to him on the bus yesterday," offered Nana.

I looked Osmond in the eye. "What happened to you on the bus?"

"I fell asleep."

I waited. "And?"

"And I didn't wake up until we got back to the boat because with Margi's collar bracing my neck, my head wasn't flopping all over the place. Best nap I've had in years."

"If Dick had been wearing one during the presentation on Chateau Gaillard today, he wouldn't have almost broken his neck when he nodded off," charged Grace.

"They're an excellent deterrent against whiplash," agreed Tilly.

"And Osmond's experience proves they promote longer, more uninterrupted sleep," added Alice.

"So we're startin' a daily lottery to see who gets to wear 'em," said Nana. "But Margi only brung three with her, so the odds of winnin' aren't real good."

I narrowed my gaze at today's lucky three winners. "Well, that's a relief. You're wearing them for show rather than for any therapeutic purpose. When I saw you, I thought—" I hesitated. "I don't really know what I thought, but I'm glad you're all right."

"Do I look taller?" asked Helen as she lifted her chin off the foam rubber. "I feel so much taller with my head so high off the ground."

"I feel like a giraffe," said Lucille.

Osmond directed his gaze downward. "I can't see my feet. Can you guys see your feet?"

"Now that we have *that* taken care of—" Jackie scooted Margi and Bernice toward the center of the group. "The last of the makeovers are complete. What do you think?"

EH! I darted a look from Bernice, to Margi, to Bernice again. I swallowed slowly. "What have you done?"

"Margi's complexion looks *sooo* translucent," cooed Grace. "She looks like an airbrushed version of the real Margi."

"How come Bernice's complexion don't look so good as Margi's?" asked Nana.

Dick Teig grabbed his belly as he burst out with laughter. "Bernice looks like she was standing too close to a vacuum cleaner when the bag blew up!"

"Is Bernice's face *supposed* to be gray?" asked Alice.

Bernice fired an irritated look at Jackie. "My face is gray?"

Jackie smiled with all her teeth. "We're getting ahead of ourselves, people."

"Did you apply cream or powder blush on Margi's cheeks?" asked Grace. "It looks so natural."

"It's a cream mousse that's formulated especially for Mona Michelle. I chose *Baby's Breath* for Margi because of the blue tones in her skin, but it's available in eight delicious shades for every color palette."

"Why does Bernice have two black eyes?" questioned Tilly. "Is it from the eyeshadow you used or did you hit her?"

"MY EYES ARE BLACK?" Bernice's fingers flew to her cheeks. "I want a mirror."

Jackie flicked her hands away. "Don't touch. So"—she addressed the whole gang—"the object of this exercise was to demonstrate that makeup, when properly applied, can have a life-altering effect on a woman's life from cradle"—she gestured toward Margi—"to grave." She gestured toward Bernice.

"Why did *I* get stuck being the 'grave' part of your stupid demonstration?" griped Bernice. "Margi would make a better dead person than me. I used to be a magazine model!"

"I know," said Jackie. "I understand why the camera loved you. Your bone structure makes your face a canvas that just screams out to be painted. No offense to Margi, but you have the more perfect skeletal structure to illustrate the magic a makeup artist can wield with a corpse."

Bernice sidled a smug look at Margi. "Hear that? I'm going to look better than you when I'm dead."

"That's what you think," Margi shot back. "I might just decide to have a closed casket. So there."

"I don't wanna be sportin' two black eyes when I'm laid out to rest," said Nana as she studied Bernice. "It don't look healthy."

"Dead people aren't supposed to look healthy," hooted Dick Stolee. "They're supposed to look dead."

"There's some folks what's died what don't look dead at all," argued Nana.

"More than likely due to the efforts of a *great* makeup artist," gushed Jackie.

"Marion's quite right," Tilly agreed. "Some corpses appear so robust, they look as if they could rise from their coffins."

"They're called *VAAM*pires," Dick Teig wisecracked in a Count Dracula vibrato.

"There's no such thing as vampires," scolded Lucille. Then more skeptically, "Are there?"

"Okay, Mrs. S.," said Jackie, "the charcoal eyeshadow and liner might not work for you, but I wanted to use it on Bernice to create a mood. I wanted her to look hopelessly sullen and bereft—you know, like she wasn't really happy about spending the rest of her life dead."

Nana gave a little suck on her teeth. "You done a good job of that."

"Would you write down the exact products and color combinations you used on Margi?" asked Grace. "I'd like to be waked with my face looking exactly like hers."

Margi swiveled her torso around to make a face at Bernice.

"I could do that," explained Jackie, "but for your sake, I'd prefer not to."

"Why not?"

"Because Margi is wearing our makeup line that allows a woman to transition seamlessly from daytime to happy hour, and Bernice is wearing a slightly exaggerated version of something we recommend our clients wear to either the opera . . . or a midnight showing of *The Rocky Horror Picture Show*."

I slapped a hand over my eyes and gave my head a woeful shake.

The loudspeaker system crackled an alert for a pending announcement. Heavy breathing on the microphone, followed by, "Ladies and gentlemen, mesdames and messieurs, before we open the doors to the dining room this evening, we would ask you to assemble in the lounge so we might share with you a message of some importance. We look forward to seeing you at six thirty. Thank you."

"Should I leave my makeup on?" fretted Bernice.

"Only if you wanna scare folks," said George.

Nana peeked at her watch. "Six thirty? That only gives us a half hour!"

And the race was on.

Elbows flew. Joints popped. Sneakers squeaked. Osmond, Helen, and Lucille were last out of their chairs and slammed headlong into each other while trying to exit, tangling themselves in a hopeless Gordian knot of arms and legs. I let out another whistle that stopped the gang dead in their tracks.

"Hey! You don't have everyone!"

While Jackie and I began the task of untangling limbs, the Dicks sprinted back. "Come on, you guys," exhorted Dick Teig. "There won't be any seats left."

"Don't rush me!" sniped Lucille. "I'm trying to figure out where my feet are. I can't see them."

"Told ya," said Osmond.

"Shoot," scoffed Helen. "I haven't seen my feet since the day I snapped on my first training bra. DICK!" She grabbed her husband's hand and slapped it into Lucille's. "Now everyone else join hands. Okay, boys. Punch it."

With a Dick at either end of the trio, they shuffled their way across the deck like a Lionel train set.

"Careful on the stairs," I called after them.

Jackie clasped her hands beneath her chin, watching them with affection. "Aren't they adorable? When I'm old and wrinkled, I want to be just like them."

I drilled her with a narrow look. "Cradle-to-grave cosmetics?"

"Wasn't that brilliant? Honestly, Emily, sometimes I surprise even myself with my genius. They were so over the moon with Walt and Ed's powerpoint presentation that I knew I could figure out some way to capitalize on it."

"Are you talking about the undertakers?"

She gasped in horror. "Planning specialist consultants. Really, Emily. Undertaker is *so* twentieth century."

I rolled my eyes. "Don't people in the funeral industry hire their own staff to do hair and makeup?"

"Yes. But if *they* can offer pre-funeral planning, why can't *I* offer pre-funeral makeup? I can help people reach decisions about all kinds of difficult cosmetic issues *before* they die. Liquid foundation or pancake? Glitter eyeshadow or noncrease matte? Sheer gloss lipstick or long-lasting stain? My clients can choose for *themselves* rather than turn the decision making over to someone who might not know the difference between the seasonal palette of a summer and an autumn."

"Won't this new sideline interfere with the job you already have?"

Sparks ignited in her eyes. "There's a whole untapped market out there for Mona Michelle products, and *I'm* the one who discovered them. So if Bobbi and Dawna are planning to get rid of me the same way they got rid of Krystal, they better hurry, because I'm talking to Victor about my idea at dinner. And if they start talking smack about me again, they're going to be in for a rude awakening, because I *will not* allow myself to be mean-mouthed. I'll say my piece to Victor, then follow the example of what other truly mature females have done."

"Ignore them?"

"Write snotty things on their Facebook pages under an assumed name."

"Why would you even *want* to have dinner with them if you're so afraid they're going to kill you?"

"I'm a big believer in that famous saying."

"'Do unto others as you would have them do unto you?'"

"'Keep your friends close and your enemies closer.'"

I gave her "the look." "So what do you make of this drug overdose speculation?"

"It's not speculation. I *told* you they killed Krystal. And now we know what method they used. All the police have to figure out is how they slipped it to her and when."

"Shouldn't the police first have to determine who had access to the drug?"

"I can tell them that. Bobbi and Dawna."

"But what if that can't be proven?"

Her mouth rounded into an O. "Are you suggesting they *didn't* do it?"

"No! But how can you be sure someone didn't slip her the lethal overdose even before she left Texas? What if Bobbi and Dawna were only two names in a long list of people who might have wanted her dead?"

Her mouth snapped shut. Her eyes lit up. "*Eww.* You mean like the ex-husband who just remarried and wanted to stop his alimony payments? Or the half sister who was suing her over the family inheritance? Or the woman who was married to the man she was having the affair with?"

I stared at her, dumbstruck. "Holy crap, Jack. Do the police know about this?"

"Not from me, they don't. Remember? They didn't bother to interview me. But Bobbi and Dawna know her history, so if the police asked for background on her, the girls probably recited a whole litany of people who wished she'd disappear. Can you think of a better way for them to divert suspicion away from themselves?"

"Well, someone obviously found a way to kill her, but if it was your peroxide twins, when would they have had an opportunity to do it?"

"Dinner two nights ago?"

I crooked my mouth. "I didn't notice any sleight of hand going on, did you?"

"What about the motion sickness pill Krystal took?"

"It was a softgel. Aren't softgels pretty much tamperproof? Besides, she gave one to Woody at breakfast yesterday morning, so if she died from ingesting a lethal softgel from that bottle, Woody should be dead, too." I replayed the day at warp speed in my head. "Did the four of you pick up anything to eat in Étretat?"

"We bought bottled water, but Krystal never opened hers, at least not while she was with me."

"Who was Krystal's cabin mate?"

"No one. Victor wanted us to be able to move around without bumping into each other, so we each have our own cabin, which is an *absolute* godsend. After I hung up all my stuff, there wasn't an inch to spare in the closet, so if I'd had to share the space, my unlucky roommate would have had to hang her clothes in the bathroom. Can you imagine what that would have done to my daily shower routine?"

"Did you visit each other's cabins for any length of time the day we boarded?"

"We shmoozed in the lounge." She flopped her hand backward at the wrist. "You know, greater visibility. When you look as good as we do, you want to be seen."

I gave her a palms up. "So when do you suggest the dynamic duo slipped her the stuff? Because from what you're telling me, there was never a good window of opportunity."

"If they didn't do it, I'll eat my—" She scanned her outfit in search of edible options. "Well, it's not going to be my shoes. I don't relish getting cork stuck between my teeth." She braced her hands on her hips and trained an accusatory look at me. "Why am I getting the impression that not only are you unconvinced that Bobbi and Dawna killed Krystal, you don't believe I'm next on their hit list?"

"Because if someone in Texas killed Krystal, which is looking more and more like a good bet, we can wash our hands of the whole affair. No Internet searches. No stalking people. No having to guess who the next victim will be. No having to look over our shoulders. No standoffs. No—"

"But we *always* do Internet searches. We *always* stalk people. We—"

"And you won't get stuck having to hang out with the gang anymore because you won't need their protection! Won't that be liberating?"

"Not hang out with the gang?" Her face started wilting like a wax candle in a hot attic. "But I like hanging out with them." She lowered her gaze, looking crestfallen. "They don't act snotty to me because I'm the one person in the room who's different."

Awww. I was suddenly very proud that my little band of Iowans could show as much respect for a six-foot transsexual as they could for each other. "Of course not. Your gender reassignment surgery doesn't faze them in the least."

She flashed a quizzical look. "What does my surgery have to do with anything?"

"I'm agreeing with you, Jack. I think it's wonderful that the gang doesn't look down their noses at you because you used to be a guy."

"That's not the reason I—" She rolled her eyes. "I'm happy they don't treat me differently because I'm *beautiful*! Women can act so snotty when the new kid on the block is a real knockout, but the gang doesn't seem to mind how much better looking I am than they are. They're so accepting." She paused thoughtfully. "Either that or their cataracts are so bad they can't actually see me."

I'm not sure why I bothered to compliment Jack when she was so much better at it than I was.

"Say, when we were eating dinner with Woody the other night, did you notice the ring he was wearing?"

"I was a little preoccupied, Emily. Incoming flak by the blonde bombshells? Sustained verbal attack? Artillery fire directed at my jugular?"

"Well, I noticed it at breakfast yesterday morning because Krystal made a big fuss over it."

"Krystal? Make a fuss? Shocking."

"It's brass with a fleur-de-lis motif that shows one of the petals broken off. Woody said it's been in his family for as long as he can remember. But here's where it gets weird. The woman who hosted us on our home visit has a needlepoint piece, embroidered by her grandmother, that has the very same motif."

"Why is that weird?"

"Because the embroidery replicates a design created by a metal-smith who lived in the grandmother's village. He fabricated all kinds of brass jewelry, but he made only one ring, and it's on Woody Jolly's finger."

"I still don't understand why that's weird. Stuff gets auctioned off and bought everywhere in the world now. Craigslist, Amazon, eBay. People can shop internationally from their laptops or iPads."

"So how did a one-of-a-kind ring that was made prior to World War II become an heirloom in the Jolly family?"

Jackie tucked in her lips. "Okay, that's a little weird. The timing's a bit off."

"Way off. I was told the metalsmith never removed the ring from his finger, so he was apparently wearing it the day he died."

"Which was when?"

"The morning of D-Day."

"So his family removed the ring before they buried him and some greedy relative later sold it, which makes Woody all mixed up about the heirloom business."

"But no one ever found the ring."

"If Woody's wearing it, *someone* must have found it."

"Here's the thing. Five members of the French Resistance undertook a mission the night before the invasion. Four of them were killed. In the Allied bombing raid the following morning, their bodies were burned beyond recognition. One of them was identified by the fragments of two gold teeth, but there was no brass ring to help identify the metalsmith."

"Could the brass have melted in the bombing?"

"If it did, how did the fully intact ring leap onto Woody's finger?"

She studied me with a one-eyed squint. "So if Woody is wearing a ring that was reputed never to have left the metalsmith's finger, either the metalsmith wasn't wearing it when he died or—"

We exchanged a long look.

"Or the metalsmith didn't die," I finished for her.

"But if he lived through the mission, why would he want people to think he was dead?"

"Because the fifth member of the team was rumored to have been an enemy collaborator who betrayed the mission to the Nazis. To reward his cooperation, they might have allowed him to escape with both his life *and* his ring. And if he were smart, he would have run far, far away, where he'd never be recognized again."

"Wait a sec, Emily. Are you suggesting that good old Woody 'I Love Ketchup' Jolly was a former French metalsmith who betrayed his countrymen to the Nazis and has been living in self-imposed exile in the United States ever since, disguised as a funeral director?"

In my mind's eye I saw the excruciating pain in Solange Ducat's face as she'd peered at the old man standing before her. I heard the agony in her voice as she'd screamed her accusations. *C'est toi. C'est toi.* But she hadn't recognized Woody by his physical appearance.

190

She'd recognized him from the ring on his finger—the one whose likeness she had fashioned in embroidery thread and framed. The one she hadn't seen since before D-Day. The one that had belonged to Pierre Lcfcvre, the metalsmith whose betrayal had resulted in the death of her only brother.

"Yup." I stared Jackie straight in the eye. "That's exactly what I'm suggesting."

FOURTEEN

"As MANY OF YOU might have heard by now, the guest who died in the tragic accident at Étretat yesterday suffered a brain hemorrhage that led to her death."

We were packed in like sardines as Rob addressed us from the square of parquet flooring in the center of the lounge. The evening's discount cocktail was a supersized Bloody Mary with extra olives and celery, so while guests squeezed together on the cushy furniture, Patrice worked the room by taking drink orders, then dashing back to the bar to mix them, which shattered a misconception I had about river cruise companies.

They didn't earn the bulk of their income from tour packages.

They earned it from alcohol.

"What you might not have heard," Rob continued, "is that the hemorrhage may have been induced by the introduction of a foreign substance into her system."

Shock. Gasps. Whispers.

"What kind of foreign substance?" asked Dick Teig.

"The police are withholding that information until they're further along in their investigation."

"Did shee order the entrée that the kisshen tried to palm off as fish the other night?" Irv called out. "The menu didn't shay fish. It said poizon."

"A misprint," said Rob. "The kitchen *does not* serve poison."

"Tell that to the blonde," Irv taunted.

"I ordered the poison the other night and it didn't cause *my* brain to hemorrhage," said Tilly.

"I've got three words for you, shweetheart," slurred Irv.

"Let me guess," challenged Tilly in her professor's voice. "You. Don't. Care."

"Shtay away from cliffs."

"That's four words," said Nana.

Irv swayed slightly forward in his chair. "Closhe enough."

Rob motioned for silence. "Because of the unusual nature of Ms. Cake's death, the French police have contacted the authorities in her hometown of Abilene, Texas, so a parallel investigation is being conducted there."

I raised my hand. "Can you tell us if the police have ruled out accidental overdose?"

"Good question, and it's one I can answer. They've determined that Ms. Cake was in no way responsible for her own death. There's no evidence indicating that the substance that caused her hemorrhage was ever in her possession."

"What kind of substance was it?" Dick Teig asked again.

Rob lifted his palms in a helpless gesture. "I told you. I don't know. The police aren't saying at the moment."

Bobbi Benedict waved her Western hat in the air, drawing the attention of every eye in the room. "When you say 'foreign' substance, hon, what're you sayin' exactly? Do you mean that whatever killed Krystal came from someplace like China? Or are you sayin' that since she was in a country that was foreign to *her*, the substance that killed her was local?"

An awkward silence descended on the room.

"I don't understand the question," Margi piped up.

"She thinks Krystal was whacked by someone from China," said Bernice.

"Is it any wonder?" mused George. "Everything is made in China now."

Grace nodded. "I bet if stuff was still being manufactured in the USA, *we'd* be the first ones fingered for the crime."

"Could someone repeat the question?" asked Dick Stolee.

"It wasn't actually a question," said Alice. "The young lady was simply saying that the woman who died didn't know what country she was in."

Oh, God.

"There's no excuse for any guest to be that uninformed," declared Lucille. "Not with the amount of literature the cruise company sent us."

"Let me back up for a moment," said Rob as he attempted to regain control of the conversation. He directed his comment at Bobbi. "Simply stated, Krystal either ate or drank something that was toxic to her health."

I wondered how many times he'd have to repeat that before it finally sank in.

"Do you have any idea what?" asked Woody, who'd obviously been tuned out when Dick Teig had posed the same question twice before. Either that, or his hearing was being affected by the jingle of Virginia Martin's jewelry and the *whooshing* from Victor's oxygen. Maybe next time, he'd think twice before shoehorning himself between them on a sofa.

Choosing not to respond to Woody's question, Rob continued. "So here's what's going to happen. While the police in Abilene conduct their investigation, the French police will question a few of you to see if you can provide any new information about Ms. Cake's activities before she died."

"But the police already questioned us," protested Dawna.

Rob shot her a sympathetic look. "That's before they reclassified Krystal's death as a homicide."

"Which lucky few get to be harassed?" cackled Bernice.

"They're compiling the list now, so they should be ready to conduct interviews after dinner. To speed the process along, they've requested that all guests return to their cabins after they've finished dining this evening, so if you hear a knock on your cabin door, please answer it, because it'll be the police."

"How are they deciding who needs to be interviewed?" asked Cal.

"I can't offer you any more information than I've already given you. All I can tell you is, be cooperative, and if all goes well, we should be able to leave for Vernon on schedule." He glanced at his watch. "Any more questions before I cut you loose?"

Margi stuck her hand in the air. "Will we be issued refunds if we're arrested for murder?"

KREEEooo! Bzzt ... bzzzt ... "Ladies and gentlemen, the dining room is now open."

Rob swept his hand toward the door. "*Bon appétit.*"

I braced myself for the stampede, shocked when nothing happened. Guests continued to sit in their chairs, looking a bit rattled and not at all anxious to file into the dining room. I guess they figured the quicker they finished dinner, the sooner they'd be treated to an evening of scintillating dialogue with the French police. Even my guys were dragging their feet. They should have been long gone by now, but instead they were slowly easing themselves out of their chairs, chatting each other up, and being just plain pokey. All except Osmond, who spotted me and Jackie in the far corner and waved his arm over his head to indicate he was heading in our direction. I knew exactly what he wanted, and my heart ached knowing what I was going to have to tell him.

"Have you heard from Madeleine yet?" He inched close to me and cupped his hand around his mouth. "I didn't want to ask in front of everyone earlier."

"As a matter of fact, I *have* heard from her."

"No kidding?"

I gave Jackie the eye. "Do you want to run ahead and find a table?"

She gave me a thumbs up. "I'll save you a seat. And by the way, I checked into the ship's seat-saving policy." She cranked her mouth into a peevish slant. "There *is* no policy. Bobbi Benedict made it all up. So I hope she gives me flak again tonight, because I just happen to be packing something that's going to shut her up forever."

"Please tell me you're not carrying pepper spray."

She began rooting around in the side pocket of her shoulder bag. "Too volatile. The slightest shift in the wind and your mascara gets relocated from your lashes to your cheeks."

"Stun gun?"

"Ta-da!" She held up a small sheet of paper. I squinted at the nearly illegible scrawl.

"Gag order?"

"A note from the captain." She hugged it to her chest like a child embracing her first doll. "I can hardly *wait* to see her reaction when she reads it."

"What's it say?" asked Osmond as he readjusted his cervical collar beneath his chin.

She beamed. "I believe the abridged version is, 'Liar, liar, pants on fire.'"

While Jackie snaked through the milling crowd toward the exit, I guided Osmond to the nearest settee and sat down next to him. "You should have joined us on the walking tour, Osmond. Can you guess who our local guide was?"

"A Joan of Arc impersonator?"

"Madeleine Saint-Sauveur."

"Madeleine dressed up like Joan of Arc?"

"No, she was dressed in street clothes, but the important thing is, I was able to talk to her after the tour, and she gave me the contact information for Solange!"

His mouth rounded like a small planet. His eyes grew to twice their size. "REALLY?"

"Really."

"Wow!" He fumbled to release his iPhone from its holster. "Can you text me the information?"

"Why don't I give you the paper I wrote it down on?"

He hesitated. "I've kinda gone paperless. Can you tweet me?"

"C'mon, Osmond. You know I don't tweet."

"Email?"

I pulled my little memo pad out of my shoulder bag, tore off the relevant page, and held it out to him. "Here you go. Express mail."

He stared at the paper with the distaste of a vegan eyeing a T-bone steak. "Could you give it to Marion and have *her* text it to me? She's not one to blab other people's business to everyone. And she's probably got the fastest thumbs in the group, so I'll get it quicker."

"Right. Because my handing the information over to you this very instant is too slow."

"Well, it's not in the right format, so that can cause all kinds of technical delays."

"Okey-dokey." I stuffed the note back in my bag, wondering if, twenty years down the road, some scientist would become famous for his groundbreaking discovery of pen and paper.

He nodded toward my bag. "So what does the note say?"

"The usual contact stuff. Phone number. Address. Email."

"Did Madeleine say Solange would be happy to hear from me?"

"Of *course* Solange is going to be happy to hear from you."

He dropped his voice to a whisper. "Did she give any hint that she might know why my name showed up in her family?"

"She mentioned that specifically. Solange named her firstborn Osmond to honor what you did for the family during the war. And every generation after that jumped on the bandwagon, so the family is rife with Osmonds."

"That was real generous of them." He scratched his jaw with a nervous hand. "Did she happen to say when the first Osmond made his way into the world?"

"Late winter. After the war."

"REALLY?"

"Osmond—"

He seized my arm, punch drunk with excitement. "Emily, do you know what this means?"

"Her husband came back," I said in a quiet voice, placing my hand over his.

He blinked as if he hadn't heard, then went very still. "What?"

"Everyone thought he died in prison, but he didn't. He escaped in a bombing raid, and three weeks after you left for England, he found his way back to his family."

"He came back?" His voice was far away, his eyes distant. "But how could he come back? He was dead."

"Nazi lies," I soothed. "He returned to Solange and fathered a slew of children with famous American names. But none more famous than yours."

Dazed, he sank back into the settee cushions and knuckled moisture away from the corners of his eyes. "So ... I'm not a father after all?"

I gave his hand a reassuring squeeze. "No one can say with any authority whether you are or aren't, Osmond. It boils down to hormones and timing. But Solange's husband raised all the children as his own, and Madeleine made it quite clear that the family wants it left that way, no matter what might have happened during the war."

Eyes downcast, he heaved a sigh. "Yup. That's the way it should be. They don't need any whippersnappers from America uprooting their family tree. Solange has lived through enough. Wouldn't be right to make waves at this stage in everyone's life. Besides, chances are the little guy wasn't mine anyway. Probably one in a million."

I breathed around a sudden lump in my throat. "But you can certainly catch up with each other through email. Madeleine is going to give Solange a crash course. Think of the decades of history you have to share, and the miracle of the information highway delivering your messages across the Atlantic in mere seconds. If you're lucky, Madeleine might even show Solange how to text."

"Yup. Well"—he struggled to keep his lips from quivering—"I guess I should be heading in to dinner."

"Solange has outlived two husbands, Osmond. It's your turn to be on the receiving end of her attention now. You'll have her all to yourself, and in the months to come, I guarantee she'll make you feel younger than you have for years."

"Sure."

I helped him to his feet. "You can still invite the whole family to Windsor City. I bet they'd be thrilled to visit the States with you as their tour guide."

"That's probably not such a good idea, Emily. Not anymore."

I rubbed the space between his shoulder blades with a gentle hand. "I'm saying nothing to anyone about this, okay?"

He nodded glumly. "Thanks. See you in there."

As I watched him shuffle across the lounge all by himself, I turned toward the bow of the ship so that I could quietly brush away the tears that were seeping onto my cheeks.

FIFTEEN

"How'm I supposed to know what it says?" complained Bobbi. "It's written in French. I can't read French. And how do I know the signature is authentic? You could have paid one of the crew to sign the captain's name." She regarded the paper with suspicion. "It could be forged."

Arriving at the round table in the corner of the dining room, I was welcomed by a controversy that was already in progress.

"This seat has your name on it," announced Jackie as she angled a neighboring chair away from the table for me. She arched her brows at Bobbi. "Contrary to what *some* people might say."

"We'll see about that," Bobbi fired back. "I'll ask our waiter to translate it, and then we'll see whose turn it is to gloat."

I was less than thrilled to be sharing the table with the same group who'd ruined dinner the other night, but with Cal joining us in Krystal's absence, maybe the hostility level would decrease.

"Give me the note." Virginia held out her hand amid an annoying jangle of beaded crystal bracelets. "Victor will read it."

"Not without my reading glasses, my pet."

"You speak perfect French. And Polish. And German." She slapped the paper down in front of him. "Would you you at least try? I'm sick of listening to your blathering beauties."

He plucked it off the table and tore it in half, then quarters, then eighths, then deposited the scraps in the pocket of his dinner jacket. "In case you missed it the first time, Virginia, that was a no. And as for the rest of my fine beauties, if you choose to continue your petty squabbling, you'll be eating the rest of your meals without me, because I'll be at another table, dining with the adults."

Bobbi gave the brim of her hat an angry tug. "She started it," she muttered under her breath.

Cal shot Victor a curious look. "Where'd you learn to speak so many languages? Man, high-school Spanish about did me in, so my love affair with foreign languages ended even before it could begin."

"Victor is a gifted linguist," cooed Virginia.

Victor fiddled with the oxygen tubing in his nostrils. "The old ethnic neighborhoods made linguists of us all. But it was a long time ago. I barely remember the basics anymore."

Virginia regarded him oddly. "That's not tr—"

"But I do remember something of greater importance," he said, cutting her off abruptly. "If we can enjoy our dining experience without any more drama, I have a surprise prepared." He contorted his mouth into something that vaguely resembled a smile and patted the front panel of his jacket.

"The bonus?" squealed Dawna.

He opened his jacket to reveal an envelope tucked into the inside pocket. "The bonus."

"*EWWW!*" cried the blondes.

"What kind of bonus?" asked Cal.

"Don't go there, son," warned Woody.

Virginia glared at her husband, eyes slatted, lips pinched. "You wrote out a personal check after I expressly told you that—"

"Do *not* tell me what I can and cannot do with *my* money," he boomed out in a voice that was uncharacteristically harsh. "One more word, Virginia, and I shall rip up this check and make out another for *double* the amount. So do continue your harangue, because I expect our honoree will be thrilled to receive an additional bonus."

That was enough to silence Virginia and everyone else at the table, except Jackie, who apparently saw great marketing potential in marital discord.

"I know I'm the newbie here, Victor, so I don't expect my name to be on that check, but after what I learned today, I have high hopes for next year. Do you know why?" She struck a pose, oozing calm and confidence. "I discovered a whole new demographic for Mona Michelle cosmetics."

Bobbi stabbed a finger at Victor. "If she's talkin' about eight-to-twelve-year-olds, I wanna remind you that I recommended targeting tweens two years ago, and you pooh-poohed the idea because you were afraid the Family Research Council would complain about us turnin' tweens into tarts."

"You wanted to slap lipstick on eight-year-olds?" asked Cal.

"We wouldn't have called it lipstick, hon. We would've called it *Bare Moisturizing Sunblock with Natural Color for Tender Lips*. Kinda like Chapstick, only less affordable."

Cal frowned. "That's deceitful. It's still lipstick. You're just calling it something different and trying to get little girls hooked on makeup years before they need to wear it."

"On the other hand," Jackie broke in, "*I'm* addressing an issue at the opposite end of the—"

"You know somethin', hon?" Bobbi directed a narrow look at Cal. "I'd rather have my mind corrupted by a solid hour of MSNBC than talk cosmetics to civilians."

"Where's Patricia?" asked Woody, scanning the dining room. "I want to get my dinner ordered."

"Dad, his name's *Patrice*, not Patricia."

Woody wrinkled his nose. "What kind of damn fool name is Patrice?"

I had this one, hands down. "French?"

"Have you all finished talking?" snapped Jackie. She glanced around the table, her eyes shooting daggers. "Because if you haven't, I certainly don't want to interrupt your chitchat with any groundbreaking news or anything."

"Forgive our manners," Victor apologized. "Or lack of them. Please, continue what you were saying."

"Okay." She leaned forward with breathless abandon and framed her hands in the air. "For the woman who wants to make her last impression on earth a memorable one: Mona Michelle cosmetics for the pre-funeral set."

"*Euww*," cried Dawna.

"Hey, that's the ticket," said Woody.

"Pre-funeral set?" repeated Victor.

"It's a totally untapped market," she enthused. "Septuagenarians. Octogenarians. Nonagenarians. We provide color palettes to help them choose what they'd like to look like for their final viewing, and if they like the results, they might decide to wear it on a regular basis even before the funeral, so we're talking millions in added revenue!"

"That's gotta be *the* most disgustin' thing I've ever heard in my entire life," said Bobbi.

Woody thwacked Cal on the shoulder. "How come you never come up with innovative stuff like this?"

"No way am I'm gonna waste my time offerin' beauty advice to old ladies with liver spots and mustaches," vowed Dawna. "If the company heads in that direction, I'm leavin'."

"Me, too," threatened Bobbi.

Victor bowed his head in contemplation, his breath coming quickly and heavily. When he looked up again, he had eyes for no one but Jackie. "It's brilliant. I don't know why it didn't occur to any of my marketing people before this."

"Maybe because it's disgustin'?" said Bobbi.

"We can reformulate our products to be more face friendly to women with thinner skin and sun-damaged complexions," he continued. "We can develop softer shades to complement silver hair. We can—"

"Schedule mini makeovers for potential customers?" asked Jackie. "Because I'm way ahead of you there. I've already done them."

Victor looked shocked. "When?"

"This afternoon. While you were touring Rouen. I stayed on the boat and market-tested a few of the products I had with me on a sample group of senior citizens. You wanna see the results?"

"By all means."

She catapulted herself out of her chair and ran around the dining room for thirty seconds, returning with Margi and Nana.

"Here they are." She positioned them close to Victor's chair as if they were decoys in a police lineup. "Our first model, Margi, is all ready for her open casket at the local Catholic church."

"Catholics don't do open caskets in church," Woody spoke up. "You're thinking of Protestants. She might have to consider converting."

"She wouldn't have to if she were cremated," said Cal.

Visibly alarmed, Margi angled her head around to look up at Jackie. "Are they telling me the only way I can buy your translucent cream blush is by renouncing my faith?"

"Don't listen to them. Our policy is to accept all major credit cards regardless of religious affiliation." Jackie placed her hand on Nana's shoulder. "And this is our second model, Mrs. S., who's prepared to paint the town pink in her ivory-toned foundation and neutral eye shadow."

Uff-da! That's what had been different about the gang. The ladies had all undergone makeovers! But the change had been so subtle, I hadn't been able to put my finger on it. I studied Nana with a critical eye. *Wow.* She looked like a million bucks. Two of her chins had either been nipped, tucked, or cleverly camouflaged. Her skin tone was less splotchy. Her face looked as if it had been lifted, peeled, and botoxed, resulting in a healthy glow that made her look twenty years younger. In fact, even though she wasn't funeral parlor–ready, she looked every bit as good as Margi.

"You don't paint a town pink," drawled Dawna. "You paint it red."

"Octogenarians paint it pink," countered Jackie. "Pastels are much more complementary to them than primary colors. And may I draw your attention to the highlighter under her brow?" She trailed a finger along the arch of Nana's eyebrow. "No sign of creping whatsoever."

"What the hell's creping?" asked Woody.

"Crepin's what happens to a girl's skin when it gets so old, it's got more crinkles than a roll of them party streamers," said Nana.

Victor shifted his gaze from Margi to Nana to Margi again. "Your results are extraordinary. And you didn't even use a reformulated product. I can't begin to tell you how impressed I am, Jackie. Your methodology, your application … all outstanding."

While Jackie preened, Woody pounced. "Say, if she can have folks looking that good when they're dead, I wouldn't mind getting a piece of the action. I hired the best makeup artist money can buy, but she can't hold a candle to what Jackie's done with these two gals. Shoot, they don't look dead at all."

Maybe because … *they weren't*?

"What do you think, Victor? Are you willing to talk turkey? If I agree to buy your cosmetics, would you agree to let Jackie train an army of gals who'd make our customers look as attractive as these gals? But I'd insist that she do the training. Second best won't cut it at Jolly's."

Victor's heavy breathing eased as dollar signs appeared in his eyes. "Why stop at Jolly's? If you have a regional platform, we could work on expanding our reach until we achieved national recognition. If sales increase exponentially, we could take the company public and offer stock options."

"Whose company?" asked Woody. "Yours or mine?"

"Both!" said Victor. "How do you feel about mergers?"

Cal made a *T* of his hands. "Okay, guys. *Time out*. Neither one of you can make a decision about anything until a heck of a lot of people put their two cents in, so why don't you cool your jets before you set the price on your initial stock offering."

"My son." Woody jerked his head toward Cal. "The party poop."

"Look at you." Virginia glanced from Woody to her husband. "Two old men making pie in the sky. You just can't let go, can you? Move over, gentlemen, because no one is buying what you have to offer anymore. You're all washed up. Passé. Do yourselves a favor, would you? Deal with it."

Our waiter arrived with a tray of soup bowls and an apology. "You will please forgive that our meal this evening begins with the soup course." He opened a nearby tray jack and set his burden down. "Due to an unfortunate mishap in the kitchen, there will be no appetizer."

That gave me pause. "I hope no one was injured."

"No, madame. Only the duck."

While Jackie escorted Margi and Nana back to their table, our waiter, whose name tag read "Ivandro," proceeded to serve the soup around the table. "Our selection this evening is creamy lobster bisque with cognac."

"How come Patricia's not waiting on us?" asked Woody.

"I'm sorry, monsieur. We have no Patricia on our wait staff."

"He means Patrice," said Cal. He leveled a disgusted look at his father. "You can't even *pretend* to try, can you?"

"Ah, Patrice." Ivandro waited for Jackie to sit down before he set the bowl down in front of her. "He is tending bar in the lounge."

"Does that mean *you'll* be pouring our drinks this evening?" asked Virginia as she held up her empty stemware. "Or do we have to send a telegram to the kitchen to get our wine glasses filled?"

"*Eh.* Forgive me again." Ivandro shot into immediate overdrive and retrieved two bottles of wine from the serving station. As he circled the table again, decanting either red or white, he loitered almost involuntarily by the blondes, his gaze lingering on the provocative plunge of Dawna's neckline.

"Will we be ordering an entrée this evening," Virginia asked him in a syrupy voice, "or do we have to wait until you finish ogling the eye candy?"

"That is *enough*, Virginia!" Victor slammed his fist on the table, causing the silverware to jump and the soup to slosh.

"Not by half, Victor, dear." She raised her glass in a toast before knocking back half the contents. "Not by half."

Ivandro took our entrée and dessert orders and melted as fast as he could into the far reaches of the dining room. I tasted the soup and was immediately transported into a state of bliss. "Oh, my Lord. Have you tasted this?" I glanced around the table. "It's incredible."

"It's a gross color," mewled Bobbi.

"I think it's gone bad," agreed Dawna.

Virginia gave her soup an idle stir before setting her spoon down and shoving the bowl toward Victor. "It tastes terrible. I don't want it."

"Have you even tried it?" asked Victor.

"I don't need to try it to know I'm not going to like it."

Wow. This was just like eating a meal with my five nephews... or Margi.

Victor slid the bowl closer. "It's quite delicious, Virginia. I suspect you may regret sharing it with me."

"I doubt it."

"I wanna clear the air about somethin'," said Bobbi as she inched her bowl toward the center of the table. "If you're gonna be openin' a whole new branch of Mona Michelle, you're gonna have to put me and Dawna in charge of somethin', Victor. We've got seniority, which is a fancy way of sayin' we've been with the company a lot longer than *she* has." She nodded across the table at Jackie.

"Amen to that," said Dawna.

Victor grinned. "You've lost your distaste of the elderly so quickly, ladies? How do you explain that?"

The girls exchanged a meaningful look before Bobbi placed a reverent hand over her heart. She turned doe eyes on Victor. "We both know it's what Krystal would have wanted. She was so dedicated. So … so maniacal about her job. We can almost feel her presence with us now, can't you?"

"That's Krystal?" Jackie scanned the ceiling. "I thought it was a draft from the air conditioner."

"Krystal never would have left you in the hands of amateurs," swore Bobbi, "and neither will we."

Especially if it meant booting Jackie off a higher rung of the corporate ladder. The girls definitely had their priorities.

"Could we declare a moratorium on shop talk?" asked Cal. "I'd like to enjoy my lobster bisque without the pain of heartburn."

"You want mine, too?" asked Bobbi, nudging it toward him. "I can't get past the color."

"Me either," said Dawna. "Mine's free for the takin'. Anyone want it?"

Jackie sucked in her breath like a Hoover with a faulty motor. "Stop! Don't anyone touch those bowls! They might be contaminated."

Yup. That got everyone's attention.

"*Euw!*" Dawna snatched her hands off the table. "Contaminated with what?"

"With whatever you and Bobbi used to kill Krystal."

"WHAT?" they cried in unison.

"Don't deny it," warned Jackie. "You wanted to eliminate the top competitor to improve your odds at earning the bonus, so you whacked her."

Bobbi's mouth rounded like a knothole. "That's not true!"

Virginia eyed the girls with cool detachment. "Are you listening to this, Victor? Your fair-haired beauties may be natural-born killers."

"We are not!" protested Dawna. "There's nothin' natural about us."

Virginia settled back in her chair and smiled. "Actually, I rather like the idea. So how did you do it? Peroxide? Or were you afraid you wouldn't have enough to see you through the entire trip, so you decided to substitute something else?"

Bobbi gasped. "Are y'all gonna sit there and let her talk to us like that?"

"I'm okay with it," said Jackie.

Dawna shot an explosive look at Virginia. "If you don't take that back, I mean to tell ya, I don't care if you *are* Victor's wife. Me and Bobbi will sue you for libel."

"No, you won't," said Cal.

"Oh, yah?" challenged Bobbi. "You just watch us, sugah."

"The only way you can sue someone for libel is if the person says something defamatory about you in *print*. If it doesn't appear in black and white, you can forget about it."

Dawna flitted a desperate look around the table. "Does anyone have a pen and paper?"

"Maybe she could text you," I suggested.

"I cannot begin to tell you how inappropriate this conversation has become," said Victor as he set his spoon on the service plate beneath his empty bowl. "Have you suddenly become members of the politburo that you can throw around your accusations so freely?"

"Harmless chitchat," chimed Virginia.

"Well, I advise you to find some other topic to chitchat about."

As it happened, I knew the perfect thing.

"Woody has some intriguing tales to tell about his experiences in World War II. Maybe he'd agree to share a few stories with us."

Cal rolled his eyes. "Great. Now you've done it."

"Happy to oblige," Woody enthused. "Happy to oblige. Well, it all started back in December of '41. Pearl Harbor got bombed on the seventh, and I was first in line at the recruitment office on the eighth."

"My Grampa Potter did the same thing!" Jackie tittered. "He was a navy guy, but he eventually ended up in France as part of a Seabee unit."

"Not me. I was army all the way. Never made it to France."

"That's too bad," I lamented. "You might have run into some of your French ancestors as you pushed toward Germany."

"What French ancestors? I'm not French."

"But—" I feigned confusion. "I guess I just assumed that since you're wearing a family heirloom with a French symbol, your ancestors were . . . you know . . . French."

"I might have had a French relative a thousand years ago, before the Norman Invasion, but my family tree got its roots in British soil."

"So how do you explain the fleur-de-lis on your ring?"

"Why should I have to explain?" His voice rose a half-octave. "Like I told you before, it's always been in the family. I don't know how its original owner came by it, or how many hands it passed through to get to me, and I don't care. Neither should you."

"I've always thought the flower on his ring was a lily," said Cal. "Considering we hail from a long line of morticians, a lily would make sense. It's certainly appropriate to the profession. We do handle more than our share of lilies. But I don't have a clue why the petal is broken."

"Maybe it signifies that one of your relatives went bankrupt," offered Jackie.

"Undertakers don't go bankrupt," scoffed Dawna.

Jackie puffed up with indignation. "Excuse me? They would if they lived in a nonsmoking community where the primary interests were fad diets and yoga."

"Did you ever have a metalsmith in your family?" I asked, continuing to press the issue. "Someone who might have actually fabricated the ring?"

Virginia groaned her impatience. "Would you mind *showing* us whatever it is you're talking about?"

Woody obliged by holding up his hand and flashing his ring around the table.

"I'm not sure what all the fuss is about," said Virginia. "It's not even fourteen carat."

Bobbi pulled a face. "That's not a lily. It's an amaryllis."

"I think it looks like a snapdragon," said Dawna.

Cal grinned. "I'd give you iris or orchid, but snapdragon? Have you ever *seen* a snapdragon?"

"Shoot," jeered Bobbi. "Dawna doesn't know the difference between a tulip and a tea rose. She probably just likes to say the word 'snapdragon' out loud. Ya know? Kinda like Krystal used to like to say 'snakeskin.'"

I tossed the Jollys a questioning look. "You're not aware of any metalsmiths in the family?"

Cal shrugged. "Beats me. Dad?"

"How the devil should I know? And when would I have time to find out? Hell, I work full time."

"Then it might surprise you to learn that, prior to World War II, a metalsmith living in Solange Ducat's village fabricated a ring that's an exact replica of yours, right down to the broken petal. And the *really* weird thing is, he's reputed to have made only one. So the only way it could have gotten into your hands is if the metalsmith had placed it there himself, and that's kind of impossible, because according to the story Madeleine Saint-Sauveur told us on our home visit, he was one of the Resistance fighters who went missing after the failed mission at Pointe du Hoc. He and his ring disappeared from the face of the earth and have never been seen again. Until now."

Color leached from Woody's face. He froze in place, eyes fixed, mouth rigid.

"There's obviously a simple explanation," said Cal. "Tell her what it is, Dad."

Woody seemed unable to breathe. He bowed his head and gripped his hands together to ease a sudden tremor.

Jackie slanted a look at him. "Is he okay?"

"Dad?" Cal gripped his father's shoulder and shook gently. "What's wrong? C'mon, Dad, you're scaring me."

"Are you suggesting that Mr. Jolly could be the same man who undertook the mission to Pointe du Hoc?" Virginia asked me. "Do you know what you're saying? Because I heard Mrs. Saint-Sauveur as well as you did. If he was the man who lived through the mission, that would mean he's the man the Nazis allowed to escape because he was collaborating with them. Are you accusing Mr. Jolly of being the traitor who sold out his village to the Nazis?"

"I'd like to go back to my cabin now," said Woody in a halting voice. "I . . . I'm not really hungry."

"Geez, Dad, will you say something? Tell them this is all a bunch of bull. Tell *me* it's all a bunch of bull!"

"I'm sorry, Cal." Woody's eyes welled with tears. "I'm . . . I'm so sor—"

"*Ehhh!*" shrieked Virginia, pulling the oxygen tubing away from Victor's face as a torrent of blood began spewing from his nose. Jackie whipped her napkin off her lap and pressed it against his nostrils.

"Gimme your napkins! This is just like Krystal's."

And we all knew what had happened to Krystal.

SIXTEEN

"Do you believe me now? First Krystal, now Victor? Aren't you sorry for calling me paranoid?"

"I never called you paranoid."

"Maybe not. But you were *thinking* it."

The ambulance transporting Victor and Virginia to the hospital had departed well over three hours ago. Normally, the restaurant manager wouldn't have called emergency services for a mere nosebleed, but after we beat him over the head with the fact that another guest at our table had died after suffering a similar nosebleed two days ago, he succumbed to our pleas and relented. He could see for himself that Victor's was no ordinary nosebleed.

It was a gusher.

So amid much fanfare and confusion, Victor had been whisked off on a gurney, loaded into an ambulance, and driven off with sirens blaring.

"He was wearing his favorite dinner jacket," Jackie reflected as she peered out the wraparound windows at the ship's bow, staring mindlessly at the city bridge that loomed above our mooring place.

In a half-baked effort to put a positive spin on an absolutely dreadful evening, we had decided to meet in the lounge for a well-deserved cocktail after the police interviews ended.

"Of course, the jacket is totally ruined now. Feel free to quote me on this, Emily. Technology will never be advanced enough to develop an oxygen-boosting stain treatment capable of removing that much blood from natural fiber clothing."

I sighed. "Victor's dinner jacket is the least of his problems."

We didn't have a clue which passengers aboard the *Renoir* had been grilled by the criminal investigation unit, but all the interviewees must have been cleared, because when the police paraded down the gangway, they didn't have any suspects in tow. I'd been granted access to one of the attending officers on-the-fly, so in a quick three-minute meeting, I expressed my fear about a male guest who'd been transported to the hospital with a nosebleed that was eerily reminiscent of the one Krystal Cake had suffered prior to her death.

"Doctors at both local hospitals are very competent, madame," he'd assured me.

"Yeah, but, could his nosebleed be an indication that someone slipped him the same substance that caused Krystal's brain hemorrhage? Could whoever killed her be trying to kill him, too?"

"Did you inform the emergency medical unit of your concerns?"

"We tried, but there was a lot of commotion in the dining room and everyone ended up talking at the same time, so I'm not sure they heard us. They were mostly interested in clearing the area and treating the patient."

"Did anyone accompany the gentleman to the hospital?"

"His wife."

"She'll be questioned by the admissions staff at the hospital. If she tells them of your concerns, I promise you, they will be addressed."

"Okay, that's good to know. I just wanted you to be current with all the details."

"I appreciate your stepping forward, Mrs. Miceli. Perhaps you would be kind enough to give me the gentleman's name? For future reference if needed."

He wrote down the information I gave him, frowning slightly as he turned to another page in his memo pad. "Ah, yes. Victor Martin. I recognize the name. We were applauding the fact that a man afflicted with so many health problems had the courage to venture so far from home."

"How do you know about his health problems?"

"Are you familiar with the term: medical history form? A most helpful tool. But given Mr. Martin's age, I will tell you I am not surprised that he was rushed to hospital with acute nasal problems. For many elderly who are oxygen-dependent, it is not an uncommon occurrence."

I stirred my Bloody Mary, trying to regain my balance after having my legs knocked out from under me. "That police officer must have thought I was just another hysterical tourist with an addiction to American TV programs beginning with the letters CSI. But I swear, I never even thought about the possibility that Victor's nosebleed might have been caused by his nasal apparatus."

"If that nosebleed was caused by nasal apparatus, someone needs to redesign the apparatus. His event was *exactly* like Krystal's, minus the whining. Trust me, our killers have struck again."

"Maybe it was a polyp. I think polyps can bleed quite profusely."

"The girls have a lot of brass to target the head of the company. I think it's a sign of how delusional they are. Beautiful women think they can get away with anything."

"Or it might be possible that the air-conditioning caused his nasal tissue to dry up. I think dry nasal tissue can cause all kinds of problems."

"Emily, pull your head out of the sand. The girls are staging a takeover of the company, although I'm not sure how they plan to eliminate all the board members. There's a whole slew of them. Mostly old men with obscenely young trophy wives. I think that's kind of a Texas tradition."

"How can Bobbi and Dawna take over anything? Neither one of them is equipped to run a multimillion dollar corporation."

"Which is exactly why they're in this together! They know they can't do it alone, so they've teamed up. Two bodies, one brain. And I hate to break it to you, but their current score ain't too shabby. Benedict and Chestnut—Two. The rest of us—Nothing."

"Don't stick Victor in their win column yet. He's still alive."

"Let's hope so. But if Virginia was too traumatized to give the paramedics some background on what's been happening around here with toxic substances—" Her voice grew gravelly with emotion.

"The police assured me that the hospital staff would pump her for information, so I expect she'll give them a full history, even though she and Victor *do* run kind of hot and cold."

Jackie exhaled a dramatic sigh. "He's such a sweet man. So Old World and mannered. The last of a dying breed. But I'm still puzzled about why the girls hit *him* instead of me. I mean, wouldn't it have made more sense for them to get rid of their closest competition and *then* hit the bigwigs? That's the way I'd do it, but then again, I'm not blonde." She sniffed delicately. "I feel as if Victor took a bullet for me."

I drained my glass and set it down on a side table, casting about for explanations. "Maybe it was a question of opportunity and timing. You were holed up with the gang on the boat all day while Victor hung out with Bobbi and Dawna on the port walk. So they literally had unrestricted access to him all day long."

"See? *Why* is it taking you so long to admit I'm right?"

I frowned. "But that doesn't really wash because we didn't stop for anything to eat while we were touring. We were too busy dodging raindrops."

"They could have eaten after the tour ended. I didn't see them in the dining room at the luncheon buffet, so they must have stopped someplace on their way back to the boat. In fact, Bobbi and Dawna were probably lobbying to eat in some fancy little bistro so they could set the wheels in motion to take out Victor."

Weary from all the mental calisthenics, I slumped in my chair and scrubbed my face with my hands. "My head's going to explode. I dunno, Jack. I get the feeling we're missing something obvious, but I can't figure out what."

She clasped her hands to her chest, her eyes brimming with nostalgia. "You know what *I* miss?"

"Your old external plumbing?"

"Twinkies. I was so crushed when Hostess stopped making them. I know they're supposed to make a comeback with another company, but I doubt they'll ever stack up to the originals."

"When did you start eating Twinkies?"

"When I became a vegetarian. Sponge cake and artificial cream filling are *so* much better for you than red meat."

At the sound of voices, I glanced over my shoulder to find Patrice setting another cocktail in front of Irv. Man, if the only thing Irv wanted to do on this trip was drink, he could have saved himself some money by having his bender at home. If he kept this up, he might not even remember *taking* the trip. I wondered if he'd mentioned his struggle with alcoholism on his medical history form. Probably not. He might even deny he *had* a problem. But thinking about the forms prompted another thought.

"Do you know how the police chose the guests they wanted to interview?"

"Well, they didn't interview *me*, so whatever process they used, it's flawed."

"They read all our medical history forms."

She gasped. "They can't do that, can they? I thought the only agencies authorized to spy on Americans were the NSA, CIA, FBI, ONI, INR, IRS, online advertisers, and Facebook."

"They *did* do it. So if the police were interested in what we wrote on our medical forms, do you realize what that means?"

The answer seemed to strike her like a lightning bolt, causing her to bounce excitedly on her chair. "I know, I know. Handwriting analysis!"

"What?"

"They analyzed everyone's handwriting to see whose penmanship best fits the profile of a killer. It's possible, Emily. The way we form our Bs and Fs can speak volumes about our potential for criminal activities. And capital Gs? They might as well be neon arrows."

I stared at her, deadpan. "They reviewed our medical histories because they wanted to check out what drugs we're carrying! If whatever killed Krystal came in prescription drug form, they'd want to interview anyone using the same drug to verify that the guest still had enough medication to treat his or her condition for the remainder of the trip. If someone demonstrated an obvious shortage, it would raise a flag, right?"

She twitched her lips. "I suppose. But if you ask me, the value of handwriting analysis is grossly underrated."

"A shortage would have to be explained. And if a guest couldn't offer a reasonable explanation as to why he'd failed to bring enough medication with him, the police would probably haul him off to the station for further questioning. Agreed?"

"Personally, I think it's regrettable that the French police could jail someone for being absentminded, stupid, or both."

"But that didn't happen. The police didn't haul anyone away, which means, if Bobbi and Dawna were questioned, they passed muster, and if they *weren't* questioned, it was probably because they weren't carrying the drug in the first place."

Jackie sat very still, looking disappointed, but not yet willing to give up the fight. "Just because the girls didn't list the drug on their medical histories doesn't mean they weren't carrying it."

"Look, if they'd planned to kill Krystal from the get-go, they might have had a reason to omit it from the list. But if they killed her because of the bonus, like you suggested, let me remind you that *none* of you knew about the bonus before you left home, so there was no reason *not* to include it."

"Listen, Emily," she huffed, "you might think you're making sense, but you'll never convince me that—"

"Neither one of us saw them tamper with Krystal's or Victor's food, Jack. How did they dole out their deadly doses with everyone watching? Krystal gave one of her supplements to Woody, but other than that, no one has shared a single morsel of food with anyone else." An image suddenly tumbled into my consciousness. "Well, other than Virginia."

The name hung in the air between us, causing us to exchange a horrified look. "Ohmigod," croaked Jackie. "The soup. She couldn't get rid of her soup fast enough at dinner. Could she have—?"

Motivations began cascading in my head. Her love/hate relationship with Victor. Her rage over the bonus check. Her contempt for Victor's bevy of beauties. Anger. Greed. Jealousy. Holy crap. It was all there in plain sight... and we'd missed it.

"Yes, she could have," I cried as I riffled through my shoulder bag for my cell phone. "And we sent her to the hospital with him. What if the only reason she agreed to go was to finish him off while he—"

"I'm really sorry to bother you ladies." Cal Jolly came up behind us on cat's feet. "It's my dad. He'd like to speak to Emily. To the both of us, actually. About the ring. He's acting pretty weird for Dad, so I'm kind of worried. It's like he blew all his internal circuits at dinner and is blathering about stuff that doesn't make any sense. I know it's an imposition, and I apologize for asking, but could I drag you away for a few minutes? It seems really important to him."

"*Uhhh*—" I froze, my hand locked around my phone, torn between courtesy and obligation.

"You go," urged Jackie, whipping out her own phone. "I'll make the call."

"But … do you know what to say?"

"Emily! I've got it." She shooed me away. "Where are you taking her?" she asked Cal.

"My dad's cabin. Number thirty-eight. I just hope he's still there. Like I said, he's not himself. It's like he's suddenly turned into an entirely different person."

———

Woody Jolly was pacing the floor when we arrived, the bluster gone from his demeanor. He greeted me with a nod before indicating that Cal and I should sit on the bed.

We sat.

He continued to pace.

"I never should have left home," he said in a voice that trembled with emotion. "But how could I know this would happen? No one ever figured it out. No one even suspected. It was my secret, and no one was any the wiser."

Acid bubbled up in my throat. Oh. My. God. My hunch had been right. It was him. He was the traitor.

"Damn ring." He tried to pull it off his finger, but it wouldn't budge.

"It's not a Jolly family heirloom, is it?" I regarded him with forced indulgence.

He shook his head.

"Why'd you do it, Woody?"

He shrugged. "I grew up thinking integrity was the most important virtue a man could have. And then, one day, I discovered it wasn't."

"What took precedence over integrity?" asked Cal.

"You have to ask?" He let out a humorless laugh. "Money, Cal. Money's the only thing that matters in this world. Without it, you're nothing."

"That's the reason you did it?" I flung out. "Because the Nazis offered to pay for your betrayal?"

He studied me with sober eyes. "There you go again. What the devil are you talking about?"

"*I'm* talking about your being a Nazi collaborator. What are *you* talking about?"

"*I'm* talking about being an imposter."

"A what?" squealed Cal.

"He's an imposter," I repeated. "He's the man who sold out his principles to the Germans for thirty pieces of silver, and his name is Pierre Lefevre."

"Who?" asked Woody.

I raised my voice in accusation. "Pierre Lefevre."

"Who's that?"

Maybe I was pronouncing it wrong. "Pierre La-FEV? La-FURV? La—"

"My name's not Pierre," spat Woody.

"Well, you just admitted you were an imposter, so if you're not Pierre, who are you?"

"Woodrow Jolly the Third!"

Cal threw out his hand in exasperation. "See what I mean? I hope he's making sense to you, because he's making *no* sense to me."

"I'm Woodrow Jolly the Third," he continued, a pained expression reshaping his features. "But I'm afraid I'm not the honorable, trustworthy guy I've always pretended to be." He hung his head as he hocked the words up from his gut. "I'm a thief."

Nazi collaborator wasn't bad enough? He was a thief besides?

"What do you mean you're a thief?" Cal fired back. "What kind of thief?"

"The kind I always taught you to condemn." He sat down on the bed across from us, shame running rampant in his eyes. "I take things from the dead."

Euww.

"Jeezuz, Dad! Are you crazy?"

He stared at his hands, shoulders slumped, voice halting. "I couldn't help myself. It started with this." He poked his ring. "I just couldn't force myself to bury it with the guy. What good would it do him anymore? It was way too nice to be locked in a casket and buried. That would have been a terrible waste. It needed to seen, admired. So I ... borrowed it."

"That's how you justified what you did? By calling it borrowing?" Cal's chest was heaving so violently, he looked to be in danger of hyperventilating. "You didn't borrow it, Dad. You *stole* it. You committed a crime!"

"It's only a crime if you're caught." A hint of a smile touched his lips. "I never got caught."

"JEEZ!" raged Cal. "I can't *believe* this!"

"I started out small," he said matter-of-factly. "A ring here, a tie pin there. But you can't get rich off men's jewelry, so I cast my net wider. The ladies were a goldmine. Necklaces, broaches, favorite dinner rings, earrings, wristwatches, evening bags, diamond tiaras."

My Grampa Sippel had been buried with his fishing pole, so I understood the concept of being interred with a bit of your favorite stuff, but still, who were Woody's clients? Royalty? "You bury women who can't part with their diamond tiaras?"

"Indeed I do. Straight into the ground they go, *after* I remove the tiara, of course. Society ladies are quite attached to their bling. Considering the extravagant way they insist on being laid out, I sometimes don't know if I'm preparing them for a wake or a charity ball."

Cal bent forward, elbows on knees and head in hands. "How long, Dad? How many years have you been desecrating the family name and reputation?"

Woody nodded thoughtfully. "Goes a long way back. Long before you were born. When I was learning the business from your grampa after the war."

"He never caught you?"

"If he'd caught me, I would've stopped."

"Who fenced the stuff for you?" demanded Cal.

"Fenced it? No one! I'm a one-man operation. A businessman with a reputation as esteemed as mine can't afford to confide in a middleman. Loose lips sink ships."

"So how did you convert your stash to cash? Or do you have it all locked away in a safety deposit box someplace?"

"It wasn't very difficult," explained Woody. "Pawn shops. Antique dealers. Online auctions. When e-Bay started up, I thought I'd died and gone to Heaven." Woody bobbed his head at me. "A little undertaker humor."

"There's not a pawn shop within fifty miles of where we live," challenged Cal. "So where are these pawn shops you're talking about?"

"How many conferences do I attend every year, Cal? Six? Seven? Las Vegas. Boston. LA. Chicago. Believe me, it's not hard to liquidate hard assets. Everyone's buying."

"*Jeeeez*," groaned Cal. "So what now, *hunh*? I just find out my father's a criminal. What do I do? Turn him in? Keep it under my hat and become an accessory to the crime by withholding information? Did you ever *once*—in the decades you've been committing grand larceny—stop to think what would happen to me, or Mom, or the rest of the family if your secret career as a felon was found out?"

He shook his head. "I thought about it once, a long time ago, but it made me so nervous I never thought about it again."

"The idea of spending the rest of your life in jail too intense for you?"

"Jail I could handle. What scared me was the thought of having to tangle with the IRS. They'd probably want to do an audit."

Cal snorted. "You're guilty of grand theft larceny, and all you're worried about is an audit?"

"You would be, too, if you never saved receipts."

"Well, I hope you made lots of money as a thief because you're going to need every red cent to pay your legal fees … *if* they don't freeze your accounts and shut down the business. Our business. *My* business. You've ruined *everyone's* life, Dad. Are you happy now?"

"I poured every penny I made back *into* the business," defended Woody. "A state-of-the-art computer system. Additional viewing rooms. New vehicles. Top-of-the-line caskets and vaults. That's where the money is, Cal. Hardware! But what do you do? Encourage *everyone* who walks through the door to be cremated. I'm surprised you're not encouraging clients to go coffin free with some kind of cockamamie green burial. I've sunk a million dollars into this business only to be sabotaged by you at every turn!"

"Million dollars?" Cal looked stunned. "Where did you get a million dollars?"

"The economic boom in the nineties. People were paying top dollar for gold and gemstones, so I was pulling in money by the bucket loads." He shrugged. "I'm not proud of it, but the truth is, I'm a damn fine thief."

Cal groaned as he buried his face in his hands again.

"Could we return to the discussion about your ring?" I asked during the lull.

Woody looked me square in the eye. "Just so you and I are on the same page, I might be a thief, but I'm no Nazi. I fought hammer and tong against the Nazis, for crying out loud."

"I believe you."

"I'm glad someone does," droned Cal.

"I realize it was decades ago," I continued, "but do you remember anything about the man who owned the ring?"

Woody nodded. "He was dead."

Cal's groans turned into a whimper.

"I understand that," I persisted, "but is there anything else you can recall about him? Age? Cause of death? Name?"

He closed his eyes and rubbed his forehead as if he were massaging a memory out of his brain. "Yup." He pinched his eyes tighter. "Pine casket, Model number P-628. No frills service onsite. Burial in Rosewood Cemetery."

I gawked at him, dumbstruck. "You remember the model number of his casket?"

"Baseball managers remember balls and strikes. Funeral directors remember caskets. We'd just purchased that line. The gentleman had the honor of being the first client to occupy one."

"First client to occupy your low-end pine caskets," taunted Cal. "First client to be robbed of his possessions. He was a man of many firsts."

"He had a closed casket," Woody reminisced. "That's what made it so easy. And there were no family members clamoring to view the body, so it was like taking candy from a baby."

"Why was the casket closed?" I asked.

"Bad car accident. No one would've wanted to see the way he ended up. He was a pretty young fella, too. Mid-forties, as I recall. Got the impression he must have been a loner because he sure didn't have many people pay their respects. The man he worked for took care of the arrangements. Angelo Agnelli. Remember him, Cal?"

"The jeweler? Sure. He kept a dish full of candy on the counter just for us kids, so we'd always stop by his store on the way to the movies every Saturday."

"The man who died worked for a jeweler?" I felt suddenly energized. *Now* we were getting somewhere. Of *course* a jeweler would work in the jewelry industry. It's what he knew! Duh?

Woody nodded. "Yup. Old Angelo turned out some of the finest pieces of jewelry I ever lifted off a corpse."

Cal covered his eyes. "*Jeeez.*"

My heart began pounding double-time. "Is he still alive?"

Woody shook his head. "We laid him to rest thirty years ago in our Mahogany roadster, Model number M-24. Our very finest casket at the time."

"Oh." That would make talking to him about his one-time employee a little out of the question then. Nuts. "I don't suppose you recall the name of the man who died in the car accident."

"Of course I do."

"REALLY?"

"A funeral director never forgets a client's name. His was Peter Smith."

Which was obviously not the name I wanted to hear. Not unless… "Is Pierre French for Peter?"

Cal shrugged. "Stuff like that is above my pay scale."

"Well, it's not above mine," said Woody. "Pierre, Pedro, Pietro. They all mean Peter."

"So if Pierre Lefevre had needed to escape France during the war, he could very well have made his way to America, started a new life, and changed his name to Peter Smith."

"Or Jones," said Cal. "That's just as generic."

I yanked my phone out of my bag. "Unless Smith isn't as generic as we think."

"Who're you phoning?" asked Woody.

"No one." I pulled up my keypad. "I'm Googling."

I typed "French Surname Meanings," found a genealogy website, and scrolled down a long list of surnames until I reached the Ls. "'Lefevre,'" I read aloud. "'A derivation of the French occupational name Fevre, which described an iron-worker or'"—my heart skipped a beat—"'smith. From the Old French "fevre" meaning craftsman.'" I glanced from Cal to Woody. "The name Smith wasn't generic to Pierre. In fact, it was probably very dear to him, because it described the profession he'd allowed to flourish in France. Metalsmith."

I inhaled a deep breath. "Gentlemen, I believe we may have just identified the traitor who escaped from Pointe du Hoc the morning of June 6, 1944."

BAM BAM BAM!

We shot looks at the cabin door. Cal stood up. "Hold on," he yelled. "I'm coming."

When he pulled the door ajar, Jackie rushed into the room, breathless with frenzy. "I wanted you to be the first to know. The police have nabbed Krystal's killer."

"Because of your phone call?" I asked expectantly.

"I never got to complete my call."

"Then how did they know to arrest Virginia?"

She fisted her hand on her hip and regarded me archly. "They haven't arrested Virginia. They've arrested Victor."

SEVENTEEN

"WHAT?"

She held up a scrap of paper and recited from it as if she were Lady Macbeth speaking through a breathing mask. "Ethyl biscoumacetate."

I stared. Woody stared. Cal stared.

I decided to pose the question that was causing all of us to stare. "What?"

"It's the drug that killed Krystal. It's a blood thinner, and Victor was taking it to prevent stroke, because he apparently has issues with atrial fibrillation."

"Victor's the killer?" I mentally picked my jaw up off the floor. "Not Virginia?"

"I'm only repeating what Rob just told me in the strictest confidence, so you can't tell anyone else. But I have to tell someone because I'm about to burst. Victor was carrying a huge quantity of the drug with him, way more than he'd need for the trip, so he had enough to take out several people. Which means ... he probably had a long hit list, and *my* name might have been next up!"

"But ... why would he kill Krystal, or *any* of you? Aside from being frustrated by your backstabbing, whining, and snarky insinuations, he genuinely seemed to like all of you."

"How should I know? Rob didn't say *why* Victor did it; he only said that the authorities have him in custody at the hospital *for* doing it. His name was on the list of guests slated to be interviewed, so the police apparently searched his cabin while he was being treated, and that's when they found his stash. They also found a miniature mortar and pestle that would have been perfect to crush tablets into powder form, so that puts another nail in his coffin."

Woody tipped his head. "Excellent analogy."

"Okay," I conceded, "but if Victor killed Krystal, who tried to kill Victor?"

"Rob said the police don't think anyone tried to kill him. They're speculating that he deliberately overdosed to throw suspicion away from himself."

Cal nodded. "The police were definitely stepping up their involvement in the case, so maybe Victor felt the noose tightening and panicked. Heck of a stunt though. Blood thinner's nothing to fool around with. He could have bled to death."

"So when's he supposed to have dosed himself?" asked Woody.

"I vote for dinner," said Jackie. "I bet he dumped the crushed tablets into his own soup."

"But no one knew the police dragnet was tightening until Rob made his announcement before dinner," I reminded them. "Victor was already in the lounge when that happened, so he had to have been carrying the stuff with him already to pull it off."

"And if that's the case ... it means he *definitely* had plans to use it." Jackie went white with the implication. "On one of his dinner companions." She riveted a look at each of our faces. "On one of us."

"But we still don't have motivation," I complained. "Even if Victor pulverized a thousand blood thinner tablets into powder, it still doesn't explain why he'd want to kill any of us, and certainly not four women whose sales efforts have kept him a wealthy man."

"Maybe it has nothing to do with wealth," offered Jackie in a tentative voice. "Maybe it has to do with the other thing Rob told me in the strictest confidence that I'm not supposed to tell anyone."

I waited a half-beat.

"Okay, I'll tell you, but you can't tell *anyone* else. When the police did a background check on Victor, they were able to verify some of his work history, but prior to 1950, they came up with nothing. Prior to 1950, there's no record of Victor Martin. It's like he'd never been born."

———

"Did you read what's on this leaflet what they slipped under our door last night?" asked Nana as she caught up with me at breakfast the following morning.

We'd set sail at midnight and were scheduled to arrive in Vernon, pronounced VerNON, in a couple of hours, where we'd board a bus to tour Claude Monet's famous lily pond and gardens in the tiny village of Giverny. I'd slept only sporadically last night, so I'd opened up the restaurant this morning, hoping to load up on enough caffeine to keep me functional throughout the day. The last person I'd expected to see at this early hour was Nana, but I was tickled for her company. She always had a way of making things seem less troubling than they actually were.

"I read it, all right," I said as she seated herself in the chair opposite me. "But that's not even half the story."

The leaflet informed us in a nutshell about the unfortunate departure of Victor Martin and his wife from the tour, but soft-pedaled the hard facts so as not to implicate Victor more than they had to. "Although Mr. Martin is expected to recover fully from the hemorrhage he suffered in the restaurant last night," the notice read, "he will remain in the hospital for observation until an undetermined date. We will keep you updated about the investigation into Ms. Krystal Cake's death as new information is released."

"What's the other half of the story?" Nana asked as she consulted the menu.

"I wish I could tell you, but I've been sworn to secrecy until such time as the information becomes public knowledge."

"Don't you fret none about it, dear. Better you keep your word. That way you don't gotta rassle with a guilty conscience." She stabbed an item on the menu with her finger. "I'm gonna order the waffle. I wouldn't mind toodlin' around the buffet, but we're gonna be doin' a lot of walkin' in them gardens this mornin', so I'm gonna pace myself."

"I'm doing the buffet. I haven't eaten anything since the soup course last night."

"Speakin' about last night"—Nana lowered her voice—"have you heard the latest?"

"Tell me what you've heard, and I'll tell you if I know."

"Victor might not be who he says he is on account of no one can find no information on him 'til a few years after World War II."

My mouth fell open. "Whotoldyouthat?" I leaned over the table, my words running into each other. "WasitJackie? Shewassupposed-tokeepitquiet. Ican'tbelievethis!"

"I run into Bernice in the corridor. She knew a lot of stuff that wasn't on the leaflet."

"How did she find out? I was assured that *no one* knew about Victor's identity problem other than Rob and Jackie." I bobbed my head. "And Woody. And Cal. And me."

"She was in a rush to get to the lounge to reserve a seat for this afternoon's watercolor lesson, so she didn't have no time to waste on a long chat. It was more like a hit and run."

"*Never* ask Jackie Thum to keep a secret," I warned, "unless you're okay with it showing up on CNN as breaking news."

"Bernice got it right then?" asked Nana.

I heaved a sigh. "According to what Rob reported to Jackie, yes, Victor's origins before 1950 seem to be in question."

Nana gave me a blank look. "So what's all the fuss about?"

I frowned. "You don't find that troubling?"

"Nope."

"Why not?"

"Because he's even older than I am, and folks back then did things different. There weren't no records in duplicate or triplicate. If the court buildin' or the local church burned, a fella might have a heck of a time provin' he was ever born. Stuff got misfiled. Clerks mighta had bad handwritin', so names got copied wrong and accidentally changed. And don't get me started on what happened to them folks what come through Ellis Island. Their names don't look nuthin' like the names they started out with before they crossed the ocean."

"So you think the French police have come up empty because of a filing error?"

"There wasn't hardly no government buildin's left standin' in Europe after the war, Emily, so the last people in the world what should be surprised by gaps in a fella's personal records are the French police."

"Did Bernice tell you that Victor has actually been arrested for murder?"

"Yup."

"Does it make sense to you that Victor would kill the woman who was probably the top sales rep in his company?"

"Nope."

"So can you understand why the police would want to delve into his background to look for clues that might explain *why* he might have wanted to kill the goose that laid the golden egg?"

"Bernice told me the only evidence them police officers got against Victor is that he had a big honkin' bottle of them blood-thinner pills in his cabin."

"Right. Enough to take out a whole host of people."

"Well, I got a little story for you. Your grampa spent so much time sittin' on his duff ice fishin' one year, he got a big ole clot in his leg, and what they give him to dissolve it was a blood thinner. Called it Warfarin. It come in a big bottle, filled to the brim, on account of the dosage changed from week to week accordin' to how much was in his bloodstream. So some weeks he took two or three tablets every day, and other weeks he took only one. But they didn't want him to run out, so that's why they give him so much. So if Victor was like your grampa, the only reason he mighta had so dang many pills in his bottle was simply because his doctor mighta wanted to make sure he had enough."

I eyed her skeptically. "You don't think he was hoarding them so he could use them to kill people?"

"If he was hoardin', it's on account of that's what the druggist give him."

"But why would the French police arrest him if they weren't sure of his guilt?"

"You ever seen them Peter Sellers movies where he played a bumblin' police inspector by the name of Clouseau?"

"Years ago. But Peter Sellers didn't portray a typical police inspector, Nana. His role was way over the top. An exaggeration."

"Don't matter. He was French. 'Nuf said."

"*Bonjour*, ladies." Ivandro greeted us with carafes of regular coffee in one hand and English breakfast tea in the other. "Coffee? Tea?"

"Tea," Nana and I said in unison.

"Have you made your breakfast selections?"

"Buffet for me," I said as he filled our cups, "and the waffle for my grandmother."

"Very good." He lingered by the table, smiling. "I hope breakfast this morning will be more peaceful than dinner last night. The gentleman is still in the hospital, yes?"

I nodded. "He may be there for a while."

"And his wife also? The maid removed their belongings from their cabin this morning, so I assume they will not be returning?"

"Apparently not." I glanced at Nana. "If they're staying behind in Rouen, they obviously can't have their stuff continuing on to Paris without them."

He leaned in over the table. "You have heard the rumor about the gentleman?"

"Which one?" asked Nana.

"That he may not be who he says he is?"

I gasped. "Does the whole ship know? I can't believe this! Who told you?"

"I do not know the names yet, madame."

"Six-foot brunette? Huge designer bag? Sucks all the oxygen out of the room?"

"She was five-feet tall. Sandpaper voice. Wire-whisk hair."

"Bernice," I hissed.

"I'm sorry, madame. Please do not take offense. I was only making conversation. When I come to work here, Patrice says to me, 'Ivandro, you may grow bored with this job, because nothing ever happens.' But since I'm here, *everything* happens. A lady dies. A gentleman is rushed to hospital. I would welcome to be bored."

"I assume you haven't been working on the *Renoir* long?" I asked.

"I have been here as many days as you. The kitchen staff was short one waiter, so Patrice put in a good word for me, and here I am. He and I cycle together on the same team, so we are what you call, good buddies."

"Are you and him trainin' for that big race where them fellas wear yellow jerseys and take dope?" asked Nana.

He laughed. "The Tour de France? *Non*, madame. We may travel the same roads, but we are not in the same class." He brandished his coffee carafe toward the ship's bow. "I scold him last night because *I* am serving the gentleman who is rushed to hospital while *he* is serving drinks to the man who has decided to camp out next to the bar. I tell him I would like *his* work schedule so I can find time to be bored.

Now I place your breakfast order, madame." He tipped his head at Nana. "Please excuse."

I cupped my hand around my mouth. "He was talking about Irv Orr," I whispered. "I don't think he's had a sober moment since he boarded."

"I seen him in the lounge all day yesterday knockin' back cocktails," said Nana. "I don't rightly know if he's even stepped off the boat to see nuthin' yet. How come the bartender don't cut him off?"

"Probably because he's not attempting to drive a vehicle. Oh, before I forget." I pulled the note with Solange's contact information out of my shoulder bag. "Could you text this to Osmond at your earliest possible convenience? He specifically asked that you do it because he appreciates your discretion and knows you won't blab to everyone."

"You bet." She studied the note. "Is this the lady what he met durin' the war?"

"Yup. I tried to *hand* him the note yesterday, but he wouldn't take it."

"'Course he wouldn't take it." She yanked her cell phone out of her pocketbook. "He's gone paperless."

As I watched her thumbs fly over the screen, I mulled over what she'd said about Victor and the mysterious gap in his background. Was it as innocent as she suggested it might be? Or had Victor Martin deliberately tried to hide something in his past? Something that might explain why he'd want Krystal dead.

My mind drifted back to Virginia Martin, who had every reason in the world to want Krystal dead, but who was under no suspicion from the police. She would have had just as much access to Victor's blood thinner as he had, wouldn't she? At least, that was *my* thinking, but I wasn't a member of the French police force.

Maybe the incompetency of Inspector Clouseau was closer to the truth than I realized.

EIGHTEEN

FROM OUR MOORAGE ON the river, Vernon appeared less historic than Rouen, less quaint than Caudebec, and less picturesque than Étretat. Nondescript apartment buildings and public parking lots fronted the river. A busy highway ran parallel to its banks, and speeding along this artery were drivers who seemed to delight in revving their engines, squealing their tires, blaring their horns, and boasting their faulty mufflers. We boarded our coach at promptly nine o'clock and, after crossing the long bridge that spanned the Seine, headed down the narrow, two-lane road that would take us to Giverny.

The countryside was similar to what we'd encountered on our way to Étretat—open fields that sloped down to the river. Shrubs giving way to a few trees. Trees weaving themselves into forests. Houses popped up alongside the road at varying intervals—houses made of stone or stucco, with steep roofs and painted shutters, sheltered behind hedges, masonry walls, split-rail fences, or decorative gates.

I sat at the back of the bus, where I could keep an eye on what was happening in front of me, because like it or not, I felt as if I needed to keep my guard up. Victor might be in the hospital, but Krystal's killer could still be among us, targeting his or her next victim. I just hoped my guys were off the killer's radar.

"We'll be arriving at the parking lot in a few minutes," Rob announced over the mike, "so I'm handing out maps to give you a chance to study them before we leave the bus." He proceeded down the center aisle, distributing sheets of white paper while he talked. "We'll be here for a total of three hours, which should give you plenty of time to tour the gardens and house, buy souvenirs in the gift shop, and pick up a cup of coffee in one of the cafés. At twelve thirty we'll meet in front of the museum on Main Street, which is marked on your maps, and walk back to the bus together. The path back to the parking lot is a little tricky, so I don't want anyone to get lost. Any questions?"

"Could you send your map to us as an email attachment?" asked Osmond.

"Sorry, folks. What you see is what you get."

"How about a photo?" inquired Alice. "If you send a picture of the map to my email address, I'll be happy to forward it to everyone."

Rob guffawed as he handed me my copy. "Come on, people. What have you got against paper?"

Ting! Ting! Ting! Ting! Ting!

"Check your inboxes," announced Nana. "I sent it JPEG, but if the image don't look clear, I can send it again as one a them PDF files."

"Mine didn't come through in color," fussed Margi.

"That's because the original is in black and white," said Tilly.

The size of a tourist attraction's parking lot is usually a good indication of how popular the attraction is with the public. Given the size of Giverny's, I steeled myself to expect crowds, which, considering our group might be playing host to a killer, could either be a blessing or a curse.

"Our bus is number twenty-one," Rob announced as our driver pulled into a space and cut the engine. "If you lose the group on your way back, don't forget that number."

We filed off the bus into the parking lot, where we began following after Rob like rats after the Pied Piper. As we passed through a pedestrian tunnel, I noticed Bernice a few paces ahead of me, and hurried to catch up.

"So, Bernice, what's the latest on Victor's condition?"

"Why're you asking me?"

"Because you seem to be the person who's dispersing all the behind-the-scenes information even before the official announcements can be made."

"I pay attention. You should try it sometime."

"Who told you? *No one* was privy to that information except for two people ... or three. Okay, maybe five, but none of them was *you*, so how did you find out?"

She regarded me sourly. "A good newsperson never reveals her sources."

"You're not a newsperson."

She waggled her eyebrows. "Doesn't matter. I'm not telling you anyway." That said, she fired up the famous afterburners that kept her a Senior Olympic five-yard sprint champ and left me in the dust.

Regardless of my opinion of Bernice, I grudgingly admired one thing about her: she'd never say anything behind my back that she wouldn't say directly to my face, no matter how rude the comment.

We followed a circuitous path to the group entrance, where we lined up like school children and filed through the turnstile without pushing or shoving. But once on the property, we faced a nearly impossible decision. What to tour first? Claude Monet's famous flower garden and house? Or his water garden and even more famous lily pond?

"I don't wanna step on no one's toes," Nana said as the gang gathered off to one side of the path, "but we're facin' one a them momentous decisions. Flower garden or water garden? So we're gonna have to vote."

All eyes flew to Osmond, who was leaning against a nearby fence, captivated by a message he was texting.

"I don't think he heard you," whispered Alice. "Maybe you should say it louder."

"CHELSVIG!" yelled Dick Teig. "I'M TAKING A VOTE!"

We watched. We waited.

Osmond continued texting.

"I still don't think he heard you," fretted Alice.

"Then he's the only one on the planet who didn't," snapped Helen. She fired a sharp look at her husband. "QUIET! This is a sacred place. Show some respect."

"This place is *not* sacred," scoffed Dick, who'd won the cervical collar lottery today and was wrapped in foam like a sausage in butcher's paper.

"It is so," she challenged. "Do you hear anyone else yelling?"

"I can't hear anyone other than *you*, Helen."

Unh-oh. This wasn't good.

"This place might not *be* sacred," soothed Lucille, "but it sure *feels* sacred. It's like we're inside a church…where everything is quiet…and hushed."

"Feels more like a library to me," said Dick Stolee, who was sporting the second cervical collar. "Without the stale book smell."

"*Shhhh.*" Lucille spread her hands wide and closed her eyes in her best imitation of a Hindi guru. "Listen to the silence."

"You better hurry before Helen starts talking again," razzed Dick.

"Do you hear that?" enthused Alice, her hand cupped around her ear. "I can hear the buzz of hundreds of honeybees."

"That's not bees," said Nana. "That's Osmond hummin' off-key."

All eyes darted back to the fence. Alice gasped. "What's he doing with his mouth?"

"Looks like he's smiling," observed George.

"He hasn't smiled for days," said Tilly. "Why do you suppose he's smiling now?"

"He's probably smiling because he's happy he's not married to Helen," Dick Teig wisecracked.

"Please ignore *Richard*," instructed Helen in a dismissive tone. "We're having a disagreement over funeral planning and, as usual, he's contributing to the discussion by acting like a dickhead."

"*Eww,* big surprise there," droned Bernice. "Like he knows how to be anything *but.*"

"I know exactly what the disagreement is about," said Grace. "*He* wants to be cremated and stuffed in a jar because it's cheaper. But *you* want an open casket with all the trimmings. Right?"

"Hey! We're not talking about Christmas dinner here," groused Dick Teig. "I'm talking about trying to prevent thousands of dollars from being poured down a six-foot hole where the return on my investment is zilch!"

"*Yeehaa!*" whooped Dick Stolee, cheering him on. "What he said!"

"Shut up, Dick," warned Grace. "You're not gypping me out of an inground burial just because Dick Teig is too cheap to spring for Helen's."

I'm not sure what this discussion said about the Dicks' fiscal ideology, but it said a great deal about the effectiveness of powerpoint presentations.

"Does everyone remember the number of the bus we're on?" I broke in in an attempt to redirect their attention.

Silence descended with an audible thud. Gazes flitted left and right.

"Do we get lifelines?" asked Nana.

"We're on bus number twenty-one," I told them. "If you think you're going to forget, write it down."

"This sounds like something we should vote on," asserted Lucille.

"Didn't we just vote on something else?" asked Alice.

"What were the results?" asked George as he tugged on his cervical collar.

"What was the question?" asked Nana.

This is where the truly adept travel escort could work her magic to reestablish order. "The water garden is thataway." I pointed them in the right direction. "Japanese bridge, lily pond, and possibly other water hazards, so watch where you're going. Looks like there are plenty of signs to guide you, so don't forget to read them. Ready?" I raised my arm like a green NASCAR flag, paused for a beat, then slashed downward. "Go!"

They took off like a herd of camels, bumping, shoving, and cutting each other off—all except Margi and Osmond, who remained behind, seemingly oblivious to their surroundings as they focused on their iPhones.

"Margi?" I stood in front of her, waving my hand to distract her. "Hello? Anybody home?"

She looked up as if surprised to see me, pulled out her earbuds, then sidled a glance slowly left and right, smiling nervously. "Where'd everyone go?"

I pointed to the path. "Water garden."

"Have they been gone long?"

"About ten seconds."

Relief flooded her face. "Shoot. I can catch up with them in no time flat." She shifted her gaze to her phone. "Right after I finish this transaction."

"You're conducting Internet business right now?"

She nodded with the kind of gusto that could cause head trauma in children. "My shopping network is hosting a special trunk show featuring designer medical scrubs, so I'm ordering one in every color except black. Black washes me out."

"But... Margi, we're in Giverny. One of the world's most beautiful gardens. Are you sure your time wouldn't be better spent touring the grounds, *then* ordering your scrubs? Remember, we're only here for three hours, and there's a gift shop at the end of the tour that's supposed to be really fantastic."

She frowned at her phone as she poked the screen. "This can't wait. I'm live-streaming the show, so it's now or never. It won't take long, Emily. I promise. I'm just waiting to see if they carry my size."

Yup. Nana had sure called that. Maybe an intervention was exactly what Margi needed, or a trip to a country without cell towers and Wi-Fi.

"Okay, I'll leave you to your shopping, but I warn you. If you have to race through the grounds at the last minute to take everything in, Bernice's pictures will be a lot better than yours, and that'll give her bragging rights."

"Gotcha." She stuffed her earbuds back into her ears and returned to her show, happily oblivious once again. I wished I could be so indifferent to the possibility of Bernice Zwerg earning official bragging rights. It might not bother Margi, but it terrified me.

I turned toward the fence and put a bead on Osmond.

"Are you planning to join the group?" I asked as I approached him.

He held up a knobby finger for me to hold that thought.

"Writing to Solange?" I whispered as I stepped closer.

He gave his screen a final poke and looked up, his face split with a jack o' lantern grin. "She's a quick study, Emily. She's already sending me email. We're both going to set up Skype accounts so we can talk face-to-face, and she's going to create a Facebook page, and... and..." Excitement filled his rheumy old eyes. "She wants me in her life again, Emily. She says she still has a lot to tell me about the war years, but I told her I knew about her husband coming back, and let her know how happy I am that she'd been able to share so many years with him. I think that was the ice breaker. It let her know I didn't want to relive the past or question anything about her family. I only want to look toward the future... with her as my very, very dear friend."

I gave his arm a little rub. "You're okay with that, are you?"

250

"Yup. I'm not one of those high-maintenance fellas, Emily, but I mean to tell you, it's sure nice being remembered, and treated not like you're a useless old man"—his voice cracked as he drew in a calming breath—"but someone special."

I flashed a wistful smile before leaning over and kissing his forehead. "You've always been someone special, Osmond." I nodded down the path. "I'm headed for the water garden. You want to tag along with me?"

"*Uhh*, I'll catch up with you right after I hear back from Solange. I just asked if she'd give me her opinion about the differences in France's geopolitical landscape under its last six presidents, so I'm hoping for an answer any minute now."

I thought he might be sending Solange messages of a more personal nature, but given what a political junkie he was, maybe a message about geopolitics *was* personal.

Leaving my two stragglers behind, I followed the path leading to the water garden and entered a world where a wood sprite might play hide and seek amid a cluster of ferns, or dance atop leaves that were big as elephant ears. The path meandered beneath a leafy canopy that rustled in the breeze and filtered light into the space below in a haze of silvery-green. A mud-brown stream flowed beside the walkway, its banks reinforced by wooden stakes that were woven together as intricately as a reed basket. I passed weeping willows whose narrow leaves drooped over the water like a mane of unbound hair, and a forest of bamboo whose stalks were growing straight as chopsticks. Clumps of purple and blue-violet flowers bunched together at the edge of the stream, while other blossoms coiled their way around tree trunks, swaddling them in clusters of bubblegum pink and fuschia. The gang had apparently dashed through this section, because they were nowhere to be seen, but I spied Bobbi and Dawna up ahead, sitting all by themselves on a bench, filing their nails.

"Have you run out of scenery to take pictures of already?" I asked as I neared them.

Bobbi eyed me with cool regard from beneath the brim of her cowboy hat. "Priorities, darlin'."

Dawna swatted an insect off her bare shoulder, nearly stabbing herself with her nail file. "Trees and bugs," she whined. "I mean to tell ya, we got plenty of trees and bugs in Nacogdoches, so I don't know why I had to get dragged here to see more."

"Because *these* trees and bugs once belonged to Claude Monet," I pointed out.

Bobbi gave her nail file a lackluster twirl in the air. "Woo hoo."

"Well, Claude Monet can have 'em," drawled Dawna. "I think they're borin'."

Nope. Couldn't let that pass. "They're not boring to the tens of thousands of tourists who pay to see them every year."

Bobbi narrowed her eyes into a squint. "Do you get paid for bein' so irritatin', sugah? I've seen you talkin' to that bunch of old geezers. Are they payin' you to babysit them or somethin'?"

"Actually, they pay me quite handsomely to escort them on trips around the world."

"You gotta be jokin'." Dawna laughed in disbelief. "You've conned folks into thinkin' they need to pay you big bucks to hold their hands while they travel?"

"Yup."

"What a crock."

"Hold on now," cautioned Bobbi, waving her fingernail file like a magician's wand. "We might be in the market for new jobs if Victor doesn't pull through."

"No way," argued Dawna. "We'll have jobs at Mona Michelle forever. Why do you think we're here starin' at trees and slappin' bugs? Because we're good at what we do. Irreplaceable even."

"We won't be keepin' our jobs at Mona Michelle if there *is* no Mona Michelle," threatened Bobbi.

"Shut your mouth," chided Dawna. "Mona Michelle will be around forever."

"Not if Virginia has anything to say about it. If Victor takes a turn for the worse and dies, I wouldn't put it past her to cash in her chips and liquidate the company. She'd do it, too. Just for spite. She hates us. We remind her of her lost youth, and she despises us for it."

"She can't do that." Dawna's face lost some of its artificial glow. "Can she?"

"You don't see our promised bonus check being handed out, do you?" asked Bobbi. "The old shrew probably tore it up on the way to the hospital. Believe me, she'll do anything she wants once Victor's out of the picture. And first and foremost she'll wanna get rid of us."

"But...how're we gonna find other jobs that pay six figures in this economy? Pretty women always get the plum jobs, but even perfect tens like us might have a hard time this go-round."

Bobbi flashed a Cheshire cat grin. "So tell me more about this job of yours, Emily. Sounds pretty cushy. Talk to the old folks. Act like you care about what they're sayin'. Take a head count now and then. Try not to lose any of 'em. Bring 'em back dead or alive. Then you get all the perks. Free plane fare. Free accommodations. Free food. Free optional tours. That sound about right?"

"Just about."

"What's the name of the company you work for?"

"Destinations Travel, based in Windsor City, Iowa."

"Where's that by?" asked Dawna.

"Windsor City is halfway between Manly and Ames."

Dawna rolled her eyes. "I was talkin' about Iowa."

"We wouldn't actually have to live there, would we?" asked Bobbi.

"Heck no," I assured her.

Bobbi smiled with the confidence of a perfect ten. "So how do we apply?"

"The owners aren't accepting applications."

Dawna yanked her bustier toward her throat and swung her hair over her shoulders. "They will after we send them our head shots. "

"I doubt that'll convince them."

"If *you* got hired," Bobbi said, looking me up and down in mock assessment, "*we* can get hired."

"I had special status."

The girls exchanged a meaningful glance. "So what'd y'all have to do to earn your special status?" taunted Bobbi. "Something naughty?"

"I married the company founder and became co-owner. Goodness, would you look at the time? Gotta run, ladies. See you on the bus."

Two things occurred to me as I ambled off. First, it seemed apparent that Bobbi and Dawna were more dependent on Victor for job security than Jackie realized, so it was highly unlikely they'd want to kill him. And secondly, the more opinions I gathered about Virginia, the more I began to wonder if my original suspicions had been correct. Who, other than someone connected to the Mona Michelle family, would want to eliminate its top sales rep *and* its president?

Not Dawna. Not Bobbi. Definitely not Jackie.

Who would benefit the most, both financially and emotionally, if the company folded?

Virginia.

Who had access to Victor's pills?

Virginia.

Who'd been a constant presence around the victims from the beginning, with numerous opportunities to tamper with their food?

Virginia.

I didn't know who owned the mortar and pestle the police had found in the Martin's cabin, but if it belonged to Virginia, I'd be willing to declare game, set, and match. Considering how many toiletries, cosmetics, and shoes a woman needed to pack for a two-week trip, why would she try to squeeze in extra kitchenware unless she had a deliberate plan to use it?

And that thought gave me pause, because I realized that by packing the mortar and pestle, Virginia may have established that not only had she committed murder—

She'd committed premeditated murder.

Holy crap. Had the police been able to piece it together yet? Had anyone even bothered *telling* them about Virginia? Or were they getting most of their information *from* Virginia?

I wheeled around and hot-footed it back to the bench. "Did the police interview the two of you last night?"

"Yah," said Bobbi. "Why?"

"Did either one of you mention how much Virginia despised you or Krystal?"

"Oh, sure," Dawna cooed. "As if we're gonna badmouth the wife of the guy who signs our paychecks. Do you know what kind of a public relations disaster that would be? We'd get kicked to the curb so fast, it'd take your breath away." She shot me a disgusted look. "What a joke. Tell the police the truth about Virginia? If they wanna know anything, they can find out from someone who's not a company gal. Shoot, just how stupid do you think we are?"

Given that she probably meant that as a rhetorical question, I thought it best not to answer. But if neither one of them had disclosed any pertinent information to the police, then *someone* needed to, else Virginia might disappear into the crowds of Rouen while the going was good and escape justice indefinitely.

Since I seemed to be the lucky individual who'd assembled all the pieces of the puzzle into a complete picture, I figured the responsibility of informing the police should therefore rest in the hands of only one person.

Rob.

This was the beauty of being a lowly escort on someone else's tour. You got to hand the ball off rather than shoot it yourself.

Now, to find him.

I hurried down the path, feeling as if I were following the yellow brick road through Oz, minus the witch and flying monkeys. Beyond more weeping willows and a dense stand of bamboo, I came upon a narrow footbridge that spanned a wider section of the stream, but crossing it would prove challenging since the gang had parked themselves all along the rail, mugging for photos.

"You need to squeeze closer together or I'll only be able to get half of you in the picture," warned Jackie, who had apparently been awarded the honor of group photographer. She stood in the middle of the walkway, framing her shot, while at her feet sat a jumble of iPhones and cameras, nested safely atop her shoulder bag. "Tall people at the back!" barked Bernice, who'd positioned herself front and center.

"We don't got no tall people no more," said Nana. "We're all shrunk to the same size."

"How about we have the men stand in back?" asked Jackie.

"I'm not standing in front of Dick Teig," growled Helen. "We're not speaking."

"Fine," said Jackie. "Stand someplace else."

"I don't want to stand by him either," said Grace. "The cheapskate."

"I'll stand in front of him," Alice volunteered.

"Good luck with that," crowed Bernice. "The only thing that can fit between Dick Teig's stomach and the rail is fresh air."

"Does anyone know the weight limit of this bridge?" asked Tilly.

Eyes drifted to the planks beneath their feet before darting to the water beneath the bridge.

"Would you just shoot the dang picture before this thing collapses?" Lucille yelled at Jackie.

"Before you do anything, can I squeeze past you?" Without waiting for a response, I stepped onto the little green bridge, sucked in my breath, and angled past them sideways.

"What was that?" asked Dick Stolee, craning his neck in every direction, his eyes shifting nervously. "It sounded like wood cracking."

"It was," said George.

They flew off the bridge in two seconds flat, everyone except George, who remained at the rail all by himself. "My leg," he said sheepishly. "I can't tell if it's expanding or contracting."

I sprinted down the walkway, past the famous lily pond with its cache of lily pads glutting the surface, and its pink and white water lilies blooming as sublimely as they had a hundred years ago. Flat-bottomed rowboats hugged the shore on either side of the pond, chained to trees that hovered over them like doting parents. Color dappled the banks in wild disarray—pale pink, deep rose, lavender, dusky pink, bright magenta, soft coral—like house paints that had spilled and been left to dry. I snapped a quick picture of the pond and Japanese bridge, then navigated through another underpass that led me back to the original flower garden.

Margi and Osmond had disappeared, but in their place were hordes of camera-toting tourists who were jamming the pathways like swarms of worker bees. Good Lord. How was I supposed to find Rob in this crowd?

I wormed my way around clusters of people posing for group photos, danced around people loitering in the middle of the path, and ducked beneath people's cameras as they took aim at the climbing roses, scarlet poppies, and towering hollyhocks. Plump pink rose blossoms twined around great iron archways that curved above the main path. Wildflowers dusted the air with wisps of color. Ornamental trees flaunted their slender trunks and miniature leaves. I tried to find an isolated spot for a Kodak moment, but tourists and their photographic equipment were everywhere, their heads invading my shot, their arms obstructing my vision, their iPads blocking my entire view.

It used to be that when people snapped pictures, they'd look into the viewfinder of a camera, frame their photo, and press the shutter. The iPad has advanced technology so much that people no longer have to place a camera anywhere near their face. Instead, they can happily hold a device the size of a mattress over their heads and shoot whatever's in front of them. Of course, no one else can see over, around, or through them to shoot their own pictures, but hey, not having to look through that viewfinder anymore is real progress.

"Can you believe this crowd?" asked Cal Jolly as he came up behind me. "I've given up trying to take pictures. Rob said the gift shop sells great postcards, so I'm doing that instead. I'm through trying to outmaneuver the iPad people. As far as I'm concerned, they've won the war."

"How long ago did you see Rob?"

"About ten minutes. He was headed for the house." Cal glanced toward the far end of the garden—at a two-story house that was as long as a boutique hotel. It was a charming froth of pale pink stucco, with dozens of green shutters and a blanket of vines and roses scaling the exterior wall. For forty-three years, it had been inhabited by Claude Monet. "They've done some work on the interior that he hasn't seen yet, so he wanted to have a look."

"Thanks much." As I made to leave, he wrapped his hand around my arm, stopping me momentarily.

"I want to thank you for listening to my dad last night, Emily, and not judging him. We're obviously going to have a mess to deal with when we get back home, and I have no idea how it'll all turn out, but at least I know what's happening now, and can try to put things to right. Dad's not a bad sort. He's just guilty of making some of the poorest choices a man can ever make, and he'll probably have to pay dearly for it." He shook his head. "I guess no matter how much you think you know a person, they can still end up surprising you."

I wondered if one day soon Victor would be making the same statement about Virginia?

I zigzagged through the crowd and took my place at the back of the queue to tour the house. Several of the second-story windows were thrown open, and since there were no bug screens, visitors were poking their heads and cameras through the openings, shooting the panoramic photos they couldn't shoot at ground level.

I kept my eyes on the open windows as I shuffled toward the entrance, and when I arrived at the stairs fronting the main door, I was rewarded with the sight I'd been looking for.

Rob.

"Rob!" I shouted, waving my arm in a wild arc over my head.

He stuck his head out the window and glanced in my direction, looking straight at me without apparent recognition, because in the next instant he drew his head back into the room and disappeared.

Well, duh? What was *wrong* with this guy? Did he have face blindness?

I ascended the stairs close on the heels of the person in front of me and, once inside the door, smiled at the docent who was directing visitors into a room on the left.

"Could I scoot up the stairs before I see the downstairs? There's someone up there I need to speak to. It's really important."

"Madame," he replied, waving me into the downstairs room.

"No, no, you don't understand. I need to go up." I pointed my forefinger toward the ceiling. "Up."

He shot me a fierce look. "Down," he said as he escorted me personally to the first room on the tour.

Nuts!

Blue smacked me in the face when I crossed the threshold. I'd entered a small sitting room where the walls were painted robin's-egg blue, the trim was painted peacock blue, and furniture boasted every color blue from cornflower to periwinkle. A blue pendulum clock stood in one corner on dainty carved feet, looking suspiciously like the clock that had sung and danced in the animated version of *Beauty and the Beast.*

I hurried through an adjoining pantry to enter a long studio where light spilled through broad open windows onto the soft wool of Oriental carpets. This was a painter's room, filled with warmth and brightness and an ambience that might inspire every brush-stroke. A chaise lounge sat behind a roped barrier. A bust of the famous painter perched near it. And filling every available space on every available wall were watercolors both large and small, square and rectangular, painted with a brush once held by Claude Monet.

But Rob wasn't in Monet's studio. He was upstairs.

I rushed back to the pantry and charged up a steep, winding staircase to the second floor. Stepping into the first room on my right, I saw that it was a bedroom modestly appointed with a lemon yellow bedstead with matching wardrobe and night stand, but what it didn't have was Rob. A docent stood by a door on the opposite side of the bed, funneling visitors into the next room, so I headed in that direction, pausing for just a moment to stick my head out the open window that overlooked the garden—which is when I saw the commotion on the path below me.

A crowd had gathered around something or someone lying on the ground. Voices rose in distress. Hands flew into the air, summoning help. "Move back!" a woman yelled in a sharp voice. "Give her room."

"Is she conscious?" someone cried.

"Call an ambulance!"

"I don't think she's breathing."

A big guy with a beard and tattooed arms swept his iPad through the air in an effort to clear people away from the immediate area. As they dispersed, I caught a glimpse of the person who was lying face-up on the ground, her body still as death as a river of blood streamed from her nose.

The bottom suddenly fell out of my stomach.

"Oh, my God. Margi!"

NINETEEN

"S'CUSE ME," I SHOUTED as I rocketed past visitors who were ambling through a bathroom that adjoined the yellow bedroom. "Sorry!" I apologized as I scrambled around a half-dozen people wandering through a smaller bedroom. I hit the main staircase at a run, clattered down the stairs, blew by the docent who was directing me to a room that glowed yellow with blinding phosphorescent light, and charged out the front door. I descended the stairs two at a time and ran toward the circle of tourists who were videotaping the event with their phones and camcorders as it played out.

"Lemme through," I cried as I bulldozed straight through them.

"You know her?" asked the man with the iPad and beard.

I fell to my knees beside her and clutched her hand. "She's my friend." Her eyes were half open and glassy with shock. "Margi? You're going to be all right. Has anyone called an ambulance?"

"*Oui,*" said an older man who was capturing us on tape.

She *had* to be all right. Krystal hadn't been lucky enough to survive her overdose, but Victor was okay. If Margi could be treated in time, she'd be okay, too. I *knew* she'd be okay. But why her? What grievous thing had Margi Swanson done that would drive someone to kill her?

"Stay with me," I begged her as I hauled a packet of tissues out of my shoulder bag.

"Emily?" she asked in a weak voice.

"I'm here, Margi. Right beside you." I began dabbing blood from her face.

"My pocketbook," she rasped.

"It's right here." Lying beside the iPhone that had apparently slipped from her hand and cracked in a dozen places. "Do you want something out of it?"

She nodded almost imperceptibly. "Hand … sanitizer."

"If this is your friend, you must know her name and address, hunh?" asked the bearded man.

I glanced up at him. "Why do you want her address?"

"So I'll know where to send the bill for my iPad." He held the device up, allowing me to see the fracture that splintered the center, and the crack that radiated out from corner to corner. He stabbed his finger at Margi. "*She* broke it, and I want it replaced. Walked right into it face-first while she was texting. *BAM*! If she doesn't start watching where she's going, the next time she runs into something, I guarantee she'll end up with more than a bloody nose."

"She walked into you?" Laughter burst from my throat like bubbles from uncorked champagne. "Her nose is bleeding because … she slammed her face into your iPad? Oh, my God!" I grabbed both of

Margi's hands and squeezed, giggling like a Valley girl. "That's the most wonderful news I've ever heard!"

The man raised his voice in disgust. "What kind of sick person says something like that to a friend? What kind of friend are you anyway?"

I regarded Margi sternly. "Promise me that this ends your love affair with texting while you walk."

"Might as well." She grappled for the packet of tissues. "The trunk sale's over."

———

I never got to speak to Rob.

By the time the paramedics had finished checking out Margi, it was time to meet up with the rest of the group in front of the museum. Her nose had stopped bleeding on its own, and she didn't display any signs of being concussed, but the medics had nonetheless cautioned us to keep an eye on her in case she started showing any unusual behavior.

I wondered if packing cervical collars for a European holiday counted as unusual behavior.

The gang was very solicitous of her on the bus ride back to the boat. George offered to give up his cervical collar if she wanted to catch a quick nap on the way back. Dick Teig lent her his iPhone so she could text a quick message to me, thanking me for my help. And Alice treated the blood on her linen top with several different fragrances of hand sanitizer that not only eliminated the stains, but filled the bus with the mouth-watering scents of hot apple pie, chocolate fudge brownie, and Christmas cookie.

By the time we returned to Vernon, we were so ravenously hungry, we decided not to wait for the lunch buffet to open, but ventured into town instead to search out a bakery, where we indulged in chocolate croissants, éclairs, macaroons, Napoleons, madeleines, fruit tarts, and an assortment of cream-filled confections. We slogged back to the boat, overstuffed but infinitely happy, and just in time for the gang to resume their scheduled activities.

"Bridge tour in ten minutes," announced Nana as we crossed the gangway. "Galley tour after that. Watercolor lessons in the lounge in an hour. Today we're s'posed to tackle them still-life paintin's."

"I love still-life painters," remarked Tilly. "Cezanne, Jean-Simeon Chardin, Giorgio Morandi. They transformed the ordinary into the *extra*ordinary. I consider myself quite fortunate to have a Cezanne print hanging over my mantel."

"*Pfffft*," scoffed Dick Teig. "I've got a plasma screen TV hanging over mine."

While the twelve of them piled through the automatic door to access the exterior stairs to the top deck, I stopped at the reception desk to talk to the purser.

"Would you happen to know where Rob is?"

"I'm afraid I don't, Mrs. Miceli, but there are one or two places he *might* be." She lifted her hand to direct me aft. "On the top deck, in the sectioned-off area at the stern. That's where we gather when we're on break. Or the dining room. Perhaps he's finishing lunch? Or, since this is Vernon, he might have walked into town for pastries. There are several brilliant bakeries just off the main street."

I checked the dining room first, finding it deserted save for a few stragglers at a couple of tables, none of whom were Rob. I ran into Ivandro on the way out.

"You know who Rob is, don't you?"

"*Oui*, madame."

"Did you see him at lunch today?"

"He was not in my section, but that does not mean he wasn't in someone else's. Although since this is Vernon, he may have escaped into town for pastry. I'm being told the bakeries here are *tres magnifique*."

I stopped by my cabin to drop off my shoulder bag before hitting the top deck to check out which crew members were taking a break in the Staff Only section.

No Rob.

The bridge tour had just concluded, so I waited while guests filed back down to the main deck for the galley tour. I didn't want to tour the galley, and I wasn't about to head back into Vernon to track down Rob, so I decided on the next best option.

I'd treat myself to a well-deserved drink in the lounge.

"Any luck finding him, Mrs. Miceli?" the purser asked when I passed the reception desk.

"He's MIA."

"I'm sorry I can't give you his mobile number, but he's expressly forbidden us to give it out. Too many non-emergency calls in the middle of the night, apparently."

I shrugged. "If you'd put a note in his mailbox, telling him I'd like to speak to him about something fairly urgent, I'd really appreciate it."

"I'll do that right away. And where will you be?"

"In the lounge. For however long it takes." I stepped in closer to the desk. "Tell him I'm wearing black capris and a pink and black striped top. Does he do better with clothing than he does with names and faces?"

She bowed her head and shielded her mouth with her hand. "He's a disaster, isn't he? He can't remember a name for more than half a minute, and on two occasions he's returned from optional tours transporting complete strangers. I have it on good authority that this is his last cruise."

I couldn't say I was surprised. "How did he get the job in the first place?"

"He and Patrice are members of the same cycling team, so Rob was offered the job on Patrice's recommendation. Patrice has vouched for many employees over the years, all who have worked out quite brilliantly. Rob is his first major failure. Absolutely ruined his perfect record. But I imagine it was bound to happen sooner or later. It was just a matter of time."

With a majority of guests touring the galley or taking an afternoon stroll around Vernon, the lounge was pretty much deserted. A woman I'd never seen before was distributing art supplies around the room—paper, brushes, water jars, paints, pencils. She'd already set up a table in the center of the lounge arranged with a ceramic bowl stacked high with summer fruit, an empty wine bottle plugged with a wax-dripping candle, and a long loaf of hard-crusted French bread. The trick for the instructees would be to *paint* the objects rather than eat them. Patrice was bartending once again, but his only customer was Irv Orr, who greeted me as I entered the room by raising his cocktail in a mock toast and motioning me toward him.

"Have a sheat," he slurred cordially. "Lemme buy you a drink. Patreesh!" He shot his hand into the air. "Another round. One for me, and one for my friend Emily." He drained his glass as I sat down in the chair beside him, and though he was obviously hammered, I had to give him credit for one thing.

Even drunk, he remembered my name.

He might have a great future as a tour director if he ever sobered up.

"What are we drinking?" From where I sat, I had a wide-angle view of the gangway, so there was no way I could miss Rob when he crossed it.

"Cu-ba … li-bre," Irv said with exaggerated slowness. "Inshpired by the country to our shouse. Cola, rum, and a hefty shquirt of lime. At a whopping fifteen pershent dishcount. We can drink all day at these prishes!"

"Did you travel to Giverny with us today?"

"Nope. Sheen one flower, sheen 'em all. I shtayed here instead, entertaining my buddy Patreesh. ISHN'T THAT RIGHT, PA-TREESH?"

Patrice waved from the bar. "*Oui*, monsieur."

"I've eshhtablished a new movement. I'm calling it, Occupy the Lounge. And all you gotta do to join is keep ordering the daily from the bar."

"Have you had anything to eat today, Irv?"

"Shure!" He began ticking items off on his fingers. "Nuts. Cherries. And I shucked on a few limes."

"You've been drinking on an empty stomach?"

He nodded. "Besht way to enjoy alcohol. All by itshelf. Did you know you can order the daily speshial shtarting at nine o'clock in the morning? And the reashon you have to wait sho long is because that's when the bartender goes on duty."

Patrice arrived with our drinks—tall highball glasses filled with ice cubes and cola, and garnished with lime and cherries. Irv fluttered his forefinger at the order pad. "Put 'em both on my tab. And keep 'em comin.'"

"Would it be possible to order some food for him from the kitchen?"

"The kitchen is closed for the galley tour, madame, but perhaps when the tour is over they might prepare something for him? Cheese? Fruit? Bread?"

"What do you say to that, Irv?"

He stuck his tongue out in distaste. "Nope. I'm not shpoiling a perfectly good highball by contaminating it with any of the major food groups. Beshides, I don't trust the food. You don't want me to end up like Victor, do you?"

"Have you had an update on his condition?" My stomach turned a slow somersault as I braced myself for news I was afraid to hear.

Irv swung his head back and forth in a lazy arc. "My shources have been abshent today, sho my reporting has been cut off. Shorry. But I'm pretty shure old Victor is shtill the shame international man of myshtery that he was yesterday. But now, Patreesh here. Patreesh is an open book, aren't you, Patreesh?"

"If you say so, monsieur."

I shifted my gaze away from Patrice as Woody entered the lounge all by himself, looking as if he were carrying the weight of the world on his shoulders. He didn't acknowledge me as he passed by, but kept his head down and gaze lowered, as if he were wishing he could disappear. He flopped down in a chair close to the bar, propped his elbow on the armrest, and braced his head in his hand, his body language signaling that if any guest dared disturb him, it would be at their own risk.

Patrice hesitated, eyeing him with some trepidation, before flashing a resigned look. He tipped his head and sighed. "*Pardonne.*"

I guess no matter how miserable a guest looked, there was always an outside chance that an outrageously expensive highball would make him feel better.

Irv watched Patrice cross the floor. "He walks pretty good for shomcone's who's been pieced back together again, doeshn't he?"

"I didn't know he'd fallen apart." Despite his despondency, Woody seemed to treat Patrice with great civility as he placed a drink order.

"Yup. He waz in a bicycle crash awhile back. Fractured his leg and broke his hip in so many shpots, they had to replace it."

"No kidding?"

"He waz out of commisshion for the better part of a whole year. But look at him now. Good ash new. He walks better'n me."

"That's because he's sober," I said matter-of-factly. "You should try it sometime, Irv. Your balance might return so quickly, you'd be able to retire your canc."

He reached out a hand to pat its carved handle. "Shobriety gives me indigestion."

An outburst of excited laughter in the reception area heralded the arrival of the art enthusiasts. They trooped into the lounge like school kids on their way to recess, a bounce in their step and confidence in their eyes, as if they were expecting the forthcoming lesson to release the hidden potential that would turn them into the next Grandma Moses. I counted eleven of my Iowans among the group, the only person unaccounted for being Bernice, who had probably found some health or safety violation in the galley and was preparing to sue the cruise company.

"Where'd all these people come from?" asked Irv as they hurried past us. "Are they with us?"

"Yup."

Nana gave me a little finger wave as she passed by. George winked. Alice held Osmond's arm, steering him around obstacles as he studied his iPhone.

"How come they don't look familiar?"

"They'd probably look familiar if you attended meals and took the optional tours."

"I took one opshional tour. One waz enough." He took a sip of his Cuba libre. "I'd rather shtay here and chat with Patreesh. Now Patreesh, he looks *very* familiar. I'd know him anywhere." He flung his head toward the bar. "Oh, look. He's hard at work. Don't you jusht love the shound of ice cubes clinking in a glassh?"

"Good afternoon once again, ladies and gentlemen," the art instructor announced behind us. "Please seat yourselves close to the supplies I've provided, and if you recall my instructions from yesterday's lesson, I would encourage you to begin. I'll come around to watch how you're progressing."

"I bet you didn't know Patreesh's family got their shtart in alcohol," Irv blathered on. "Calvadosh. That delicioush brandy our lovely hostess sherved ush at her housh."

"The one made from apples?"

"The one that's only made in Normandy."

"Aha! So that's why he's able to cycle on the Tour de France roads. Does he live along the route? Or nearby?"

"His family lives shomewhere by those D-Day beaches we vishited."

"Really? I wonder if they live in the same vicinity as Madeleine Saint-Sauveur."

"He menshioned shomeplace called Pointe...shomething or other."

"Pointe du Hoc?"

He made a pointer of his finger and stabbed it into the air. "That's it. Pointe...whatever you shaid. Good guessh."

"It wasn't a guess. Madeleine told us the story about Pointe du Hoc. Didn't you hear her? It's where the Resistance fighters from the local village were killed."

"Oh, yeah. The Resishtance fighters. His grandfather was a Resishtance fighter."

A frisson of alarm sent a chill rippling down my spine. "I didn't realize that." I glanced toward the bar as Patrice delivered a Cuba libre to Woody. "Did Patrice tell you anything else about his grandfather?"

Irv nodded. "Yup. He gave me the whole hishtory. He died on D-Day. At that Pointe dew whatever place."

The picture came together in that instant with the impact of a multiple car crash. Of course. Of course! *Oh, my God.*

I launched myself out of my chair and raced across the room. "Don't drink that!" I yelled, slapping the glass out of Woody's hand just as the rim touched his lips.

"What the hell?" he boomed.

The glass flew onto the floor, splashing cola onto every dry surface and shooting ice across the carpet like hockey pucks.

"What'd you do that for?" he barked.

"It's you!" I cried, firing my accusation at Patrice like a bullet from a .45. "You saw his ring!" I jerked Woody's hand upward and flashed his ring finger. "You know its history. It's why you want to kill him!"

Eyes big as plates, Patrice backed slowly toward the bar. "I don't know what you say, madame." He stretched his hand out in warning. "You should mind where you step. The ice. You might slip."

"I couldn't figure out the one detail that connected all the events, but it was you. *You* were the connection."

I heard loud thumps and scuffling as the gang stampeded across the room to form a wide circle around me.

"It's him what's been doin' the killin'?" asked Nana.

I nodded. "It's him. When the police analyze the contents of the highball he just mixed for Woody, I suspect the jig will be up."

Woody snorted his outrage. "He put something in my drink?"

"Blood thinner," I said. "Warfarin. Most probably left over from the hip replacement surgery he underwent last year. The drug that killed Krystal. The drug that sent Victor to the hospital."

Patrice took another step backward, chest heaving, eyes skittish. He shook his head. "A mistake. A terrible mistake. I did not mean for the girl to die. I did not mean for the gentleman to suffer."

"Then why did they?" I demanded.

"The mademoiselle. It was a terrible confusion. The day she died, she ate the food I intended for *him*. *Cochon*," he spat at Woody.

Woody looked stunned. "You mean to say, if I'd eaten Krystal's breakfast, I'd be dead?"

"That was the idea," snarled Patrice.

"How did the order get mixed up in the first place?" I urged. "They both ordered the same thing, so—"

"Two omelets," snapped Patrice. "One for the man in place setting one, and one for the mademoiselle in place setting two. *She* should be alive. *He* should be dead. So I ask, what happened?"

"They switched seats," I said, recalling breakfast that morning. "Krystal complained about having to sit in the sun, so Woody offered to change seats with her. If you'd been the one who actually *served* the food, you might have noticed the switch, but, as I remember, you conveniently found someone else to do your dirty work for you."

He had the decency to look sheepish. "What can I say? The dining room was very busy that morning."

"Let this be a lesson to all you men," Helen blasted. "Giving up your seat to a lady might save your life one day. YOU HEAR THAT, DICK?"

"Krystal didn't complain to anyone about the food tasting funny?" I pressed Patrice.

"She would have no cause. The drug has no taste, no odor. And when mixed into the horseradish-infused sauce for the omelet, it would have been undetectable. But again, it pains me greatly that she died. She was not my intended target."

"And what about Victor? How did you make a mistake with him?"

"The Bloody Marys last night." He trained a damning eye on Woody. "I placed the drink directly in his hand, but what does he do? He sets it on the table so close to Monsieur Martin's cocktail that the other gentleman picks it up and drinks it." He thrust an angry finger at Woody. "Why are you so hard to kill? You belong in Hell with the scum who executed my grandfather on the morning of D-Day!"

275

"That wasn't me!" raged Woody. "I didn't kill your grampa. I wasn't anywhere near Normandy on D-Day. If you wanna kill the real owner of this ring, you're way too late, son. He died years ago, and the reason I know that is because I'm the one who buried him."

Patrice narrowed his eyes with suspicion. "My grandmother wore a brooch with the same fleur-de-lis design. She told me stories of Pierre Lefevre and his signature jewelry. If you are not Pierre Lefevre, how is it that you wear a ring that Pierre Lefevre never removed from his finger?"

Woody gnawed on his lower lip, his cheeks and nose turning scarlet. "It's a little hard to explain," he choked out.

I didn't condone what Woody had done, but neither did I condone his having to face any more public humiliation than what he'd be facing when he returned home. "I don't know how you dispose of personal property here in France," I spoke up, "but back home we have something called an estate sale, where possessions that people have held dear can be purchased by perfect strangers. Isn't that right, Mr. Jolly?"

Woody coughed self-consciously and bobbed his head.

"They're listed in the newspaper every week," I continued. "Some folks are so addicted to them, they'll attend two or three a day."

Patrice shook his head, disbelieving. "You are Pierre Lefevre. The traitor of D-Day."

"Honest, son, I'm Woodrow Jolly the Third, newly retired funeral director of Jolly Funeral Home, born and bred in the good old US of A, and that's the God's honest truth."

Doubt filled Patrice's eyes. "It is not possible."

"Show of hands," announced Osmond. "How many people think the old guy is who he says he is?"

"No voting!" I cried.

"If you are not Pierre Lefevre," rasped Patrice, his vocal cords straining against his throat, "then I have—" He gasped for breath as the magnitude of what he'd done played out on his face in anguished waves. Horror. Fear. Regret. Fusing into a primal need to run.

Hemmed in on three sides, he bolted around the end of the bar.

"Do *not* follow him behind there!" I warned as Dick Stolee made to give chase.

"Move away from the bar," ordered Patrice as he assumed a central position behind the counter, barricading himself behind a stack of cocktail napkins and bowl of nuts. He stared at us. We stared at him. Nobody moved.

"Did you mean that as a threat?" asked Tilly.

"*Oui*, madame."

"Move away from the bar or else ... what?" questioned Dick Teig.

Patrice dropped his voice to a menacing pitch. "You should move away for your own good."

He made googly eyes at us. We made googly eyes back.

Nana raised her hand.

"*Oui*, madame?" Patrice nodded, giving her the floor.

"I don't wanna slam your escape plan or nuthin', but you don't got no leverage. If you was plannin' to make threats, you shoulda taken a hostage."

"Nana!" I chided.

"I'll be his hoshtage," volunteered Irv, "if he lets me camp out behind the bar with him."

As if recognizing the wisdom of Nana's words, Patrice snatched up an industrial-size corkscrew and pressed it to his throat. "If you do not move away, I will drive this corkscrew into my throat, and for the rest of your lives, *all* of you will have my blood on your hands."

"Not if we keep standing where we are," said Margi. "I think we're far enough out of range to avoid splatter."

George scratched his head. "I hate to bring this up, son, but the notion behind taking a hostage is to threaten someone *else's* life, not your own."

"My life?" wailed Patrice. "It is worth nothing now. I will kill myself, and you will all watch!"

A trickle of blood streamed down his throat as he prepared to make good on his threat.

"Okay!" I yielded. "We're moving back. Put the corkscrew down. C'mon, everyone." I began shuffling backward, motioning the gang to move back with me. "Nice and slow. Everybody back."

"Faster!" yelled Patrice. He grabbed something off the bar and hurled it toward us.

A shot glass bounced off Dick Stolee's shoulder and hit the floor. "Ow!" he howled. "Hey! Cut that out."

Lucille ducked as the bottom half of a cocktail shaker sailed toward her. "Take cover!" she cried.

A martini glass crashed onto a table and shattered. A champagne flute hit a vertical column, spraying glass everywhere. We took refuge behind chairs and sofas as Patrice unloaded his arsenal, pelting us with margarita glasses, wine glasses, highball glasses, lowball glasses. A bottle of Tanqueray flew over my head and smashed upon landing, exploding like a homemade bomb.

"SHTOP!" screamed Irv. "Not the booze!"

"Who's got a phone?" I shouted out.

"I do," they all replied from their hidey holes.

"I'd prefer not to talk about it," sniffed Margi from beneath a nearby table.

"Call the police," I instructed.

"What's the number?" asked Dick Teig.

"Try one-one-two," said Tilly. "That's a general emergency number for Europe."

"Can't we just call the boat and let *them* handle him?" asked Grace.

I poked my head above the armrest of my chair, diving to the deck when I saw a projectile hurtling toward me.

BOOM went the bottle as it burst over the floor.

"Waz that Crown Royal?" shrieked Irv. "Do you know how expenshive that shtuff is?"

"Hello?" Dick Teig said into his phone. "I'm trying to call the police. Po-lice. POLICE."

"Does anyone know the phone number for the boat?" asked Grace.

"Are you speaking English?" snapped Dick. "It doesn't sound like English." He waved his phone above his head. "Anyone else wanna give it a try? I can't understand what she's saying."

"Slide it this way," Margi urged from beneath her table. "I'll try out my new language skills."

"FIRE IN THE HOLE!" shouted Dick Stolee, who'd slithered his way across the floor to reach the bowl of fruit. He lobbed a cantelope through the air toward the bar.

CRASH! Boom! *Tinkle, tinkle, tinkle.*

"*Où est la bibliotèque?*" Margi asked into Dick's phone.

Patrice retaliated with a bottle of Jim Beam, followed by a handful of nuts and a bowl of pimento-stuffed olives.

"Why is Margi asking directions to the library?" inquired Tilly.

"Hold it right there, mister!" Lucille huffed as she plucked one of the nuts off the carpet. "Do you live under a rock? These things are dangerous! You ever heard of peanut allergies? Just being in the same room with one of these little buggers can be enough to kill some folks."

"I wish he'd throw some maraschino cherries," said Nana.

"Ask him," I prodded. "Maybe he'll take requests."

Dick Stolee started rapid firing a volley of missiles that sent Patrice scrambling for cover. Grapefruit. Apple. Pear. Naval orange. Peach, or maybe a nectarine. I couldn't tell which. Muskmelon. BOOM! *Bam.* CRASH. *Splat!*

"*Écoutez et répétez,*" recited Margi in a singsong voice "*Bonjour, Jean.*"

"Ready or not, here I come," Bernice yelled above the mayhem.

I peeked around my chair to the entrance side of the lounge to find Bernice dressed in a short tie-belt bathrobe ... and nothing else. *Holy crap!* Where were her clothes?

On a brighter note, her makeup looked quite spectacular.

"What the devil's going on?" she crabbed as she studied the devastation. "Is this lesson about Monet ... or Picasso?"

She shrieked as Patrice catapulted over the bar and went airborne, accidentally clipping his foot on the counter and landing on top of her with a rib-rattling *OOOFF,* flattening her beneath him. "Oh, my God!" I cried. "Bernice!"

"Don't let him get away!" whooped Dick Stolee.

Patrice shot his head up and boosted himself onto his hands as if preparing to flee.

"Not sho fasht," Irv slurred as he lifted his cane and thwacked Patrice across the back of his head. "I'll forgive your other transgresshions, but I'll never forgive you for deshtroying perfectly good Crown Royal. It jusht happens to be my favorite."

TWENTY

Two DAYS LATER WE found ourselves moored alongside an embankment in Paris, in a nondescript section of the city bounded by roads, bridges, and an empty parking lot. Upon arrival, we'd cruised far enough up the Seine to shoot photos not only of the Eiffel Tower, but of the small-scale replica of the Statue of Liberty that occupied a tiny island in the middle of the river. Yesterday evening we'd enjoyed a night cruise of the city, where we *oohed* and *ahhed* at the sight of Gustave Eiffel's tower, illuminated with a million lights, and twinkling like a giant Independence Day sparkler. Today, it was still fairly early, so we were sitting on the top deck, dithering about which optional tours we should sign up for.

"I'm leanin' toward the Louvre," said Nana as she consulted her travel brochure. "I wanna check out the competition, just in case I ever paint somethin' that makes a big splash in them fancy art circles." The water color instructor had been so complimentary of Nana's work that Nana was actually talking about continuing to paint when she got back home, and exhibiting her work in either the

Senior Center lunch room or a contemporary art gallery. Since Windsor City didn't have an art gallery, she figured she might have to resort to building one herself on the north end of Main Street. Property values were cheaper on the north end, so she imagined she could do it for a song. Maybe less than ten million.

"I don't feel like battling the museum crowds." Jackie snapped her makeup mirror shut and recapped her lipstick wand. She batted her eyelashes flirtatiously. "I'm hopping on the Metro and heading into the city. You'll never guess where I'm going."

Nana regarded her with a long, unblinking stare. "The eye doctor?"

"Guerlain," I said. "Or Chanel. Or Lancome. Or—" I ran out of names.

"Don't forget Esteé Lauder. I'm going shopping for cosmetics!"

"No kiddin'?" asked Nana. "You don't got enough already?"

"Mrs. S., a woman can *never* have enough cosmetics, especially in my profession. You can't imagine all the products I've gone through in my attempt to show you guys how hot you can look with your complexions buried beneath a ton of foundation."

"Well, you sure done right by Bernice. I never seen her look so good as she did the other day."

Jackie splayed her hand over her heart. "Bernice is one of my great success stories."

I nodded. "I'll give credit where credit is due, too. Her face looked amazing before Patrice fell on her."

Jackie canted her head, staring off into space. "She was my masterpiece. She wanted to be to Mrs. S.'s art class what Mona Lisa had been to da Vinci. But sadly, smear-proof lipstick and volumizing mascara were never product tested beneath the weight of a 160-pound Frenchman."

"I've gotta hand it to her," I said, recalling what had happened when we'd pulled Patrice off her. "I was astonished she wasn't embarrassed by her rather blatant overexposure when her bathrobe fell open. I would have been mortified."

Nana rolled her eyes. "You wasn't the one what was plannin' to surprise the art class by posin' in the buff 'cuz you thought 'still life' meant 'naked person not movin.'"

"Count your blessings," counseled Jackie. "At least she wasn't hurt. And her threat to sue the tour company scored her a voucher for a free cruise at some later date. Kinda makes me wish I'd had a 160-pound Frenchman fall on top of *me*."

Patrice had been led off the boat in handcuffs, destined to face an uncertain future in the French prison system. If only he'd taken the time to discuss the history of Pierre Lefevre's ring with Woody. If only he hadn't tried to avenge past wrongs by committing new ones.

"So what's on your schedule, dear?" asked Nana.

A fluttery sensation tickled my breastbone. "I'm going to sit on this very spot and wait for a call from Etienne. His seminar is over, so he should be phoning me up any minute now."

Jackie stood up. "I'm off, then. What about you, Mrs. S.?"

"I've only got a couple of hours before the bus leaves, so I better go, too."

I stared out over the empty parking lot. "The bus isn't even here yet, Nana."

"I know, dear, so if I get in line now, there won't be no way I'll miss it."

I removed my cell phone from my shoulder bag and set it on my lap, willing it to ring. A few guests were doing laps around the deck, some walking, others jogging, but it was pretty quiet up here this morning. It kinda made me feel as if I were the only passenger on the entire boat.

"There you are, Emily. I ran into Jackie downstairs. She was kind enough to tell me where you were. I hope you won't mind the intrusion."

"Victor!" I popped out of my chair and ushered him to the chair Nana had just vacated. His oxygen tube was secure in his nostrils, and he was still supporting himself on his cane, but he looked surprisingly hale considering what he'd just been through. "I hope you're feeling as good as you look."

He laughed. "Flatterer. But the hospital stay did me good. I don't know what those IVs were pumping into me, but I no longer feel like a two-hundred-year-old relic. I feel more like a mere pup of perhaps seventy or eighty."

"Are you rejoining us for the remainder of the trip?"

He nodded. "I'm making arrangements to accompany Krystal's remains back to Texas, so until that happens, I'll continue sightseeing with you. Besides, I'm feeling much too frisky to remain on my back any longer. I might even surprise Virginia and decide to climb to the top of the Eiffel Tower."

I flashed a concerned look. "Are you sure that's wise?"

"Just kidding." He trailed his fingertips along the carved handle of his cane. "I'm told the ne'er-do-well who tried to poison me has been arrested."

"Did the police give you details?"

"Enough to satisfy me for a while. What no one has bothered to tell me is why I'm still alive and young Krystal is dead. How is it that the person living in this decrepit body of mine could defy death? Why is she dead, while I live?"

"Actually, I was curious about that myself, so I nosed around the Internet, and I think I found the answer. Do you remember Krystal's battle with motion sickness? She was so prone to the condition that she took daily supplements to ward it off. Massive doses of ginger. According to the information I found, ginger can amplify the effects of blood thinners to dangerous levels. Fatal levels. So I suspect that's why she died and you didn't."

He shook his head sadly. "Life is so unfair. No one as beautiful as that lovely woman should have to die so young. And for what? For nothing." He opened his jacket to observe the envelope containing his twenty-five-thousand-dollar bonus check. "Upon copious reflection during my hospital stay, I've decided to award my much-anticipated bonus check to no one, but instead make a contribution in Krystal's name to a worthy cause. What do you think of that idea?"

"I think it's a wonderful idea." Although I doubted Bobbi or Dawna would share my opinion.

"Good. I'm glad you agree. You didn't spend much time in Krystal's company, but from what little you observed of her, did you get any sense of where she might want a donation of this size to end up?"

"The NRA?"

He frowned. "I don't think so." He closed his jacket and patted his lapel. "I'll give it more thought."

"Could I ask you something, Victor? I might be way out of line, but I'm really curious."

He invited my inquiry with a palms up. "Please."

"Why do you travel with a mortar and pestle?"

"You heard about that, did you?"

I shrugged. "Word gets around."

He smiled. "They belong to Virginia. She uses them to pulverize her vitamin E softgels, which she applies to her face daily to maintain her flawless complexion. I've told her there's no difference between vitamin E in liquid form and what's contained in her softgels, but she doesn't believe me. So wherever we go, so too go her mortar and pestle."

"She does have a lovely complexion." I touched my fingers to my cheek. "Maybe I should hop on board with her beauty tip."

A faraway look crept into his eyes. "Virginia is indeed lovely, but I think no woman will ever match the incomparable beauty of Solange Spenard."

I regarded him curiously. "You say that as if Solange were an old acquaintance."

"I never had the pleasure of meeting the lady until a few days ago."

I frowned. "Then how would you know—"

He held up his hand. "I saw her picture many years ago. Her husband hid it beneath the insole of his shoe to secret it away from our jailers, because, as you might imagine, the Germans were rather stingy about allowing their prisoners to indulge in creature comforts. And I ask you, what greater comfort would there be for an imprisoned man than a photo of his wife?"

I sat statue-still, the unexpectedness of his admission taking my breath away. "You were a prisoner with Solange's husband? In Amiens Prison?"

"*Ah*. You know of Amiens. You've heard the story then?"

"Madeleine told me."

"Then you know of the bombing raid. Many prisoners escaped, but many were tracked down and dragged back. Henri Spenard and I were fortunate. We eluded capture, but we lived in constant fear."

"You escaped together?"

"We survived together. In the cold. In the snow. In the rain. We fled into Belgium, and from there, realized we must part company. Henri vowed to return home to Solange and his family. I had no home to return to. The Nazis had burned my village. Executed my family. So I started walking south, and ended up in Genoa." His eyes grew wistful. "I regret that after all these years, I still don't know if Henri ever made it home."

"He did," I said happily. "He and Solange were together for over fifty years and raised seven children."

He smiled. "Henri was a good man. I'm glad he was able to return to the life he loved so much." He thumped his fist on his sternum and coughed. "I'm afraid mine has been rather hampered by health issues, none of which were helped by a prolonged stay in a German prison cell, or a five hundred-mile trek to the sea."

"How did you hike five hundred miles through occupied Europe without getting caught?"

Victor shrugged. "I chose my path carefully. Through forests. Along streams. Over mountain passes. I *had* to choose my path carefully. I carried no identity papers, so if I'd been asked to present them, my brilliant escape and journey would have been for naught."

"You weren't stopped in Genoa?"

"In Genoa, I found a sympathetic priest who falsified identity papers for me, and a sympathetic member of the Red Cross who provided me with a valid passport. I officially became Victor Martin at that moment, and I've been Victor Martin ever since."

Which explained a great deal about why the police had run into a stone wall while looking into Victor's past. "So you became Victor Martin. Where did you go?"

"Argentina. The priest paid for my passage, which I have repaid many times over with an annual contribution to his church. From Argentina, I eventually made my way north, to the United States, where my skills as an apothecary were, thankfully, in great demand."

"You were a pharmacist in France?"

"I was, but I no longer wanted to formulate medications. I wanted to formulate a product that would help people recover from their war wounds and scars. I wanted to create something that would help people, especially women, to feel good about themselves in the postwar world. So I developed Mona Michelle, the cosmetic line that would allow every woman an opportunity to look as beautiful as the photo of Henri's wife. I've never forgotten her face, you see. It's haunted me for years."

I stared at him, awestruck. "Is this your first trip back to France since the war?"

He nodded. "I never wanted to come back. Too many painful memories. But Virginia insisted so . . . here we are."

His tone made me suspicious. "Is Virginia aware of anything you've just told me?"

He grinned. "Virginia thinks I was born and raised in Connecticut. She's never asked questions about my origins because she's not interested in my past history. As long as I continue to provide for her in the manner to which she's accustomed, I could be a fugitive from Krypton, and she wouldn't care."

"If Virginia doesn't know about your past, why are you sharing it with me?"

"Because I like you. You've been gracious to me without expecting anything in return, and given my status, you don't know how rare that is." He graced me with a soft smile. "Believe it or not, Emily dear, after all these years, I was feeling a need to tell someone, so I chose you."

"I don't know what to say."

"Nothing," he suggested. "To anyone. If you'd be so kind."

"Of course. But still—"

Victor heaved himself to his feet with more strength than he'd displayed over the entire trip. "Now that I've said my piece, I'll take my leave before Virginia has a chance to convince herself that she actually misses me. Will I see you at dinner, my dear?"

"You bet."

"Good. Our table needs the diversity."

"Victor, would you answer one more question for me before you leave?"

"If I'm able."

"Why did you select the name Mona Michelle for your company?"

He smiled enigmatically. "When people ask, I tell them quite simply that I liked the name. But to you, I will tell the truth. Mona Michelle was my mother's name."

"And what was yours?"

"Richard. Richard Michelle. But my family saddled me with a pet name. Dick. I actually like Victor much better."

He disappeared behind the wheelhouse, having provided me with the answers to so many unanswered questions. Why he'd refused to talk about where he'd fought in the war. Why he had spoken to Solange with such familiarity. Why—

"Cigars for everyone!" cried Osmond as he appeared at the rail. He held out a stogie to a man jogging past him. "Cigar?"

The guy grabbed it and kept running.

"Cigar, Emily?" He waved a fistful in my direction.

"What are you celebrating?"

He raced over to me like a stick figure in an animated short. "I'm a father!" He shoved a cigar at me, a goofy grin on his face, the rest of his body doing a little jump around.

"Oh, my God! How do you know? Did Solange tell you?"

"She didn't need to."

I spoke to him in a gentle voice. "Osmond, if she didn't tell you, how can you possibly be sure?"

"Because the apple didn't fall far from the tree."

"What do you mean by that?"

"She's been writing to me all morning about what her kids do for a living."

"And?"

"And her son Osmond? He's a political pollster!"

THE END

© Photo Express

ABOUT THE AUTHOR

After experiencing disastrous vacations on three continents, Maddy Hunter decided to combine her love of humor, travel, and storytelling to fictionalize her misadventures. Inspired by her feisty aunt and by memories of her Irish grandmother, she created the nationally bestselling, Agatha Award–nominated Passport to Peril mystery series, where quirky seniors from Iowa get to relive everything that went wrong on Maddy's holiday. *Fleur de Lies* is the ninth book in the series. Maddy lives in Madison, Wisconsin, with her husband and a head full of imaginary characters who keep asking, "Are we there yet?"

Please visit her website at www.maddyhunter.com, or become a follower on her Maddy Hunter Facebook Fan Page.

WWW.MIDNIGHTINKBOOKS.COM

From the gritty streets of New York City to sacred tombs in the Middle East, it's always midnight somewhere. Join us online at any hour for fresh new voices in mystery fiction.

At midnightinkbooks.com you'll also find our author blog, new and upcoming books, events, book club questions, excerpts, mystery resources, and more.

MIDNIGHT INK ORDERING INFORMATION

Order Online:

• Visit our website *www.midnightinkbooks.com*, select your books, and order them on our secure server.

Order by Phone:

• Call toll-free within the U.S. and Canada at
1-888-NITE-INK (1-888-648-3465)
• We accept VISA, MasterCard, and American Express

Order by Mail:

Send the full price of your order (MN residents add 6.875% sales tax) in U.S. funds, plus postage & handling to:

Midnight Ink
2143 Wooddale Drive
Woodbury, MN 55125-2989

Postage & Handling:

Standard (U.S. & Canada). If your order is:
$25.00 and under, add $4.00
$25.01 and over, FREE STANDARD SHIPPING

AK, HI, PR: $16.00 for one book plus $2.00 for each additional book.

International Orders (airmail only):
$16.00 for one book plus $3.00 for each additional book

Orders are processed within 12 business days. Please allow for normal shipping time.
Postage and handling rates subject to change.

Dutch Me Deadly

A PASSPORT TO PERIL MYSTERY

maddy HUNTER

DUTCH ME DEADLY
Maddy Hunter

As a travel escort for seniors, Emily Andrew-Miceli has led her feisty Iowa clan all over the world. This time, they're off to see historic windmills and Dutch art in Holland—if they can ever unplug from their smartphones, that is. Joining them is the class from Bangor, Maine, celebrating their 50th reunion, which is divided by old rivalries. Emily's hopes for a 100% survival rate on this trip are dashed when an important member of the tour suffers a tragic (and highly suspicious) accident. Then the saucy seniors' wild night of drug-laced desserts and risqué shows in Amsterdam's red light district gets even more mysterious when one reunioner—the class bully—goes missing.

978-0-7387-2704-2 $14.95

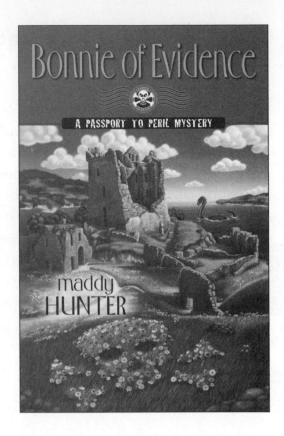

Bonnie of Evidence

A PASSPORT TO PERIL MYSTERY

maddy HUNTER

BONNIE OF EVIDENCE
Maddy Hunter

Emily Andrew-Miceli, travel escort extraordinaire, is leading a group of Iowa seniors on a tour of Scotland. And to make the trip even more fun, Emily and her foxy husband, Etienne, have organized a high-tech scavenger hunt. But when one team's underhanded strategizing brings a cursed dirk into their hotel on Loch Ness, Isobel Kronk—a member of the tour group—ends up dead. Was it the curse of the dagger, as hotel proprietor Mrs. Dalrymple believes? Was it an allergic reaction? Or is there a flesh and blood killer on the loose?

978-0-7387-2705-9 $14.99